Paisley
Wolf

Paisley Wolf

Copyright © 2018 by B. S. Todd.

Printed in the United States of America

Editing by Teri@editingfairy.com
Book Formatting by Derek Murphy@Creativindie.com
Bookcover image@pixabay.com

Paperback ISBN : 978-0-9991169-3-7
Ebook ISBN: 978-0-9991169-4-4

Library of Congress Control Number: 2018907920
First Edition: 2018

10 9 8 7 6 5 4 3 2 1

Paisley

Wolf

A CLOVERLY WOLVES NOVEL

B. S. TODD

Prologue

Tucker

Tucker spent most of his days scouting the mountainside. Coming home exhausted and physically drained, it usually helped him sleep at night. It had been two months since leaving Cloverly and still he was haunted by the choices he'd made. *What's done is done.*

He walked into the kitchen and leaned against the counter. "Mom?" he said, unable to mask the concern in his voice. He wanted to be there when the doctor came that morning, but securing the eastern ridge where his father had fallen two months ago, was top priority.

As the unspoken question lingered between them, Lucia carried a pot of water from the sink and placed it on the stovetop. "Dr. Ward said your father has healed nicely and with a little therapy to work the shoulder, he will be back to normal in no time." She reached over and squeezed his hand. "I told you not to worry. We may be older, but we still heal."

"He has no business scouting the eastern ridge alone. He's always telling us to go in pairs yet he doesn't follow his own advice," Tucker groused.

"Well, after this scare, I think he's learned his lesson." Lucia turned to search through the pantry as Lily Rose raced into the room.

"Tucker!" The tiny voice that greeted him after a long day's work was music to his ears, and he pushed away from the counter.

"Peanut!" His excitement matched hers. Scooping Lily into his arms, she giggled when he spun her around and then placed her back on her feet.

At seven years old, Lily was the youngest of the Wilson clan and stood a whopping three feet tall. She was the runt of the family and Tucker's favorite. "Stand up here and let me see how much you've grown."

Lily stepped back and curtsied, her pink tutu flaring out over the purple tights that matched the purple-striped shirt she wore.

"Wow, before long you'll be as tall as me," Tucker said, knowing she would never reach his six-foot-six stature.

"Lily, get your chores done before supper," Lucia said and Lily's brows lifted.

"Better do as you're told before Mama Bear gets riled," Tucker snarled as he planted a kiss on top of her head and she hugged him around the neck.

"I love you!" Lily giggled with his tickle.

"I love you back," Tucker said, turning to his mother after Lily ran out of the room. "I think I'm gonna take a walk. I'll be back in time for supper." Breathing in the crisp mountain air as he walked out the backdoor, he wondered why anyone would ever want to leave such a beautiful place.

Spending the afternoon visiting with friends only reinforced the idea that he needed to get it together if he planned to settle down. Tucker wanted a family like the one he grew up in; but to have that, something had to change. He was a nice person by everyone's standards, but being nice only got you so far. And that was a mistake he would definitely learn from.

He looked up at the sky to gauge the time before heading back toward the house. That was until he heard a familiar laugh and he ducked behind a tree while motioning for Sawyer to head home.

Katherine didn't see him as she strolled down the street, her long, blonde hair catching the breeze. She was royalty in the making with her snobbish ways and uppity attitude. Coming from one of the wealthiest families in the mountain area, she expected to mate with a male of equal or higher standing, but Tucker wasn't planning to be her golden goose. He groaned as she waved to her friends just outside the alpha house. Like vultures waiting for their next meal, it had become a daily occurrence since word got out that he was back in Tennessee.

"Come on, we'll be late." Sawyer laughed as he ran across the street, leaving Tucker at the mercy of the tree.

Sawyer was younger than the females that stalked his older brothers, but with promises of passing messages for them, they treated him like he was their best friend. He was sharp when it came to she-wolves and although he said he would never be mated to one, he had his eye on a little strawberry-blonde down the road.

Pulling the hood up over his head, Tucker waited for Sawyer's distraction. He'd done well avoiding the pack females for the past two months, and if it hadn't been for his brothers, they would have caught him weeks ago.

Hayden motioned him forward from the safety of the front porch while Sawyer raced across the yard, heading off the group of catty females. Pointing off in the distance, maybe tipping them to Tucker's whereabouts, Tucker slipped past without being noticed.

Hayden laughed and slapped Tucker on the back when he ran up on the porch. "It's a good thing we like you because they look starved for attention."

Tucker didn't look back as he walked into the house. He shrugged off his jacket and hung it on the coat rack just inside the door. "I owe you," he said when Sawyer walked in behind Hayden. His little brother, almost as tall as he, grinned.

"Man, those females are getting restless. I have messages for you both but I'm not sure I should repeat them. Talk about graphic." Sawyer bounced his eyebrows waggishly.

Tucker followed behind his brothers as they bounded up the stairs—the messages instantly forgotten. With five minutes to wash up, he stood against the wall of the two-story cabin and looked down at the large dining room below. The open floor plan was perfect for pack meetings, and when he and Hayden were younger; they liked to hide upstairs and peek through the spindles.

"Hurry, you only have a minute," Hayden said,

descending the stairs two at a time.

Tucker rushed into the bathroom and turned on the faucet as he grabbed a bar of soap. He could hear the chairs sliding across the wood floor and he quickly lathered up before rinsing the suds down the drain. Shutting off the water, he dried his hands and hurried down to supper.

As the family gathered around the large dining table that seated twelve, Tucker smiled, remembering his thoughts from earlier. Glancing up at the hallway, he easily pictured himself snickering while Hayden shot spitballs through a straw at the females that dared to look up. He had great memories of his home life and it was times like then that he questioned his decision to train as the alpha for the Berkley pack, an extension of the Kinsley pack.

"So have you decided when you're going back to Kentucky?" Alpha Wilson asked from the head of the table. His dad, equally as tall, had been the alpha of the Smoky Mountain Pack for the past thirty-five years, a very much sought after role which he would soon hand down to Hayden.

"No, but I'm here as long as you need me," Tucker said. He still had to decide what to do once he returned to Kentucky. Maybe eliminating the negative energy that hung over him, threatening to destroy his world, would be a good start. His thoughts turned to Jesse, and had he not denied their bond, he could have introduced her to his family, and they would have loved her.

He glanced around the table at his siblings. Hayden was the oldest and then Tucker, with Sawyer coming in at fifth place. Between them was Alyssa and Jaylee, and the youngest three were Miles, Paige, and Lily Rose. "What?" Tucker asked when he realized they were all staring. "Is my hair messed up?" The giggles and snickers that filled the room warmed his heart.

By ten that night, most of the family had gone off to bed except for Hayden, Jaylee, and Alyssa. Joining them on the porch, they talked about the pack and everything Tucker missed while he was away. It was nice hanging out with his siblings, something he always looked forward to when he lived at home.

"Tucker, did you see Katherine today?" Alyssa asked and glanced over at Jaylee, her virtual twin, even wearing the same hairstyle. Their chestnut brown hair hung past their shoulders and both wore it pulled back in a ponytail.

"Well, I saw her, but I didn't talk to her," Tucker said, taking a seat on an old driftwood bench that sat next to the front door. The mountain cabin was the only home he'd ever known before moving to a smaller version in Cloverly.

The females laughed as Jaylee picked up were Alyssa left off. "You know, she's twenty-one now, and plans to bond with a Wilson male. I told her not to hold her breath."

"Congratulations, big brother," Tucker teased and punched Hayden in the arm when he walked past to the swing.

"Whatever. I'm not the one she's infatuated with. She's pining after the dread-head and that's not me." Hayden smirked knowingly.

"Good to know because after tonight, it won't be me either." Tucker laughed when his sisters squealed, unable to hide their excitement. It wasn't the real reason he wanted to cut his hair, but better than explaining why he needed a change.

"Do you know how happy that will make Mom? She always said you had the prettiest hair," Alyssa reminded him.

Tucker rolled his eyes as his sisters ran into the house to gather everything they needed to cut his hair. He was quite aware of why his mother didn't like his dreads. She was a fan of his natural curly locks, and often referred to them as beautiful. But for a young stud of seventeen, beautiful wasn't a word that boosted his ego. Now he was twenty-two and a lot wiser, he needed to move past that teenage mindset. He had more important things to worry about besides how he wore his hair.

His thoughts drifted...

Not only had Jesse attracted his attention, but that of his wolf as well. By breaking the bond they shared, he freed his wolf but did little to ease the heartache he later endured. Closing his eyes, he could still see the smile on her face when he dipped her on the dance floor before whispering into her ear. He knew she wouldn't hear the three words he spoke, but at least he had said them.

"How short do you want your hair?" Jaylee asked as she snipped the scissors in the air, startling him.

"Eh, I don't know. Collar length?"

"This is so epic!" Alyssa's enthusiasm was terrifying if he were being honest. He cringed at the first snip, but once they started, there was no turning back. He looked down at the thick cords piling around the chair—his head feeling ten pounds lighter. "Now comes the fun part," Alyssa taunted as she pulled a rat tail comb out of her back pocket.

It was well after midnight by the time Tucker cleaned up the mess and headed to bed. Tiptoeing up the stairs, he quietly opened the bedroom door and kicked off his boots. As he crawled into bed and lay back on a pillow, he stared at the plastic, glow-in-the-dark, stars pasted to the ceiling. He couldn't help remembering the day he and Hayden glued them there, and they got into so much trouble. He was eleven, Hayden twelve. They tried hanging the stars with the sticky-putty stuff that came in the package, but ran out after about ten stars. So doing what most normal males of that age would do, they glued the remaining stars to the ceiling. It worked out great until his mother decided to repaint his room. When she realized what they'd done, she gave them each a paintbrush and told them to get busy. The job took several days to trim around each of the fifty-three stars, plus the planets and comets that shot across the ceiling. He chuckled to himself as he rolled over.

Night time was always the worst because his thoughts tormented him. Visualizing Jesse standing before the town council, he did his best to stay in the background, listening while she made her case against the pack. She was afraid of them, thanks to Travis, and because of that, he questioned how a bond between them could work. She didn't know who the wolves were, but she assumed they were all dangerous. The more he listened, the worse he felt, knowing she would never settle for someone like him. That was what he told himself before walking out the door and breaking their bond forever.

Maybe if he'd stayed in Tennessee, he could eventually forget about her. There were plenty of pack females that would jump at the chance to become his mate. And since he had denied the bond, maybe he would get lucky and bond with another. It sounded good, but the niggling in the back of his mind said he would never be happy. He closed his eyes, praying sleep would come easy.

The following morning, a light peck on the bedroom door roused him from his sleep. Instantly recognizing the knock, he called for Lily to enter. The smell of breakfast drifted in the air when she pushed open the door and bounded across the room. She jumped up on the bed and he narrowed his eyes, confused by the frown she wore. "What's wrong?" Tucker asked as she scanned the outline of his face.

"Your hair is gone." She lifted a tiny finger to point, and he smiled and ran his fingers through his hair. He suddenly realized she'd never seen him with anything but dreads, so he could imagine her surprise.

"Do you like my new haircut?"

She rose onto her knees and looked over his shoulder before settling back on the bed. Her eyes sparkled as a toothy grin spread across her face. "You have hair like mine."

"I do, and in a few days, it will curl just like yours, and then we'll be twins," he said, tickling her ribs. When the squeals and giggles stopped, he sent her down to the kitchen. "Don't tell Mom. It's a surprise."

Lily did a pinky swear and then headed out the door.

Tucker hurried into the bathroom, eager to get the day started. Being able to wash his hair and massage his scalp felt great, and he stayed in the shower until the water ran cold. Then he dressed and within minutes, dried his hair and was on his way downstairs to breakfast.

When he walked into the kitchen, everyone grew quiet except for the snickers shared between Alyssa and Jaylee. He pulled out a chair and joined them at the bar, meeting their grins.

Finally, his mother turned from the stove, waving a spatula in the air. "All right, what is going on here?" she asked, suspicious at not hearing their normal chatter. Upon seeing Tucker, her eyes lit up and she stared for what seemed like minutes before laughing. "What a wonderful sight to see this morning!" She tossed the spatula into the pan and walked over to comb her fingers through his hair.

"Oh, Mom, it's just hair." Tucker swatted her hand away, only to draw more snickers from his sisters.

After breakfast, Tucker and Hayden headed out to repair the roof on the family's small cabin that overlooked the mountainside. He welcomed the work; it occupied his mind, plus; it kept him out of sight of the females that sought his attention. But driving across town to pick up supplies, Katherine was the last person he expected to see. Tucker quickly turned his head. Surely without the dreads, she wouldn't recognize him—or so he hoped.

"Tucker, is that you?" Katherine called out, waving happily from across the street.

Tucker patted down his pockets because it was too late to run back to the store for ear plugs. That was his automatic reaction and one of the reasons he avoided her. Her singsong voice teetered more on the annoying side than it tottered on cutesy. He glanced around for Hayden, but it was apparent he wouldn't be running interference, and was probably somewhere hiding, laughing at his expense. He drew in a breath and turned, knowing Katherine would be wearing a catty grin.

"I knew you were coming back. I was telling Nancy that just the other day. You love the mountains and finding a single worthy female in a small pack would be like finding a diamond up a goat's rear end." She sidled up beside him and promptly changed the subject. "Are you going to the bonfire this weekend? It will be fun. I don't have a date if you care to escort me."

"Yeah, Tucker, she doesn't have a date and neither do you." Hayden winked as he walked past the two, carrying a bucket of nails. *Traitor.*

"It depends on how Dad is feeling." Tucker hated using his dad to escape her clutches, but desperate times called for desperate measures and if that's what it took to dissuade her, he would apologize to his dad later.

"Oh, I heard about his accident. Is there anything I can do?"

"No, but thanks for asking. We practically trip over each other as it is." It was hard to believe she would offer her time, and Tucker looked up, expecting the sky to fall.

"Well, then, I'm sure they won't mind if I take you out of the way. One less body they'll have to trip over. I'll see you Friday night." She smiled and sashayed back across the street.

Tucker scowled when Hayden walked around the truck and laughed at the sour expression on his face. "It's not a death sentence. It's just a bonfire, so lighten up. You're a good match."

"Well, this match has already been lit, and it wasn't on her bonfire."

"Whoa there, little brother! Are you admitting to

sparking firestorms in Cloverly?" Hayden's brows rose to his hairline, and Tucker blushed.

"Shut up and get in the truck," Tucker said, ignoring his brother who was now grinning like a loon.

The roof repair took up most of the day, giving Tucker very little time to spend with his father that afternoon. He liked to sit and listen to him talk politics, as well as the responsibilities an alpha had, and what was expected from the pack.

That night after his dad went to bed, Tucker headed upstairs to his room. His mind had been preoccupied with Jesse ever since he'd broken the bond, and he was surprised he'd heard a word his father had said. Standing in front of the open balcony door, the cold, dark night sent a shiver through his body as he watched a lone star streaking across the sky. "I love you, Jesse." His heart shattered.

Startled by the little hands that pulled on his shirt, he looked down at the soft, brown eyes blinking up at him. "Peanut, what are you doing out of bed?"

"I thought you might like to tuck me in," Lily said, and he grinned at the precious, little princess.

"I would love to." Gently scooping her up in his arms, he carried her to her room and placed her on the frilly, white daybed. Taking the time to tuck the covers snugly around her, he leaned down and kissed her on the forehead. "It's going to be a cold night; stay under the covers."

"Tucker," Lily said when he turned to leave. "Who is Jesse?" He looked down at her questioning eyes. "You were talking to her when I came in your room."

Tucker smiled and kneeled down beside the bed.

"She's a female I met in Cloverly, but you don't know her."

"Can I meet her? What's she like?" Her excitement made him chuckle, and he sat down on the floor, resting his elbow on the bed beside her.

"Well... she's like a sunrise, eager to greet the day. She has dark brown eyes, almost black, that sparkle with her smile. Her jet-black hair flows down to her waist, and is full of curls just like yours," he said and tweaked her nose—she giggled. "But I don't know about meeting her. She's human, and I'm not sure how she feels about us."

"Then she would love me because I don't have my wolf yet."

The innocence of her words weighed on his heart, and he cleared his throat as tears rimmed his eyes. "You're right. She would love you, and you would love her."

Lily reached out from beneath the blanket and touched his cheek. "Don't worry, she'll love you too."

"One day, maybe," he said as he tucked her hand back beneath the blanket.

The next morning, Tucker moped around as Lily's words echoed in his head. If only things were as simple as they were to a seven-year-old, life would be grand. The thought of leaving and not seeing her little face every day was almost enough to keep him at home. But as the weekend drew nearer, he grew restless.

Tucker dreaded the thought of going to the bonfire with Katherine, to the point of feeling ill. Not eating breakfast that morning was a red flag that not only caught the attention of his siblings, but his mother. Once everyone was up and about, his mother called him back into the kitchen where she had just finished wiping down the stove.

"Tucker, what's bothering you?" Lucia pulled out a chair and sat down at the bar, motioning for him to do the same. "Something's been bothering you since you got home and I think it's time we talked about it. I know you better than anyone and your heart is hurt. What happened?"

"I screwed up. I walked away from the one female that was perfect for me. I denied our bond." He rested his elbows on the table and shoved his fingers into his hair.

"Why? The bond is there for a reason. You know that." Worry creased her brows, and she reached over and pulled his arms down.

He looked up.

"I know, Mom!" Filled with guilt, his stomach churned. "I'm sorry. I didn't mean to raise my voice. It's... a long story, but it doesn't matter now. It's done." He closed his eyes to hide the tears that threatened to fall.

"Is it?" She squeezed his hand, and he opened his eyes, the pain of his decision etched on his face.

"Yes. I broke the bond by choice." He shook his head as his mother's thumb lightly rubbed over his knuckles. It was a comforting gesture, and one he didn't deserve. He was a fool for giving up on himself, his wolf, and Jesse. *You are no alpha!* He swallowed the razor sharp thought that ripped through his heart.

"Then why haven't you moved on?"

"I wish I could let her go as easily as my wolf did, but I can't. Everything reminds me of her, and I feel like I'm suffocating." He huffed and pushed up from the chair. Shoving his hands into his pockets, he leaned against the counter.

"How well did you know this female?" Lucia turned to face him.

"Well enough to know she was in a relationship with another."

"Oh, Tucker." His mother sighed. "As much as I love having you at home, I want you to go back to Cloverly this day. Forget about the bonfire. Katherine will have plenty of time to find another date, and if not, I'll send Hayden in your place. If what you're saying is true, the bond may not be intact, but your heart is. You owe it to yourself, and to her, so tell her how you feel. Until you do, I don't think you'll get past this."

One

Jesse

It was early autumn, Jesse's favorite time of year, and just her luck, she'd feel like crap. Sneezing and shivering, a girl couldn't catch a break. She wiped her nose and tucked the tissue into her pocket as Brian walked up on the porch and asked, "How's my best girl today?" The words alone made it sound like he had a harem of ladies all eager for his attention, which at that moment, was kindly being bestowed on her.

"Tired," she grumbled when he sat down beside her and toed the swing back and forth—his grin reflecting in his eyes. He was good looking, clean shaven, and the perfect candidate for a fireman-of-the-month calendar. She smiled weakly as the sun cast his blond hair in a soft golden glow, reminding her of fresh apple cider. Add a slice of pumpkin pie along with the glorious smell of dried leaves that lingered in the air, and she briefly closed her eyes to savor the moment.

"You feel warm. It's a good thing there's a doctor in the house." With his hand pressed against her forehead, his smile faded when he noticed her glassy eyes. "You don't look so good. You should probably be inside." Brian locked his knees to stop the swing.

"And waste a perfectly good afternoon?" Jesse asked, but she startled when the tornado sirens wailed. Testing the sirens on a daily basis was like a dinner bell to the locals, and she didn't think she could ever get used to hearing that earsplitting racket. "Is that necessary?" she yelled and then continued when the sirens wound down. "Despite what you think, this is my ideal weather. Not too hot, not too cold."

"And that right there is exactly why we could never get along." Brian grabbed an afghan off the rocking chair that was catty-corner to the swing and draped it over her shoulders.

"Ha! Don't blame failed relationships on the weather. We all know you're pig-headed and bossy." She unclipped her raven hair, allowing the curls to cascade down her back.

"Only because you're the most stubborn person I know."

"Oh, that's rich. Are you the pot or the kettle?" She narrowed her eyes, impressed they could last a total of five minutes before the war-of-words started. Then she clenched her jaw as a stabbing pain shot through her thigh. Admitting he was right made her nauseous, but as more aches assaulted her body, she caved. "And just so you know, I was getting ready to go in when you first came up. So there."

"I'm sure you were." Unable to hide his smirk, Brian laid the afghan over the back of the swing and took hold of Jesse's arm. The coolness of his hand seeped through her sweater, and she shivered when he pulled her out of the swing and opened the front door. "Can you make it up the stairs? Or shall I carry you?" he asked, walking her across the foyer.

"I'm sure I can manage on my own." She rolled her eyes when he flicked his brows, suggesting something she didn't want to imagine.

"Manage what?" her grandmother asked when she walked into the room with a dusting rag draped over her shoulder.

Jesse pivoted on the step and glared down at Brian—a silent warning to keep his mouth shut.

"Jesse has a fever and isn't feeling well."

So much for keeping his mouth shut.

"Thank you, Dr. Edwards." Jesse didn't know whether to spit or hiss, and the sarcasm in her voice didn't go unnoticed. Brian's grin widened, and he winked. He most definitely had a death wish. "Gramma, it's nothing an aspirin and a little sleep can't cure."

"Well, your dad won't be home until next week, but I can call Dr. Fisher if need be."

"That won't be necessary. I'm fine." Jesse was furious, and as soon as her grandmother left the room, she slipped off her house shoe and chucked it at Brian's head. "I can't believe you did that. You know how much she worries."

"Come on, Jess. You know I'm only looking out for

your best interest." Brian picked up the shoe and carried it up to where she stood, scowling. His breath brushed across her cheek when he leaned in and whispered, "You could save yourself a lot of trouble if, for once in your life, you did as you were told."

"Yeah, you would like to think that," Jesse hissed. "Give me my shoe." She yanked it from his hand, which only made him laugh harder as he backed down the stairs.

"Get some rest, and I'll check on you tomorrow." Again he winked, and she flipped him the bird.

Exhausted from stomping up two flights of stairs, she dropped down on the bed and kicked off her shoes. "Best interest, my butt!" She pulled her favorite fuzzy blanket up to her chin and rolled over on the pillow.

Staring at the black-and-white picture pinned to her corkboard, she whispered, "I'm sorry." Jesse never admitted to anyone that she bawled like a baby the day Tucker left Cloverly. Or that she kept the red roses he gave her until the petals turned brown. She also never imagined he would be interested in someone like her. A chunky lump of stupidity that couldn't see what was right in front of her eyes. Had she known…?

Her heart ached with his memory. *His smile was amazing, and the connection between them as they danced, nothing less than magical. Yeah, too bad you scared him off.* The thought twisted like a knife in her chest, and she turned, facing the front window as Brian backed out of his driveway.

He was probably on his way over to rescue Annie by changing a lightbulb or opening a jar of pickles. Annie was a devious, little nymph with long, flowing hair the color of sunshine. The stick-thin blonde knew exactly how to play him; Brian just wasn't smart enough to see it. He was a sucker for a damsel in distress, and Annie was always in some sort of distress. But Jesse ignored them as best she could. She didn't need Brian to save her, and she definitely didn't need him to open her pickle jars. She closed her eyes and eventually drifted off to sleep.

The bedsprings creaked with each toss and turn, the mattress bordering on the lumpy side. Jesse wasn't sure how long she'd been in bed, or if she'd slept, due to the intense itching of her left hand. She leaned up on her elbow and glanced over at the glowing numbers on the alarm clock. It was five in the morning, too early to get up, yet she was wide awake. Shoving the blanket to the side, she yawned.

It had been months since she'd gotten a good night's sleep and she blamed that on the weather. As the air cooled, and the trees dropped their leaves, she swore she could hear animals burrowing in the woods—a slight distraction to her already cluttered mind. She sat up, and her toes instantly curled into the plush beige carpet. Glimpsing a light through the lace curtain, she pushed it to the side. Brian's porch light was still on, which meant Annie had duped him into an all-nighter. *Poor widdle Annie.*

As she turned away from the window, she caught a glimpse of the tree line that ran alongside her house. Her body quivered, and she drew in a deep breath, banishing the urge to run to the back of her mind. She wasn't afraid of the woods even though she was well aware of the night prowlers that roamed the area. And although they were friends, a wolf in the dark was still a wolf.

Jesse pulled off her sweater and dropped it to the floor. The room was unusually hot, so she propped open the side window, allowing the cool air to blow over her sweat-soaked skin.

A low hiss brought her attention to Moose, who had just hunkered down beside the window seat. "What's the matter, boy? Did you hear something?" She bent down and picked up the bristling, gray tabby. "It's okay. I won't let the mean, old wolves get you." She kissed the top of his head, but Moose wasn't having any of her sweet talk and without warning, he extracted himself from her arms and darted beneath the bed. Moose wasn't a fan of the wolves and anytime they were near, he copped an attitude. She chuckled, knowing it wasn't that long ago that she felt the same way.

After exposing the secret of Cloverly, most of the townspeople thought it was a hoax, but the select few that knew the truth finally agreed to embrace the wolves in the community. It was a big to-do that day, and Jesse left the council meeting feeling like a complete failure, or idiot, depending on which side you were on. Then she realized after talking with her dad, that the wolves provided most of the security for the town, so how bad could they be?

Resisting another strong urge to run, she shook that silly notion out of her head. She wasn't the athletic type, and although it was a great way to stay fit, the only thing she would gain from running was probably a sprained ankle. She sauntered over to the closet and opened the door, searching for something lightweight to wear—and dry She quickly dressed in the first things she grabbed—a navy tee and a pair of red and black boxers—before heading downstairs to the kitchen.

Not wanting to wake her grandmother, she stepped lightly to avoid the creaky floorboards as she tiptoed into the kitchen. After drinking down a tall glass of water, she splashed a handful over her face. The wetness instantly cooled her skin but did little to ease the heat that roared through her veins. She dried her face and tossed the hand towel on the counter as she looked back towards the hallway.

Maybe her grandmother had turned on the furnace, which would explain why the house was so hot, considering it wasn't that cold outside. She opened the backdoor, allowing cooler air to freshen the room.

Jesse quietly stepped out onto the porch as the heat from an invisible rash trailed up her arm. She closed the door, and looked up at the moonless sky where even the faintest of stars sparkled like tiny crystals. Allowing the crisp morning air to cool her body, she sucked in a hissing breath and aggressively rubbed over her left hand—the itch burning to the bone. It had been two months since the straggly mutt nipped her, leaving behind a small bruise that refused to heal. *Stupid dog!* She frowned and glanced over at the oak tree that stood in the corner of the backyard.

The large, twisted, branches haunted her, reminding her of the night she was attacked by a member of the Kinsley pack. It had been three months since Travis lured her into the backyard. From what she understood, it was part of his strategy to take over the pack. Instead, he broke pack law and was dealt with accordingly. The details were vague, but she wasn't a pack member, or privileged to that information.

A prickling sensation from head to toe set her mind in

a whirl as a bout of dizziness swept over her. Stumbling across the porch, she toppled down the wooden steps, landing face first on the cold, hard ground. As melting frost soaked through her clothes, she struggled to sit up. When she finally gathered her bearings and the ground beneath her stopped moving, she stood on unsteady legs and staggered across the yard.

The oak tree with its web of branches welcomed her, pulling her into a world that was new, yet terrifying. She cocked her head and listened. The slightest noise piqued her curiosity and her body swayed as she stepped onto the dirt trail. *Do you really think this is a good idea?* Ignoring her own question, she ambled up the path where dried leaves crunched beneath her bare feet. It wasn't the smartest thing she'd ever done, but at that point, common sense eluded her. Tucking a strand of hair behind her ear, her vision blurred.

It was a different world, darker, more mysterious even, but somewhat familiar. Unable to work through her confusion, pain shot from her core as a thunderbolt exploded behind her eyes. She gripped her head as black splotches clouded her vision, the sudden change pushing her to her knees.

Shreds of clothing drifted to the ground, her body now covered in a thick layer of black fur—she inhaled a gasping breath. Her heart raced and her vision cleared, and she threw her head back—the howl sounding more like a muffled growl. Sniffing the air, she hunkered low—searching. It was surreal, dreamlike, and as the urge to run pushed her forward, she shot through the woods in the faint morning light.

Two

Jesse

Jesse stretched and yawned, enjoying the cool breeze that caressed her body. Lost in the relaxation of the deep sleep that had consumed her, she wasn't ready to release the Sandman of his duties, not quite yet. She was waiting for that promised dream of a sexy man sweeping her off her feet, but the images that flashed behind her lids were anything but. She arched her back and stretched again, apparently the dusting prankster had deserted her!

Burrowed down in a pine-needle nest, she blinked sleepily as she stared up into thick, bristled branches—the pine scent teasing her nose. "What the...?" She bolted into an upright position and rubbed the sleep from her eyes. The rapid movement caused her muscles to throb and had she not been in the woods, she would have sworn she'd been hit by a city bus. Rubbing down the gooseflesh that raced up her arms, her eyes widened when she realized she wasn't wearing any clothes. Afraid to move or breathe, a slow tremor worked up her spine, and she pulled her knees up to her chest. Unable to catch her breath, her vision grew dark and all she could hear was the buzzing in her ears. Not knowing where she was, or more importantly, where her clothes were, her stomach heaved and she clamped her hand over her mouth to keep from throwing up.

She swallowed down the bile that inched up her throat, and slowly counted to three before drawing in a shaky breath to clear her mind. Why did everything bad always happen to her? Fighting off another bout of dizziness, she grabbed an overhead branch and hoisted herself off the ground.

Still a bit queasy, and somewhat fearful, she gradually eased out from beneath the branches, and scanned the area while her mind sorted through sketchy memories from the night before. She was in the woods, obviously, but how she got there was a total mystery. Her face flushed with humiliation as she tried to figure out how to get home, unseen, while in her current condition.

Jesse glanced down at the dirt trail, barely visible beneath a thick layer of dead leaves. Jack once told her she had to head downhill to get home, so she crossed her arms over her chest and set out through the woods.

Nothing about the path seemed familiar, and the thought of being kidnapped by a deranged lunatic hastened her steps. But that lasted a total of two minutes before she remembered why she didn't jog. Being a big-boned girl with curves to match, running was pure torture. Slowing her speed, she finally had to stop to stretch her shoulders. Oh, what she wouldn't give for a sports bra!

With a silent curse on skinny chicks, she started down the trail again, going much slower than before. She had no idea of the time, but based on the temperature drop and the sun sitting so low in the sky, it had to be late afternoon. Heat radiated around her neck, warming her face. Apparently, the fever was back, and that bothered her for some reason. Maybe it was because she overexerted herself, not being used to so much exercise. Even that sounded better than her grandmother saying, "You'll catch your death!" It was her way of politely telling Jesse she needed to dress properly for the weather.

Entering the clearing at Sallee's Rock, her breath hitched when she recognized the landmark formation. Being just two miles into the woods from where she lived, it was a welcoming sight. Having made the hike many times over the summer, she was more than elated to see it. Her chest swelled with joyous emotion and she swallowed down her fear. Now much more at ease with her location, she slowed her pace but kept moving steadily down the trail. Rounding the bend where the path leveled out, her skin prickled and she jumped behind a tree and listened. The silence was unnerving and the longer she stood there, the more certain she became that she wasn't alone.

Run! She screamed in her head but her feet were already moving. Being caught so close to home, oh, hell no! She raced down the trail faster than she believed possible, and didn't dare look back until the oak tree came into view. Choking down a sob, she quickly ducked behind a maple tree to weigh her options.

Rushing through the backdoor of her house was doable, but she quickly dismissed the idea. Her grandmother's eyesight wasn't too bad for a seventy-two-year-old but seeing her granddaughter waltzing through the door bare-assed would probably cause her heart failure. Jesse frowned, refusing to be responsible for that medical emergency.

Then a car door slammed, directing her attention to the front of the house as Brian slowly backed out of his driveway. A plan began forming in her head. *Breaking and entering is only a crime if you get caught.* The thought, although incorrect, made sense to her weary mind as she mulled over the idea. It wasn't like actually robbing him; she just needed to borrow a few clothes. Plus, if she got in and out fast enough, she could return the clothes before he came home, and he would never even know.

With her mind made up, and daylight dwindling, she sprinted back through the woods and ducked beneath a large pine tree that concealed a narrow trail that led to Brian's backyard. It wasn't an open, established trail like the one leading to Sallee's Rock, so she didn't expect to encounter anyone along the way.

Emerging from beneath the pine branches, she walked the final stretch to the privacy fence that surrounded Brian's yard. Peering through the open gate, Brian was gone, but Jesse was certain he kept a spare key hidden near the sliding glass doors. Tired and hungry, she ran straight toward the cast-iron lizard perched next to a flowerpot at the edge of the patio. She stooped and flipped the lizard over, exposing a shiny, black key holder.

With trembling hands, she quickly inserted the key into the lock and turned. The lock clicked, and she pulled back on the door, but the door didn't budge. "What the hell!?" She glared down at the security bar that prevented the door from opening. What was the purpose of the spare key?

Out of options, she sat at the patio table and bit her lip until she tasted blood. Maybe Brian had been right all along, and if she'd listened to him, karma wouldn't be gnawing so hard on her ass right now. But she wasn't one to back down when she truly believed she was right, and at the time, she thought exposing the wolves was the right thing to do.

She ran her fingers through her hair, removing a few pine needles in the process. If nothing else, at least she was out of those damn woods! It wasn't much of a bonus, though, and once Brian came home, he would most definitely have something sarcastic to say about her situation. She groaned and grabbed a seat cushion to shield her body when the neighbor's backdoor opened and a series of snorting grunts trailed the fence row.

"Hurry up, Bones," Mr. Tully grumbled at the little pug who was now barking in her direction. Jesse sunk lower in the chair as the old man walked to the back corner of the yard. Doing her best to ignore the yappy canine, a slow smile spread across her face and she peeked over the back of the chair. She lived in a neighborhood that was mostly comprised of elderly people, and where there were elderly people there were always clotheslines.

Her knee bounced as Mr. Tully called Bones back into the house before closing the door. Tossing the cushion to the ground, she hurried over to the fence and peered between the wooden planks. Positive she could sneak over and snatch the paisley tablecloth off the clothesline—she skirted the yard and slipped through the gate in a matter of seconds.

The sun was all but a memory as she cautiously moved along the fence, and around to Mr. Tully's yard. A nervous chuckle escaped her, knowing the longer she stood there, the darker the shadows grew. Ignoring a slight quiver that threatened her sanity, she grabbed the tablecloth off the line and wrapped it around her body. Draped in autumn colors from her armpits to ankles, she ran back to the gate and peeked up at the house before darting across the yard.

Grateful to finally be on her way home, Jesse reached to unlatch the front gate but paused when headlights turned into the drive. *Just my frickin' luck!* She cringed when two doors slammed, followed by high-pitched laughter. She silently continued watching through a crack in the fence as Brian handed Annie the house key.

"I'll get your bags," he said and walked around to the passenger side of the Jeep.

Jesse gnawed her lip, nervously. How long could it take to pull a few bags out of a vehicle? She glanced over her shoulder when the kitchen light came on, and a deep rumble settled in her chest. Watching Annie remove the security bar and then open the door, her jaw clenched. Of all the things that could have happened at that moment, it had to be the prissy blonde walking out onto the patio! It was bad enough to think Brian might catch her there, but Annie catching her would be twice as traumatic.

"I'm out here," Annie yelled as she turned toward the open door.

Jesse stooped behind a small, prickly bush and pulled her hair over her shoulders in an attempt to hide her face. What the heck were they doing outside, anyway? She frowned when Brian walked out the door and pulled Annie into his arms, groping her in the process.

You lying dog!

For months, he'd been telling her he didn't want a serious relationship with Annie, yet what she saw him doing now looked pretty damn serious to her.

"Wow, you really missed me." Annie giggled, tugging down her dress.

Jesse closed her eyes to avoid witnessing their impromptu make-out session, but from the way Brian kept grabbing Annie, he was just getting started.

"You get a fire going and I'll mix us a drink," Annie said, and Jesse's eyes sprang open. Annie's sweater dress had fully captured Brian's attention as she danced her way across the patio. "What are you waiting for?" She seductively smiled, and within seconds he was chasing her back into the house.

What a tool!

Taking advantage of Brian's distraction, Jesse bolted out the gate, fleeing the imminent smooch-fest that would surely take place as soon as they returned. Focused only on getting home, she dashed across the street to the back of the house.

All she wanted was to go to her room and hide away from the world, but apparently, the universe had other plans. Stealing a glance in the kitchen window as the headlights lit up the backyard, she was happy to see Gramma at the kitchen table talking on the phone. She never understood why her grandmother insisted on keeping the landline, when cell phones were more convenient, but now she was glad she did. The pocket phones, as Gramma called them, were more technical than she preferred, and internet service was non-existent until Jesse and her dad moved in.

"Jesse!" Megan yelled from Jack's driveway, but Jesse pretended not to hear. She only had a few minutes if she planned to get inside the house before her grandmother hung up the phone, and she wasn't about to waste them. So snubbing her best friend, she raced back around the house, hoping Megan wouldn't follow.

Standing on the front porch, she cracked open the door to listen, before tiptoeing across the foyer. "It's just me," Jesse yelled and rushed up the two flights of stairs

Pausing just inside the bedroom door, she slumped against the wall, and glanced around the dimly lit room. Noticing the jeans and sweater laying on the floor, she pushed off the wall and picked up the sweater, placing it on the window bench—her mind instantly tracing back the time. She remembered changing into something cooler, but for the life of her, she couldn't remember what. "I must have amnesia." The soft whisper sounded plausible to her mind. What else could it be? She rolled her eyes. It still didn't explain why she woke up in the woods naked.

Jesse dropped the tablecloth and stumbled into the bathroom and flipped on the light to start a tub of water. Adding a coconut bath bomb, she then turned to the sink to stare at her tear-stained reflection. *What a mess!* With her hairbrush in hand, inch by inch, she worked the twigs and pine needles from her *mane?* She scowled at the mirror. Frustrated that she couldn't remember the events leading up to her waking in the woods, she stepped into the tub and immersed her body into the heated water. Resting her head on an inflatable pillow, she closed her eyes, allowing the soothing coconut scent to carry her away to a peaceful paradise where tension and anxiety didn't exist.

Once the water cooled, Jesse got out of the tub and walked over to the mirror hanging on the bathroom door. She reached for a towel while studying her curves. Her skin was smooth, her body firm, but something was very different. Pinching her thigh, her belly, even her... she looked up and blushed. Her eyes seemed brighter, sparkling beneath the incandescent light. She lifted her hand. The itch was gone, but the small bruise remained. It was odd nonetheless, but as with everything lately, she had no words to explain it.

Slipping into a pair of flannel sleep pants and a long sleeved t-shirt, she deftly twisted her hair up in the damp towel and walked into the bedroom. She was mentally exhausted from the day's events, so she crawled into bed and pulled the blanket up to her chin before fatigue took over and she drifted off to sleep.

Her dream state kept her on her toes as she raced through the woods in the predawn light. *Standing alone on Hunter's Ridge, she stared up at the early morning sky—a serene calm embracing her. She licked her paw and then rolled over and wiggled her rump in the gritty dirt, shifting slightly to the left to relieve an itch. It was familiar territory, yet something ominous, and much darker, settled there. Her ears perked up when a shot rang out.*

Jesse's eyes snapped open, and she stared up at the

ceiling until her body stopped trembling. Slowly, she scanned the darkest corners of the room, but couldn't shake the feeling she wasn't alone. She clamped her jaws shut to keep her teeth from chattering. The dream seemed real enough, and she wiped the sweat from her forehead as troublesome thoughts entered her mind.

You were a wolf.

Three

Megan

Megan hurried into the cabin, a bit dismayed when Jesse brushed her off. Jesse had been acting rather peculiar lately, and she had no idea why. It wasn't like her to not answer her phone, but Megan had already called her twice and both calls went straight to voice mail. Hanging her purse on the coat rack next to the front door, her fingers trailed over Jack's favorite recliner as she walked to the kitchen.

The small one bedroom cabin was cozy, but once she and Jack officially sealed their bond, they would live in a newly built cabin that overlooked the Green River. Excitement fluttered in her belly when she thought about the title their bonding would bring—being mated with an alpha. It was surreal and exciting, and her heart somersaulted as her thoughts drifted.

Staring across the river, she closed her eyes and tilted her face to the sun. So warm and peaceful. But hearing a disturbance, her eyes flew open, and she jumped up off the bench as a flash of fur shot past, followed by two others.

"That will be enough!" She didn't mean to raise her voice, but honestly, they were supposed to be working. Still, it wasn't smart to interfere when male wolves had a tussle, but she instantly recognized the black wolf, and he knew better.

"Jason!" she snapped, stunned that Jack would be sucked into such childish behavior. With her arms crossed over her chest, she tapped her toe and waited until the three wolves turned and sauntered over to where she was standing behind the bench.

As she stared down the black wolf, he lowered his head, and if she weren't mistaken, he was laughing. Her eyes narrowed, and he looked away. He was most definitely laughing.

The gray wolf? Well, he just stared. He wasn't giving an inch. This was a wolf she'd never seen before, and clearly, he wasn't accustomed to any female scolding him. Megan rested her hand on her hip and tapped her toe harder until even he looked away.

A sneeze from the third wolf eased the tension, and she cracked a grin. The deep auburn brown fur could belong to none other than Tucker, and even when clad in fur, he had a way of making her smile. He sat stiff and tall, but unlike the others, he never looked away. Instead, his tongue lolled to the side, and for a minute there, she thought he rolled his eyes. He was hilarious.

"Would someone care to explain your behavior?"

The three wolves leaned in as if whispering before sitting back on their haunches. Megan met each of their eyes—beautiful blue, hazel, and warm brown. She suspected they were up to something, but before she could throw out a warning, they phased.

Holy macaroni! Her cheeks blushed with the heat of a thousand suns, and she slapped her hand over her eyes and turned away. "That is not funny!" Her jaws ached from grinning. Just because she was part wolf, didn't mean she was comfortable seeing the males in all their naked glory. Heck, she didn't like seeing herself naked, even in the privacy of her own bathroom. "You'll get used to it," Jack often said. She huffed out a breath that lifted the curls off her face. Hearing chuckles and movement behind her, she assumed they were getting dressed.

"We're decent now," Jack said, and she turned, aiming her glare directly at him. Side-glancing the other two, her blush deepened.

"I take it you've never met Alpha Cooper's wolf." Tucker said with a laugh.

Megan smiled as the memory faded. So many things had changed in a short amount of time. And if it weren't for Travis attacking her, jarring her memory, she would still be meandering through life as if something were missing.

She continued over to the refrigerator.

"Is anyone home?" A familiar voice called out from the front door, and Megan raced back into the living room and slid to a stop. "What's wrong?" Tucker seemed concerned and reached out to steady her when she teetered back on her heels.

"When did you get back in town?" That was the only

thing she could think to say since her mind was still reeling from the sudden shock of seeing him.

"Two minutes ago." He smiled and pushed his fingers through his hair.

"You nearly gave me a heart attack!" Megan placed her hand over her heart to emphasize her words. "You look so different without the dreads, but I love it." She motioned him into the kitchen. "I bet you drive the girls wild with all those curls."

Reaching for the loaf of bread on top of the refrigerator—her five-foot height didn't stretch that tall. She stuck out her tongue when Tucker smirked before handing her the inaccessible loaf.

"I figured Jack would be here."

Megan placed the bread on the table, not expecting the change of subject. "I'm on a food run. He's helping our newest member get settled into Tracy's old cabin." She moved over to the sink to wash her hands while glancing over her shoulder.

"And they wouldn't let you help?" Tucker lifted a brow, and she couldn't tell if he were seriously asking that question.

"I'm the designated sandwich maker since no one's had supper." She grabbed the dish towel hanging on the oven door and glanced up at the stove clock. It was seven-thirty P.M. but her stomach didn't care about the time.

"Do you need help? I'm pretty handy in the kitchen," he said when she placed several packages of lunchmeat on the table.

"Sure. It's nothing fancy." Her smile faded. Something about Tucker confused her. He was fidgeting, *nervous,* she thought, and not his normal easygoing self.

"You know, a candle and flowers could make it fancy." He walked over to the sink to wash his hands.

"Oh, really? Do you dine the ladies by candlelight often?" She sucked in her jaws to keep the impish grin off her face.

"Nah..." He reached for the dish towel, avoiding eye contact.

Megan tilted her head, studying his movements. Not up for chit-chat, she assumed, but whether he liked it or not, she would have him talking. She pulled open the fridge and grabbed a jar of mayo and a plate of tomato slices, which she placed on the table. "So... you're a mountain wolf from Tennessee..." She grabbed a tray off the shelf behind her and placed it on the table.

"Yeah, but I was born across the river in Kinsley. My father is from Tennessee." He looked up, and she nodded, prompting him to continue. "He's the alpha of the Smoky Mountain Pack and he met my mother while visiting the caves here in Kentucky."

"So you're from Tennessee, but born in Kinsley. I'm sure there's a story there somewhere." Spreading mayo on a slice of bread, she looked up at his frown.

"My parents were visiting my uncle before he became the alpha. I was unexpectedly early." He picked up a package of lunchmeat and chuckled when Megan placed her hands on her hips and stared at his hulking frame.

"A preemie? Why do I find that hard to believe?" She grinned when he shrugged and placed two slices of turkey on a piece of bread. She knew something was there, on the tip of his tongue, but he clammed up. Not wanting to intrude on his thoughts, a comfortable silence fell between them and within minutes, they had a nice assortment of sandwiches stacked neatly on the tray. Finally, unable to hold her tongue any longer, she blurted out, "Don't you even want to know who's moving into the cabin? From what someone told me, at one time, she was sweet on you." Megan grinned and opened the napkins, placing a stack on the edge of the tray.

Tucker leaned against the counter and crossed his arms over his chest. "Let me guess. Gina finally weaseled her way across the river."

"So it's true? Do you like her?" The thought of playing Cupid made Megan giddy. "She's cute. A little coy, but she seems nice enough."

"I liked her better when she lived across the river." His bluntness threw her off her game but when his brow creased and he turned to look out the window, what came next stunned the daylights out of her. "Have you talked to Jesse lately?"

Her brows shot up and she looked past Tucker, out the window, expecting to see Jesse in the backyard. "I saw her but didn't actually talk to her."

He glanced over his shoulder, disappointment evident on his face.

"You like her, don't you?" Megan asked, opening the can of worms she'd been dying to dig into since the town council meeting. Things had changed, and Jesse refused to answer any of her questions. Like, who really sent her the flowers? Why did she and Brian split? Or what happened between her and Tucker the day he left Cloverly? "I noticed a few subtle glances between the two of you, but I didn't say anything because... well, I..." She fumbled for words.

"Because Brian was your friend, and they were

dating."

"It's stupid, I know, but I thought they were happy." Her face flushed. She honestly thought Jesse and Brian made a great couple, and it wasn't until after the dance when she realized there was trouble in paradise. "They're not dating now," she said, and his hands fisted.

"When did they split?" He stifled a growl, the air between them growing uncomfortable.

"Well, you saw what happened at the dance. That pretty much sealed the deal. I think. They just couldn't seem to connect after that." A sinking feeling settled in her stomach when he turned back to the window—his expression troubling. "What was that?" she asked, not hearing the words he whispered. But when Tucker turned to face her, she knew whatever it was, it wasn't good.

"I had a bond with Jesse," he said, and her hand shot up to her mouth. "I never mentioned it because I wasn't sure of the relationship she had with Brian. It was hard to watch them together, and if he'd been a wolf, I'd have taken his ass out." His jaw ticked as he turned and tossed the empty meat wrappers in the trashcan. "I know he's a good friend of yours, but he treated her like she was his property."

"Wow. That was not what I was expecting." Megan stared across the room. Brian was one of her best friends, and as much as she didn't want to believe what Tucker was saying, she knew it was the truth.

"Of course it wasn't. No one saw Brian for what he was. A fireman, way bigger than life, and hometown boy that had everyone fooled. He was a jerk!" Tucker's anger spiked, and Megan took a step back. "I knew it, and I should have confronted Jesse at the dance. I wanted to steal her away." With the shake of his head, it was obvious he was fighting an internal battle. "The bond between us was strong. She deserved much better than Brian." He rubbed his hand over his face. "The next time I saw her, she was at the town council meeting and terrified of us. Wolves, I mean."

"Despite what you think, it's not too late. You can tell her now." She tried to sound upbeat and hopeful but judging by the way he hung his head, he had already given up.

"I know you're trying to be optimistic, but anything that could have been is over, and it's all on me."

"Whatever," Megan said not understanding. "I saw the hurt in her eyes when you walked out of the council meeting. Had I told her that morning what I was, she would have never tried to expose us. So I guess that makes it my fault, not yours. But putting all that aside, she realized that day you were a wolf, and later that night, her dad explained everything to her and her grandmother. They're okay with us. She's not so shallow she'd look down on you because of what you are."

He squeezed his eyes shut and turned back to the window. "I denied the bond that day. It's over."

"Oh, no!" Tears welled in her eyes. "Do you have to have a bond? I mean we all saw how Tracy chased after Jack."

"No, but my wolf would never recognize her as its mate without one. You should know that."

"But you control the wolf," she reminded him as she walked around the table to join him at the sink.

"You know as well as I, at some point even the wolf has to be mollified."

"Maybe, but you should tell her how you feel. We don't know what causes a bond to form, and who's saying it can't reform?" Megan bounced her brows, hoping he would crack a smile. "You know there will be a Halloween dance at the park. She'll be there. It would be the perfect place to bump into her... accidentally."

"That was my intention when I came back to Cloverly, but now that I'm here, I don't think so. What we could've had is gone, and it's time I moved on."

"So just like that, you're giving up? Wow, I definitely had you pegged wrong." Megan paused at the scowl on his face. *Too bad.* If he didn't like what she had to say, he could go back to the mountains. "Jesse has a picture of a wolf hanging on her wall." She turned and leaned against the counter, an impish grin on her face.

"So? A lot of people have pictures of wolves on their walls." Tucker turned, but Megan caught hold of his arm.

"It's you. She has a picture of *your wolf* hanging on her corkboard. That has to mean something." She smiled as he pushed away from the counter and walked over and stood in the doorway. He was mulling over the idea, and clearly not ready to actually move on.

"No way could she have a picture of my wolf... it can't be me. There's no possible way it could be me."

"Oh, it's you. I know what your wolf looks like even if the picture is black and white. I don't know how she got it, and I didn't ask, but I assume she knows it's you, considering it's hanging with the ribbons..." Her words trailed off, and she shot a glance over her shoulder before facing Tucker again. "Wow, suddenly everything makes sense!"

"Good, maybe you could shed some light for those of

us who don't reside in your head."

She snarled at his snarky comment. "It was you! You're the one that sent the flowers. That's why she wrote below the picture 'Never deny that which is in your heart for it too shall walk away.' She knew the flowers were from you."

"Well, Sherlock, even if I believed it was me in that picture, it's still too late. I gave up without a fight and now I have to live with my decision."

"First off, it's not too late if you don't want it to be," Megan scolded. "Second, the worst that can happen is you end up right where you are now. And third, don't think about it. Just get your costume ready. I expect you'll be at the party, and I'll tell Jesse the truth about why you left town if you don't show up." She grinned wickedly causing him to frown. "You really don't want me to tell my version of the truth."

"There's nothing to tell." He narrowed his eyes, and she laughed at his attempt to intimidate her.

"Obviously, you've never been the target of my imagination." Megan shoved her hand into her pocket, fishing for the vibrating phone. "It's probably Jack," she said and answered without looking at the screen. "Slow down, I can't understand you." She glanced out the window. "I'm on my way." Ending the call, she looked up at the apprehension in Tucker's eyes; he knew.

"Jesse?" His nonchalant attitude seemed out of place, and she shoved the phone back into her pocket.

"Yeah, I need to go over there so if you're done pretending to be an ass, would you deliver the food across the street?" Megan didn't usually lose her cool, but he was seriously starting to tick her off.

"Whatever. It doesn't matter to me one way or the other." Tucker reluctantly picked up the tray and glared her way. "I'm not trying to be an ass. I'm just tired of being the nice guy."

Her jaw dropped as he walked out of the room.

Four

Megan

Megan waited until Tucker was across the street before heading out the back door. The last thing she needed was for him to find out Jesse was upset because Brian and Annie had gotten back together. Walking across the yard, she glanced up at the attic window. She understood why Tucker denied the bond with Jesse, thinking he was protecting her, but that only made her feel worse for not telling Jesse the truth about the pack. Had she, maybe Tucker and Jesse would have sealed their bond and been happy, instead of being miserably alone.

She thought about her bond with Jack as she stepped up onto the porch. Everything she wanted out of life revolved around their bond, and she couldn't imagine what it would be like if Jack had denied her. She exhaled a slow breath as she reached for the doorknob.

The old, two-story farmhouse was familiar to her, its occupants, an extension of her Cloverly family. Saying a quick hello to Gramma when she walked in the back door, she hurried out of the kitchen, and up to the attic, tapping lightly on the open bedroom door.

Balled-up beneath a pink, fleecy blanket, Jesse's hair splayed across the pillow, barely visible in the dimly lit room. Tiptoeing across the carpet, following a hiccupping breath, Megan eased down on the edge of the bed. "I got here as fast as I could. What's wrong?" she asked when Jesse rolled over and poked her head out from beneath the blanket. Her face was red and splotchy, and her eyes were swollen from tears.

"I think I'm going crazy." Jesse wiped her eyes with her sleeve. "I had a dream that I was a wolf, and it freaked me out."

"Oh, Jesse, I'm sorry. I know you've been worried about the whole town council thing, but everyone understands why you exposed the pack. If I were you, I would have done the same. Please stop being so hard on yourself." Megan leaned in and kissed her on the forehead. "I don't like seeing you this way. It makes me sad."

"It's not that." Jesse hiccupped as another tear slid down the side of her face. "So many things have changed since then, and I don't understand what's going on with me. I don't remember how I got into the woods," she whispered the last part, causing Megan to scowl.

"What are you talking about? Jesse, I can't help you if you don't tell me what's going on. Does this have anything to do with Brian?" Megan crisscrossed her legs and sat up at the end of the bed.

"He wishes I'd cry over him." Jesse sniffled and sat up across from Megan. "I think he was at Annie's last night." She cast a glance toward the front window.

"Then what happened?"

Jesse's face twisted with a change of emotions. Fear. Disgust. Humiliation. She reached over and turned on the bedside lamp. "I don't know. That's the problem." She hiccupped again. Apparently, she didn't miss the skeptical look Megan gave her and quickly continued. "I woke up in the woods this afternoon, with pine needles in my hair. I don't know how I got there, and I don't know what happened to my clothes."

Megan startled when Jesse jumped off the bed to pace the room. It was clear she was telling the truth, but none of it made sense. If it had been a full moon night, she may have suggested Jesse phased, but that was two weeks ago, and Jesse wasn't a wolf. "There has to be a logical explanation. Just come back over here and sit down. You're making me nervous."

"I can't help it. I'm so ashamed." Jesse took a seat on the edge of the bed, wringing her hands. "What if I did something... you know? What if I was with someone?" She side glanced at Megan before swiftly looking away.

"Surely if you were with someone, you would've remembered." Megan placed her hand on Jesse's and lightly squeezed. "Were you at a party? Maybe someone drugged you." It was the only thing Megan could think of off the top of her head. "You read about these things all the time." She pursed her lips, knowing that probably wasn't the case.

"Yeah, in big cities but this is Cloverly! Plus, I was sick. I had a fever and went to bed after Brian left."

"I thought you said he was with Annie last night."
Again, nothing made sense, and it was hard for Megan to
keep the scowl off her face. Jesse was acting weird, or
weirder than normal, and she was determined to find out
why.

"Please. You know Brian better than I do. He was
making his rounds." Jesse rolled her eyes. "But this isn't
about him. He's been relegated to the past."

"Good. I was hoping you weren't having a change of
heart." Megan shot a glare at the front window.

"I'm not jealous of Annie if that's what you're
thinking. As a matter of fact, she's with him right now.
They're probably three sheets to the wind and a tangled
mess of limbs." Jesse stood and started pacing again.

"How do you know that? I'm supposed to be the one
that gets all the gossip."

"That's what I'm trying to tell you," Jesse huffed,
annoyed. "I woke up in the woods, naked. I ran home and
waited behind that old maple tree, just inside the tree line.
When I heard Brian leaving, I got this brilliant idea to go
to his house and borrow clothes. But owing to my usual
luck, I couldn't get the door opened and ended up sitting
on his patio until the sun went down."

"Naked?"

"I wasn't totally naked. I had a chair cushion." Jesse
glowered and swatted Megan's leg as she paced past her.
"Old Man Tully came outside and Bones started barking."
She turned and snarled. "Am I amusing you?"

"Sorry. Continue." Megan rolled her lips but couldn't
hide her smile.

"Anyway, I ended up swiping a tablecloth off Tully's
clothesline, and when I cut back across Brian's yard, they

pulled into the drive. Thankfully though, they were too consumed with each other to notice me there. But you can bet your ass as soon as they went inside, I got the hell outta Dodge. I wasn't about to make it a threesome."

Megan couldn't contain her giggle as she fell back on the bed and covered her eyes. "I did not need that visual."

"Keep it up and I'm not going to tell you anything else." Jesse smirked when Megan sucked in her lower lip and sat up on the bed. "I woke early this morning. It was hot, so I went outside and stood on the back porch. After that, things get sketchy." Jesse glared when Megan cleared her throat of one last snicker.

"Honestly, it sounds like you were sleepwalking. You did say you hadn't been sleeping well." Still there was something about Jesse's demeanor that Megan couldn't decipher. "Maybe it's catching up with you."

"Maybe, but that doesn't explain what happened to my clothes."

"Sleepwalkers have been known to drive cars, so getting undressed is a valid possibility."

"And there's the silver lining. Great!" Jesse palmed her forehead.

"Well, it's better than thinking something bad happened." Megan pulled Jesse down on the bed. "Plus, I don't think sleepwalkers sleepwalk every night."

"Maybe not, but if Dad finds out, he'll kill me." Jesse glanced toward the bedroom door. "I'll be grounded for life."

"He's a doctor. I'm sure he's dealt with sleepwalkers before."

"Yeah, but I'm *his* sleepwalker." Jesse groused and wiped her nose.

"Until you move out..." Megan smiled knowingly and Jesse grinned, excitement flashing in her eyes. "So when's the big day?"

"My birthday of course. A celebration of sorts."

"So your first night in the apartment will be Halloween? That's spooky."

"It's my eighteenth birthday present to me. It seems fitting, don't you think?"

"Speaking of Halloween, have you decided what you're wearing to the party?" Megan didn't want to distract her from the issue at hand, but talking about Jesse's birthday and the apartment seemed to calm her. "I'll tell you, if you tell me."

"It's here in the closet." Jesse walked across the room and Megan took that opportunity to inch closer to the corkboard. Glancing up at the picture of Tucker's wolf, it was clear there was a connection between them, based only on the memorabilia.

"Can I see? I promise I won't tell a soul." Megan made a crisscross over her heart.

"You can have a peek but you better not breathe a word to anyone. If Lori finds out I showed you and not her, she'll be pissy," Jesse said, but before she could get the dress off the hanger, Megan was bouncing on her toes.

"That looks dangerous. Did you make it?" Megan asked, trailing her fingers over the thin material.

"No. It's a vintage nightgown I bought online." Jesse held out the full-sweep skirt and said, "I love the way silky nylon flows, and I added leather and sequins to the bodice so it would stand out. And also hide the fact I won't be wearing a bra."

"It's not sequins that will make it stand out." Megan

directed her eyes down to Jesse's chest and then back up. "Some of us need sequins, some of us don't. Do you have any leftovers?" She lifted her chest and looked down. "Do fairies have big boobs?"

"You're asking the wrong person. That's a question better suited for Lori."

"Yeah, I guess." Megan grabbed the tablecloth off the floor, trying to imagine Jesse wrapped in the festive material. She giggled softly and laid it over the end of the bed while Jesse returned the costume to the closet. "So, are you supposed to be a sexy witch?"

"Not hardly." Jesse walked out of the closet, and Megan's eyes widened.

"Okay, that is a little on the creepy side." Megan shivered. "What the heck is it?" The black mask Jesse wore was perfect for Halloween, but Megan wasn't sure she wanted to touch it. "Exactly what are you supposed to be?"

"Let's just say my costume matches my mood."

"Boo. I told you what my costume was." Megan pouted as Jesse pulled off the mask and grinned.

"No, you asked me if fairies had big boobs. I, on the other hand, showed you half of my costume. If you can't figure it out, that's your problem." Jesse sashayed across the room, the grin on her face suggestive of the secret she kept.

"Fine," Megan huffed. "But I've got a little surprise of my own, and you will have to wait until the party to find out what it is." She returned the grin.

"You had better not scare me. It will be freaky enough being alone in an apartment, over an empty warehouse. I would hate to be that person who puts a crimp on your love life, so soon after your bonding ceremony. But if you trick me, you might as well get ready to kiss lover boy goodbye because you *will* be spending the night," Jesse warned.

"Oh, I wouldn't call it a trick, more like a treat." Megan cackled wickedly and Jesse glared.

Five

Megan

When a special pack meeting was called on a full moon night, it usually resulted in a bonding ceremony. A time when all the wolves gathered under the full moon as the lucky couple stood before the pack and accepted their bond mates. It wasn't necessary, but having a ceremony allowed the bonded pair to run with the pack, uniting them as a family.

With the help of Jack's mother, Megan finished dressing and waited inside the front door as the pack gathered in the front yard of the alpha house. "You look just like your mom," Reva said as she tied the silk ribbon at Megan's back.

Jesse and Lori—unable to attend the ceremony—designed the dress she wore. The ivory gown hung down to her ankles with a satin white ribbon tied at the waist.

Tiny orange and burgundy flowers decorated the bodice, trailing down one side, like leaves falling from a tree. At Lori's insistence, she wore burgundy lace beneath the dress and white heels that did little to add to her height, standing next to Jack who stood a foot taller.

"Thank you," Megan blushed as a tear rolled down her cheek. She was nervous but eager to have the bond she shared with Jack sealed by the alpha, especially after being raised outside the pack. She peeked out the door and Tracy winked. It wouldn't be long before she and Randy would follow in their footsteps and she could hardly wait.

Catching sight of her parents, she gave a pageant wave, elated they were there. Normally, humans didn't attend bonding ceremonies unless that person was the mate of a wolf. But because her adopted parents made a promise to her birth parents, and kept her safe, the elders made them honorary members and they gladly accepted.

"It's time. Are you ready?" Reva opened the door as Megan inhaled a calming breath.

"Settle down, everyone," Alpha Cooper said, standing before the crowd.

Jack and Tucker ran up on the porch, taking their place to the right of the alpha. Dressed in black slacks and white, button-down shirts—their sleeves rolled up to their elbows—they were both a bit dressier than the others but that was to be expected.

Alpha Cooper lifted his hand, and waited for the chatter to die down. "Thank you all for joining us here tonight," he said, gaining control of the crowd. "Before we get things underway, I'd like to announce that Jack has completed his training and is now the official alpha of the Cloverly Pack." Handing Jack the key to the newly built alpha house, his father congratulated him with a hug.

"Thank you," Jack said, flashing his newly inked tattoo to the well-wishers in the pack.

"Also," Ben added, "Tucker will train for the alpha position in Berkley. Anyone interested in joining his pack will have thirty days to contact the elders for placement." Tucker nodded, ignoring the catcalls. Being an unbonded male in an alpha position made him a prime target for all the single females in the pack. And Megan expected there would be plenty to sign up before the moon set.

As the group silenced once again, Alpha Cooper walked over and met Megan at the door. "For those of you who don't know Megan Smith, she has been a member of our pack since the day she was born, and I'm proud to announce that she and Jack share a bond."

Intense heat rose up her neck as Alpha Cooper walked her across the deck. Blocking out the crowd, she focused on Jack, her best friend since childhood and the only man she had ever loved. With her memories restored, she cherished every moment of their past and was ready to make new memories for future reflections. Jack grinned as tears welled in her eyes. Now standing beside him, he took her hand, and they turned toward the alpha.

"Do you, Jackson Cooper, accept Megan as your bond mate, uniting the two of you until your time on this earth is over?"

Jack turned toward Megan and she squeezed his hand. He winked. "I accept Megan as my bond mate. Now and throughout eternity." She melted beneath his gaze.

"And do you, Megan Smith, accept Jack as your bond mate, uniting the two of you until your time on this earth is over?"

Averting her eyes from the smile on Jack's face, lest she forget her words, she stared deeply into his eyes. "I accept Jack as my bond mate. Now and throughout eternity." Her face flushed when he flicked his brows.

Ben nodded his approval before turning toward the pack. "As the alpha of the Green River Region, let it be known, Jack and Megan Cooper have duly sealed their bond. May their union be blessed and may they bring new life to our pack."

Megan practically swooned when Jack pulled her into his arms. Lost in the moment, her breath caught when he drew her into a passionate kiss. Her heart strummed with his nearness, the kiss weakening her knees. It was soft, gentle, and when he nipped her lower lip, a low growl rumbled in her chest as heat spread through her body. He was the fire in her soul, and everything right in her world. She wrapped her arms around his neck, enjoying the feel of his body as whistles and cheers filled the air. "I love you," she whispered against his lips.

"Love you too," he whispered back before drawing her into another toe-curling kiss. Alpha Cooper cleared his throat, and Jack looked out at the pack, a slight blush on his face. "Let's get this run started." Unbuttoning his shirt as the pack headed into the woods, he draped it over the porch rail. "We'll need our clothes to wear home."

"By all means," Megan said and a ripple of excitement sparked in her belly. Jack flashed a grin and stepped out of his pants, his blue boxers matching his eyes. "No need to stop there." She blushed at her boldness, but had no intentions of backing down. Their time had come, and she wanted it to be a night he would never forget. She returned his wink as she reached back and untied the ribbon at her waist. With her gaze locked on his, she allowed the dress to slip off her shoulders.

"That's it? Just a ribbon?" He stepped forward, never taking his eyes off her.

"You can thank Lori for that. She said you would like it." Megan passed the dress to Tracy, who stood with her hand out.

"Well, she was right about that." Jack's smoldering gaze dropped to the burgundy lace bra. "I like it a lot which is why you need to put the dress back on. I don't want the others to see your... damn!" His voice droned in her ear as he pulled her against his chest.

"Really? I thought you said it wasn't sexual," she reminded, dousing his fire.

"Seeing you without clothes isn't. We see that every time we phase. It's the lacy package I don't want them fantasizing about." He snaked his arms around her waist and kissed her ear.

"Sorry, I'm not stripping naked in front of everyone, so they'll just have to be content to see my lace." She pushed away and glided down the steps—flashing a smoldering glance his way.

"I think you've met your match." Tracy laughed as Jack jumped down the steps, following Megan.

The night was cool, the woods unfamiliar, but Megan stayed by Jack's side as he led her around the property. Four of the five hundred acres were nothing but forest and her wolf was delighted to be there. They ran for miles, the entire pack, coming together to celebrate her bonding with Jack. It was empowering, exciting and truly a night she would never forget. Running along the riverbank, she and Jack phased as the others continued past.

"Look, there's our cabin," Jack said and Megan stared across the river—the lights from the cabin reflecting on the water below.

"It's beautiful, but it looks so big."

"Yeah," he said almost wistfully. "It'll keep us busy." His eyes flared, and she sucked in a sharp breath.

In that brief instant, she felt bold, confident, and dare she think it? *Spontaneous.* "Tracy said whatever we do on our bonding night when the moon is at its fullest, is what we will do the most throughout the year." Her sultry gaze settled on his lips and then rose to meet his eyes.

"Is that so? Well, then, maybe we should get started and consummate our bond." His whispered breath brushed across her cheek and she nodded her consent.

It was at times like that when she had to remind herself he was real. He was there. He was her mate. Tears filled her eyes when he pulled back and lifted her chin, their future reflected in his eyes.

"You know," he said, taking a seat on the grassy riverbank and pulling her into his lap. "When I realized who you were, I was afraid to sleep for fear of waking up and discovering you were only a dream." His body quivered as he breathed in her mossy scent. "I never thought this day would come." He lifted her around until she was straddling his lap, his hands resting on her waist. "I love you so much, my heart hurts." His blue eyes, darker than usual, reflected the moon.

"You'll always be here," she said, placing her hand over her heart. "And I love you back." Fresh tears welled in her eyes as her finger traced the tattoo on his chest.

"Good, because I don't plan to ever let you go."

The heat they shared clashed with the autumn breeze,

and a blazing chill settled deep in her belly. She needed him and what he offered, more than the air she breathed. Wrapping her arms around his neck, he nuzzled her hair, before carefully reclining her back onto the grass. His earthy pine scent was soothing, and she drew in a deep breath.

Goosebumps trailed behind his fingers as his hand moved down, resting on her hip. "We don't have to do this... here." His whispered words and subsequent caresses set her body aflame with a longing so strong, she ached for more.

"I'm not the fragile little girl you once saved on Hunter's Ridge." For years, she felt alone and lost, but with Jack, her inhibition shattered and waiting was no longer an option. He was the missing link in her life for far too long, and now that they were officially bonded, she was eager to shed her innocence. "I've waited long enough."

A soft growl rumbled in his chest, sending a jolt of electricity to her core. The skin on skin contact united their souls, but it wasn't until he nipped her neck that her desire spiraled out of control. Lost in a sensual haze as her body melded with his, she arched against him.

Jack and Megan spent the rest of the night right there beneath the full moon. Tangled in each other's arms, her head rested on his chest as she traced patterns of circles over his belly. Knowing their bond was intact and nothing could ever come between them, she smiled and closed her eyes as he sang softly in her hair. It was magical, and he was everything she knew he would be. "Thank you for never giving up on me," she whispered, and he rolled her over and trailed kisses down her neck.

She fisted her hands in the overgrown grass as goosebumps traveled up her arms. Adjusting his body, he looked up and grinned when she opened her eyes. The mischievous gleam that flashed in his eyes had her biting her lip in anticipation of what he was about to do. "Don't stop," she pleaded and then squealed when he growled against her belly.

It was sunup by the time Jack and Megan walked up on the porch and quickly dressed. Side glancing as he buttoned his shirt, a deep pink tinged her cheeks with the memory of their bonding.

"You ready for the meet and greet?" he teased as he took hold of her hand, leading her into the house. "Relax; we didn't do anything different from what they did on their bonding night."

Megan grinned and looked up through her lashes.

The early morning crowd was lively as they waited for breakfast to be served. Following Jack across the room, she took a seat next to him at the alpha's table. Her belly fluttered when he ran his hand up her thigh, a promise of what would come later. Her blush deepened. How did he expect her to get through breakfast with his teasing? He removed his hand and pulled her chair closer to his.

"I'll behave. For now," he whispered, flashing a smile that brightened the entire room.

Being away from the pack for sixteen years, Megan felt awkward and out of place, but after their run, she realized the pack was where she truly belonged. She glanced around the large dining area where smiles greeted her at every turn. Some faces were unfamiliar but a lot of them she remembered. She was at peace with Jack being an alpha. And as his bonded female, life was sure to be interesting.

She loved the idea of splitting the larger pack into smaller ones, which were all connected by a Regional Alpha. After what happened to her years ago, the security of knowing something like that could never happen again eased her mind.

Smiling across the table at her extended family, she was the lucky one. They were her people, her peers, her friends, her family, and she was more than excited to see where her new life would lead.

"Aren't you hungry?" Jack asked, placing strawberries on her plate beside the eggs and bacon.

"I was just thinking," she said and picked up a strawberry.

"About?" He moved his hand back up her thigh and she gasped, causing him to chuckle.

"It's nice to be home."

Six

Jesse

"Happy Birthday to me!" Jesse sang out of tune as she pushed open the front door of her spacious one-bedroom apartment.

Megan had assisted her in moving, most of the day, and understood her uncertainty about living alone. But since the sleepwalking incident had been a one-time occurrence, Jesse chalked it up to stress.

Thrilled to be officially living on her own she sauntered across the room to the kitchenette and took a soda out of the refrigerator and popped the top.

"Moose," she called out, knowing he wasn't there. It was a habit she would eventually have to break now that he was the proud owner of a large farmhouse and Gramma was his official caretaker. Her grandmother was overjoyed when Jesse suggested leaving Moose with her.

They had become best buds, hanging out together and watching the evening news.

With plans of celebrating her new life as an independent woman, Jesse took a quick sip of her soda and then set the can back in the fridge. There was plenty of work to be done, starting with the unpacking of all her boxes, and adding her own personal touches to the apartment. But first, there was a Halloween party she anxiously wanted to attend. With no curfew, and no one waiting for her to get home, she planned to dance the night away, and afterward? Who knew?

Rushing into the bedroom, she pulled off her clothes and threw open the closet door where the dark angel costume awaited its first unveiling. Having worked on the costume since midsummer—and solving three mishaps with the wings—she was pleased with the end result. She was, in a word, frightful.

After applying dark eye makeup, Jesse carefully dressed and took a glance at her reflection in the mirror. The large black wings, rising two feet above her head, looked delicate, yet dark and dangerous. But the eeriest part of the costume was definitely the black mask which covered most of her face. Long tendrils coiled in all directions like snakes slithering around her head. After smoothing down the black gown that touched the floor, she adjusted the leather bodice. It held everything in place, pushing her cleavage to a whole new level. *Perfect,* she thought as she unclipped her hair, allowing it to hang loosely between the wings.

Jesse moved over to watch from the bedroom window as couples in coordinated costumes entered the park. Unlike them, she had no companion, and it sucked.

Lowering her eyes, she applied lotion to her hands and her thoughts slipped to Tucker. Again. *He was a wonderful dancer and if only she'd known at the time that he was the one leaving her flowers, she would have definitely reconsidered her relationship with Brian.* She tried to banish Tucker from her head. There was no need to rehash the past. Nothing good could come from it.

Closing the blind, she ambled over and checked her costume once more before shutting off the light and heading downstairs.

Her footsteps echoed off the walls as she walked across the empty warehouse, to the side door to click on an overhead light. The sixty-watt lightbulb wasn't the brightest, but certainly better than entering the building in total darkness. She peeked out the door before stepping out onto the sidewalk.

Walking in the shadows, something she would never have dared to do four months ago, she bobbed her head to the beat that drifted from the park.

The party was in full swing by the time Jesse crossed Main Street and the first thing she noticed was the basketball court had been converted into a temporary dance floor. Also greeting the ghoulish crowd was jack-o'-lanterns with candlelit faces perched atop straw bales, placed randomly around the park. Refreshments were being served from a small gazebo at the center of the park, and picnic tables were gathered to form a rest area for anyone who was not on the dance floor. It was nice; the city did a great job with the decorations, and judging by the number of partygoers, they really appreciated it.

Jesse scanned the crowd and instantly spotted Lori wearing a glitzy, purple-and-gold belly dance costume that matched Steve's Arabian knight perfectly. It was good to see Lori smiling, and she and Steve were a cute couple. But since he moved to Oklahoma to attend college on a full scholarship, they rarely saw each other anymore.

Then she noticed Brian doing what he did best— chatting up old friends. She wrinkled her nose and ducked behind a tree. Dressed as the God of Thunder, once his laughter faded, she assumed he had walked the other way. But when she stepped out from her hiding spot, surprise! There he stood.

"You look... amazing," Brian said, his eyes following the feathers out before dropping down to her chest. "Would you like to dance?" He was the last person she expected to ask her to dance, but he was also the first, so she bit the bullet and followed him to the dance floor. As a slow song played, she mentally rolled her eyes. *At least you're not sulking in the shadows*, but by the way Brian kept looking at her cleavage, that probably wasn't a bad idea.

Where were her two best friends when she needed them most? Ignoring Brian, she glanced around the dance floor. Two songs later, she abandoned any hope of escaping Thor's grasp. She smiled awkwardly because the compliments he was pitching teetered on the obnoxious side. If only she had the big hammer thingy Thor carried, she would have pounded him into the ground.

"Are you busy next weekend? I was thinking we could catch a movie, or hang out at my place, if you want," Brian asked. He was unsure and with good reason, but that didn't stop him from asking, which only proved how clueless he really was.

"You know I'm not much for movies." Her brow

lifted in unmasked suspicion.

"Which was why I threw in hanging out at my place. We could've been good together, and now that you're not chasing fairytales, maybe we could pick up where we left off."

"Where we left off was us agreeing to be friends! And I may be wrong, but your girlfriend isn't too thrilled right now." Jesse nodded towards the prissy blonde, ironically dressed as an angel.

Brian glanced over at Annie and winked, making her smile.

Jesse groaned. *Geesh, what a tool!*

"She's not my girlfriend. I told you we're not serious," he said, shooting another glance towards Annie.

"Brian, despite what you say, she thinks she's your girlfriend and although you don't think it's serious, apparently, she does. You really should consider her feelings before you ruin the relationship." When the song ended, Jesse made a quick exit, hoping Brian would get lost in the crowd. After everything they'd been through, she couldn't believe he had the audacity to ask her out.

On a frickin' date!

In her haste to escape Brian, she darted around the gazebo and ran right smack into Dracula. And if he hadn't grabbed hold of her arm, there was no doubt she would have landed on her feathers.

"Excuse me," she said, feeling like a klutz.

Dracula bowed at the waist and then offered his arm, smiling to expose his fangs. Jesse stared at the ominous creature-of-the-night, and although he never said a word, he seemed vaguely familiar. Taking him up on the offer was the least she could do, and how could she go wrong?

He kept his mouth shut and only made casual eye contact without drooling over her boobs. She smiled and placed her hand on his arm, allowing him to lead her back to the dance floor.

As the music ramped up, Jesse tried to get a closer look at Dracula's eyes, but he quickly turned away. He was avoiding her, which meant he was trying to keep his identity hidden for as long as possible. Unable to place the hottie behind the white mask—which blended with his white painted face—she grinned and spun around, her black feathers fluttering in her wake.

"Dracula, you've got some mad skills on the dance floor." She laughed, feeling totally at ease dancing with the black-caped bloodsucker.

"I ahm Count Drraculah. Ziss iz vhaat I do. Eez better zhan drrinking bluhd," he coughed to clear his throat. "Okay, that didn't come out the way I intended it to." His laughter made her giddy, but his striking, gray eyes sparkling beneath the overhead lights, made her breath hitch.

"Seth!" Jesse squealed, but before she could say another word, a hand latched onto her arm, spinning her away.

"Whoa, sister!" Lori exclaimed, her eyes taking in the enormous wings.

Jesse turned and gave Dracula her best *I'm sorry* look, and he winked.

"Excuse me; did Dracula just wink at the dark angel?" Lori pointed between the two.

"Shh!" Jesse looked back, and he winked again. "You're gonna get me in trouble."

"Honey, you can't blame me for this." Lori fanned her

hands in the air. "I'm not the one dressed to kill, which sucks, by the way. Can I be you?"

"Just one more dance," Brian cut in, ignoring Lori who stood behind him, glaring. He was definitely treading on dangerous ground, and she wasn't the one to cross.

"Sorry, but I promised this dance to another." Jesse smiled and grabbed Lori's hand, dragging her into the crowd.

"What the hell was that about?" Lori asked as she shot a dirty look over her shoulder. She was a wildcat, and had no fear of taking Brian clean out of the picture, even though he was three times her size. She was fierce when she got pissed, and once she started spewing swear words, all bets were off.

"You don't want to know," Jesse said before she asked, "Where's Steve?"

"He's around here somewhere." Lori flicked her wrist, looking unconcerned and grinned when the music started to play again. In all her glory, doing what only Lori would do, she broke into her version of the hamster dance. Jesse snorted. Lori had no qualms about being the center of attention. "What are you waiting for? Let's dance!"

"Um... that would be a no." Jesse laughed, shaking her head. "Not happening." And as she spun away, her eyes landed on a dark-haired guy standing near the gazebo. Wearing a black tuxedo, his hulking frame and the way he moved instantly reminded her of Tucker. Her heart paused for a brief second. *It's not him,* she scolded, yet willing him to turn so she could see his eyes. A slow rumble vibrated her chest when a gorgeous blonde cozied up to him, stopping him before he could look her way. Jesse averted her eyes. Even her dark angel couldn't compete with the skimpy, little barmaid costume that was intentionally designed to attract attention.

"I ditched my date to dance with you. So get to it or I'm going up on stage and singing happy birthday," Lori yelled over the music.

"You wouldn't." Jesse cringed, but she knew her best friend would hold true to the threat. She laughed as other dancers moved in and followed Lori's lead. Heck, she was in costume, after all, and it was Halloween.

Jesse doing the hamster dance while dressed as a dark angel was comical if not awkward. The weight of her wings when she hopped back caused her to stumble, and she bumped into the person behind her. She spun around, her face red-hot. "I'm so sorry," she said, meeting Randy's grin.

"Badass, birthday girl." Randy's enthusiasm lit his eyes and Jesse faked a swoon, remembering the night he gave her a ride home on his motorcycle. He was extremely good looking and a player at heart. She glanced down at his lips and he smirked as if he knew what she was thinking.

"So, what rabbit's hole did you crawl out of?" She laughed, and he winked. *Still a tease.*

"It was her idea." He nodded towards Tracy who was distracted by her wings.

"I love your costume," Tracy gushed, reaching out to touch the feathers.

"Are you kidding me?" Jesse looked between the two. Tracy, dressed in all black, was stunning. From her buckled knee boots to the tight, little mini dress and matching top hat that screamed, "Look at me!" But it was Randy who ramped up the sizzle factor. His long legs displayed a pair of red-and-black striped hatter pants. And the white shirt collar with a green bowtie, fastened around his neck, made his well-defined chest hard to miss. And for a brief moment, even she was enchanted. Her eyes drifted up to the sparkling, orange top hat that matched Tracy's hair. "Girl, you'd better keep an eye on him."

"Don't worry. I keep him on a short leash." Tracy chuckled as she wrapped her arm around his waist.

It was easy to see why Randy and Tracy were a couple because they complemented each other perfectly. Watching them dance, Jesse smiled when they laughed. Why couldn't she get that lucky? Once upon a time, she thought Brian was the real deal—but she was so wrong.

"Are you having fun yet?" Megan asked, and Jesse turned to see the little trickster grinning like she had just swallowed a canary.

"Actually, I am," Jesse replied, noticing the subtly arched brow that Megan flicked at Jack. The little gypsy was up to something, and the big, bad gangster was her new partner in crime. "Nice costume, although I expected to see you dressed as a fairy."

"I never said I was coming as a fairy. I just asked if they had big boobs. You, on the other hand, are wicked cool."

"What she said," Jack added as his eyes trailed over the wings. "I don't know if I should be impressed or terrified."

Megan laughed a little too loud, putting Jesse on edge and her scalp prickled. It was an eerie feeling of being watched and déjà vu. She scanned the crowd and whispered, "Megan, who's the guy in the tux?"

"He's the best man." Megan smiled at Jack, a silent message passing between them.

Red flags went up, and Jesse glared through squinted eyes. "Megan," she warned and took a step back. The grin on Megan's face was proof she definitely had something up her sleeve and Jesse wasn't sticking around to find out what that something might be. Bumping into Brian, in her haste to escape, she released the breath she was holding.

"Just the person I was looking for," Brian said without realizing his timing was perfect.

"I could say the same about you." Jesse took hold of his hand and pulled him deeper into the crowd. Putting distance between her and her bubbly best friend still didn't ease her mind. She hated when Lori or Megan kept secrets from her because it usually ended with her humiliation. She looked around for Lori, who was now dancing with Steve. She turned back to Brian and asked, "So why aren't you dancing with Annie?"

"She said her wings were too heavy, although they're like an eighth the size of yours." Brian looked up. "She's not too big on dancing."

"And you are?"

"Just trying to make up for past mistakes."

Awkward!

What Brian considered a mistake, Jesse considered a blessing in disguise. But afraid if she said anything it would bruise his ego, she glanced over at Megan who mouthed "Happy Birthday!" Oh yeah, she was definitely up to something if the toothy grin she eagerly displayed were any indicator.

She rolled her eyes.

It happened so fast that if Jesse hadn't been watching

Megan, she may have noticed the Best Man tapping Brian on the shoulder, ending their dance. She stared up at the golden flecks sparkling in Mr. Tuxedo's eyes, and her knees grew week. "Tucker?" she questioned breathlessly as her vision distorted. Inhaling the woodsy scent that could only belong to him, she fell into his arms as a silent sob rocked her body. "You're back."

His hold was gentle but firm and his smile strained. "It's me, Jesse," she said, unsure if he recognized her behind the mask. But after exposing his pack at the town council meeting, she wasn't stupid enough to believe he came back to Cloverly just for her.

Tucker lifted her chin and gazed into her eyes as he removed the mask from her face. Jesse wasn't sure what he saw, when he whispered, "It can't be," and she frowned. Was she that repulsive? Had he really not known it was her?

She glimpsed over at the blonde bombshell that was standing on the sideline staring daggers her way. She wanted to scream, "he's mine," but before she had a chance, Tucker turned and walked away.

Jesse stood speechless and hot tears stung her eyes. With the embarrassment of rejection smothering her, she looked up to see the barmaid chasing after him. Rushing off the dance floor, she bolted for the straw bale nearest the road as pain exploded behind her eyes. Nausea swirled her stomach, and she clamped her hand over her mouth when sweat dripped down her forehead.

"Jesse, are you all right?" Megan asked, grabbing for her hand, but Jesse pushed her away. "I'm sorry. I didn't think seeing him again..."

"Leave me alone!" Jesse rested her head on her knees,

hoping the dizziness would pass. Her cheeks burned red; she was mortified when Tucker walked away, again. *What the hell did I do this time?* It was obvious he didn't care about her, not the way she did him. The first time he walked away left a hole in her heart the size of Texas. This time, seeing him with another female, she couldn't breathe.

When she first moved to Cloverly, her world was perfect. Now, everything was spiraling out of control, and there wasn't a damn thing she could do to stop it. Her anger spiked, and at that moment, she wanted to punch something. Coincidentally or not, the barmaid was at the very top of her list.

Seven

Tucker

Tucker ripped off his mask and flung it to the ground as he stormed across the park. Cutting through the crowd so none of the others would notice him leaving, he kept his head down. *This can't be,* he thought as he stepped between two cars and crossed the street. He wasn't trying to hurt Jesse by walking away, but knowing how strongly his wolf would react, especially after denying a bond with her the first time, he feared his wolf would emerge and demand its mate.

Her dark eyes were brighter than he remembered, electrifying even, and it made his heart soar until he realized what that meant. "Sleepwalking, my ass," he whispered as he continued down the street to where his car was parked. Jesse may have fooled Megan, but Tucker wasn't that gullible. Frustration filled his thoughts as his mind reeled, going in a million different directions.

"Tucker, wait up!" Gina called out, running to catch him. He had been back in Cloverly for a few weeks and already Gina was stalking him like Tracy used to stalk Jack. She was cute, and a lot of the males liked her, but she wasn't exactly his type.

Tucker didn't want to give her a ride home because he knew she would take it the wrong way. Based on how she clung to him at the park, he agreeing to give her a ride there had been a big mistake. "Fine, but I'm in a hurry." He pulled open the driver's door.

A low rumble vibrated his chest when he drove past Jesse sitting on the straw bale, her wings folded in, shielding her from view. He swallowed hard, debating whether or not to go back. *Are you crazy?* It was a mistake to walk away from the one person that held his heart, but what he saw when he looked into her eyes scared the shit out of him. He should have stayed in Tennessee. It would have been safer there. Deep down, however, he wanted to be wherever Jesse was. "Dammit!" He slammed his hands down on the steering wheel, causing Gina to jump.

As he turned onto Cabin Run Road, Gina finally spoke, pulling him from his thoughts. "Would you like to come in for some coffee? It's still early."

Tucker frowned. "No, thanks. I've got other plans." He pulled over in front of her cabin and waited for her to get out of the car, but instead, she turned in the seat.

"Are you going back to see that witch you were dancing with?" It was an innocent enough question, but he didn't miss the hateful swipe. He was best friends with

Tracy and whether Gina knew it or not, he was well aware of what she was doing.

"Which one?" It seemed the only witch he had danced with was her.

"The female dressed in that hideous black costume. Talk about desperate! Her boobs were nearly up your nose."

Tucker looked down at the black-and-white barmaid costume Gina wore. Her chest practically bubbled over the white ruffled trim, and he expected if she moved the wrong way, all the padding might fallout as well. But the worst sight was when she bent over, which she did quite often. Her matching white thong didn't cover nearly enough skin to justify wearing it.

"The dark angel was a lot of things, but desperate wasn't one of them."

"Whatever. It's not like you haven't seen the female body before. We do phase without our clothes," Gina smartly replied.

"Yeah, that's unfortunate. I find modesty much more attractive than a bare ass." Tucker looked out the side window to hide his disgust. When he finally turned to face her again, she struggled to keep her smile in place. "I need to go," he said dismissively.

"I could change clothes and go with you. I have nothing better to do." She unfastened her seatbelt, and surprised him when, without warning, she suddenly straddled his lap. "We could make a night of it. It would do you good to relieve all that stress." He gripped her waist as she peppered kisses down his neck. "We can sneak away, and no one would know."

Wrong. His wolf would know. He originally planned

to stay home and skip the party entirely, but since Hayden went to all the trouble of bringing him the tuxedo, against his better judgment, he went. His plans were only to move on with his life and find another mate, and until then, maybe a female to hang out with. Gina had been coming onto him for the past two weeks, but was he *that* desperate? However, after seeing Jesse again, his wolf was even more determined to keep Gina at bay.

"I can smell your desire," she cooed, continuing the slow, torturous grinding of her hips. His body responded in a big way but not for the reason she believed. "I can make you forget all about the witch." Okay, maybe she did know.

"That's not necessary." He grabbed her arms and lifted her off his lap before placing her unceremoniously back in her seat. "I don't need anything from you," he said, waiting for her to open the door. The wily she-wolf was annoyingly persistent and more than eager to overstep her bounds. She spun in the seat. He made a mental note to remember to use bleach wipes before anyone else sat there. He could see the anger in Gina's eyes when she finally got out of the car, but his wolf was in no mood to play the game Tracy had managed to perfect. Tucker wasn't as nice as Jack when it came to pushy females, and Gina was ten times worse than Tracy.

"Your loss," Gina sneered and slammed the car door, providing more proof why he shouldn't get involved with her. She bounded up the sidewalk, her short skirt exposing more flesh than he cared to see. And when she stepped up on the porch, she snubbed her nose.

Tucker pulled away from the curb, more than glad to be rid of Gina. He turned into the drive and got out of the car, his mind wandering back to the first day he saw Jesse. *Standing with her hands pressed against the window of the flower shop. She was breathtaking. The way her long hair, lifted by the breeze, reached out to him.* She was a human, he a wolf, and although they shared a bond, she had no clue about him or the pack until Travis attacked her. How could he expect her to be with him if she basically feared him? He couldn't. That was why he denied the bond and walked away.

The thought of whiskey crossed his mind, but he wasn't a drinker and Cloverly was a dry county. Based on previous limited experience, he concluded the hype wasn't worth the headache that followed the next morning. He pushed open the door and walked into the cabin, not bothering to turn on the lights.

The small cabin was comfortable but nothing compared to his family's cabin in Tennessee. There it was lively with the chatter of his siblings, another reminder of the loneliness that gripped his heart. Changing clothes, he looked out the bedroom window and pictured Jesse there. Her dark angel was so beautiful, silently speaking to his heart. He combed his fingers through his hair and exhaled loudly, turning from the window. The memory of how she felt as he held her close was enough to stir the wolf within. *Sorry, buddy, she's off limits.* He denied their bond two months ago and shouldn't have felt anything towards her, but the pull was stronger now, even more so than he remembered—nearly knocking him on his ass.

Lying back on the bed, he counted the ceiling boards, trying to shake the unease that filled his heart. Jesse's eyes were bright and happy—then muddled and almost unseeing—but when the haze lifted, he panicked, staring into the eyes of her wolf. It was wishful thinking on his part, but deep down he hoped it was real. *Travis could have changed her,* he reasoned, but surely Jack would have known. He closed his eyes and rolled over onto his side, taking his frustration out on the pillow. His head hurt from all the scenarios bombarding his brain, but eventually, he drifted into a troubled sleep.

Tucker wasn't there the night Travis attacked Jesse, but for some reason, her memory played in his dreams. His eyes shot open and his teeth gnashed as his wolf rumbled deep inside his chest. "It was just a dream," he told himself, but he couldn't deny how terrified Jesse was, and Travis was practically lapping up her fear. He got out of bed, his rage building.

Stomping through the cabin, he yanked open the backdoor, his wolf simmering just beneath the surface. He needed to let his wolf run off steam, but first, he had to gain full control. He sucked in a deep breath to keep his wolf at bay as he stepped out of his jeans. The night air was much warmer, carrying the smell of murky water up from the river. He took another deep breath to clear his head of the horrid visions his eyes refused to un-see. Anger consumed him, like poison to his soul, and his wolf bristled—threatening the wolf that no longer existed.

He phased.

Not wasting any time, Tucker cut across the ditch and raced to his favorite spot ten miles away. It was a nice plot of land, three hundred acres or more, and surrounded by rivers on three sides. The old, two-story cabin that was nestled back in the trees was somewhat rundown, but he often imagined it as a nice place to fix up and raise a family. When he arrived at the abandoned cabin, he phased in the trees and walked over to the weathered, wooden porch. He sat down as a barge pushed its tow upriver, and although the run did calm his wolf, if Travis had not been killed by Jack, he would have gladly done the deed.

He studied the area.

A faded for sale sign that was nothing more than a piece of plywood with red painted letters laid in the tall grass, hidden from view. He once considered buying the property since he needed a place to live as soon as he finished his alpha training. It had potential, being in Berkley, and although it wasn't nearly as big as Jack's cabin, it had plenty of room for add-ons. His excitement stirred, and he lay back on the porch and stared up at the moon.

Thinking back, Tucker had no intentions of confronting Jesse at the party. Their lives were no longer connected, and he didn't need the reminder of what he voluntarily gave up. His mother wouldn't be happy about that, but it was his life and his decision. But when he glimpsed her dancing with Brian, it ignited a firestorm in his veins, and he wanted to rip them apart and claim her as his. That was the reason why he ignored her every time she looked his way. She had obviously made her choice, again, and he would make his, even if it were Gina in his arms. Then Megan informed him that it was Jesse's eighteenth birthday, and he should at least give her one dance. Yeah, she shamed him into doing it. So after saying he would never go there, he gladly tapped Brian's shoulder interrupting his and Jesse's dance.

He had never heard of a bond re-forming, but when he took Jesse into his arms, and she met his eyes, undeniable electricity sizzled beneath his skin. He stood before her, stunned by the possibility that everything he thought he knew was wrong. The bond was back and his mind tried to understand what it believed impossible. *Fate is never wrong*, he argued, but the bond that formed between them wasn't his.

He exhaled a heavy breath.

This is wrong. It has to be.

He closed his eyes, trying to picture Jesse as a wolf. She was a healthy female, and her wolf would most definitely reflect that. Her coat would be black, salt-and-pepper or gray—thick and silky. But it made little sense she would be a wolf and no one would know. She had to phase at some point, and more than likely, the pack would've encountered her in the woods, or scented her there. Damn, he needed to push her out of his head before he went crazy. He opened his eyes and counted the stars until he eventually nodded off.

"Tucker, you came back," Jesse said as she slowly approached the cabin. "I didn't think I'd ever see you again."

"What are you doing here?" His voice sounded a bit edgy, but even that couldn't stop his eyes from trailing down her body, to the sleep pants that hugged her hips. He wanted to hug those hips, and do so much more. She was stunning, standing there with a mass of black curls that reached her waist. He imagined fisting his hands in her hair... and shook off a shiver.

"I'm here for you." She walked over to where he was sitting on the porch, the dried grass folding beneath her feet.

"No, this isn't real." He closed his eyes and counted to

three before opening them.

"I assure you, I'm real." She smiled and stepped between his knees to wrap her arms around his neck.

"I know you're real, but this," he motioned with his hand, "this is a dream! There's no way you can be here."

"Well, if that's the case, then you won't mind if I do this." She leaned closer to kiss his neck, but pulled back, looking confused. "Is there another?"

"No, it's not what you think." His body responded with a quiver that began below the belt, and the thought of her actually kissing him made him tighten his grip on the edge of the porch. He pulled back and stared into her eyes, searching for answers, but in a blink, her dark eyes trapped him in a wolf-like gaze. He sucked in a sharp breath, afraid to admit what he was seeing. "Jesse, I... are you..." His voice wavered, and he squirmed, unable to ask the question he desperately longed to know the answer to. "It's just a dream."

"Shh..." she said, her thumb trailing across his bottom lip.

Her nearness rocked him to the core, and he fisted his hands in her hair. The heat radiating between them was proof of their attraction, and he wrapped one arm around her waist. She was everything he craved, the only female he ever wanted. "I've dreamed of you for so long, but this... is only a dream." His heart crashed into his stomach.

"You keep saying that, but it feels real. You feel real." Placing her hand on his chest, her fingers splayed. "Your skin is warm. Your heart is beating." Sadness appeared on her face as he stared into her troubled eyes. "Does it not beat for me?"

"My heart beats only for you, but it also wants what's real and this will never be real." He squeezed his eyes shut and counted to three again.

"Then let me be yours in our dream. I want this. I want you." His eyes opened to meet hers.

It sounded so simple, yet deep down, he knew it was impossible. But what if? *"If you want me, then be with me when you're awake. Be with me. Love me for what I am. If not, let me go."* He lifted her hand to his lips. *"I want more than just a dream. This bond we share, it's not mine, and it can't be yours..."*

"Jesse, are you awake?" The sudden interruption startled her and Tucker could hear a muffled male voice pulling her from the dream. His wolf bristled.

"No, don't go!" Trying to hold on as long as the dream would allow, he begged, *"Please, don't go."*

His eyes opened, and he bolted upright on the porch.

"Just a minute," Tucker heard himself saying before coughing to clear his throat of the silvery sound. He cracked open the door and scowled when he saw the smirking smile that greeted him. "What the hell are you doing here?" He coughed again.

"Checking on my girl," Brian said. His eyes traveled downward and Tucker's face heated, but not in a good way. "Can I come in?"

"Did you just check me out? Hell no, you can't come in." He folded his arms over his chest, his stance threatening.

"I see somebody woke up on the wrong side of the bed this morning. Get dressed and I'll go get us some coffee." Brian winked as the door slammed in his face.

"What the hell?" Tucker mumbled as recognition

registered in his mind. He was in Sonya's apartment, which only provided more proof he was still dreaming. But that didn't explain why Brian was there.

As he walked through the apartment, he remembered Sonya talking about selling the bookstore, but he didn't honestly think she would. Kicking boxes to the side, just to open the closet door, his eyes widened. "Whoa! Not my foot." Only once had he worn pink nail polish, and that was in the privacy of his sister's bedroom. Lily was five at the time, and being his favorite sibling, it was his way of helping her with a major life decision before her first day of preschool.

He looked down at the green shirt he wore and his eyes practically popped out of his head. Rarely did he have such vivid, whacked-out dreams. When he did, it was usually after eating extra-spicy hot wings or his dad's blistering turtle soup—but even then; he remained a male. His mind freaked as he put two and two together. He had often been called a lot of things, over the years, but a female... hell to the no! *It's a silly dream. Just roll with it.*

Apparently, trying to understand Jesse put him in her mindset, and he needed to place her in a familiar location, and Sonya's apartment was it. *I can do this,* he thought, stepping into the closet.

Sorting through her clothes, there was no way he was wearing a dress, and a low-cut blouse was most definitely out of the question—especially with Brian lurking nearby. He grabbed a blue sweatshirt and a pair of black sweatpants off a hanger and carried them over and laid them out on the bed. He had never seen Jesse wear sweats before, but everyone had comfort clothes, or at least, he did—stark naked. He grinned as he walked into the bathroom and flipped on the light.

Lifting the shirt over his head, his mouth went dry. *Holy mother of Luna!* Fantasizing about Jesse was one thing, but this? This was crossing the line. His heart raced as he tossed the shirt to the floor, and a soft beige camisole came into view. He blew out a breath. *Thank the moon.*

His mistake was assuming he had control of the dream until he looked down at the fingers working the pull string around his waist. "No! I can't see this," he warned, but as he fought to pull his hands back, the pants fell around his ankles, and a pair of red boxers took their place. "Okay, this is not fun anymore," he fussed as he walked over to the sink where Jesse's image stared back at him. "Oh, shit!" His jaw dropped when her dark eyes flared, and he realized he was seeing her world through the eyes of her wolf.

Eight

Jesse

Shutting off the shower, Jesse grabbed a towel and wrapped it around her body. She had a splitting headache, a piss poor attitude, and was not in the mood for Brian's macho bull crap.

Her first night at the apartment, she hadn't slept well, and she attributed that to the late night stragglers leaving the park.

She stomped into the bedroom and frowned at the clothes that were laid out on the bed. She hated wearing jogging pants because nothing about the way they fit suggested she'd ever jogged a day in her life. Frustrated, she quickly dressed and walked over to the full-length mirror that hung on the back of the bedroom door.

Her mind tracked back to the party, to when Tucker had removed her mask. She couldn't imagine what he saw that prompted him to storm off so quickly. She had blackened her eyes with makeup, and probably looked like a raccoon, but he had to realize it was necessary for the costume. And she couldn't think of anything she might have said that would have offended him. Or at least nothing came to mind. Then she remembered his clingy date. *He made his choice.* A low rumble rose in her throat and she beat on her chest to force out the burp. *And it's not you.* Another rumble, but still no burp. She went into the bathroom and opened the medicine cabinet, searching for the antacids. With relief in sight, she popped two chalky tablets into her mouth as she walked into the living room and grabbed her sneakers off the floor. After tying up her shoes, she snatched the hair clip off the coffee table and gathered her hair up as she headed out the door.

The banging coming from the back of the storeroom kept rhythm with the pounding in her head and she suppressed a groan. Jack had promised to work on the changing rooms, she, however, did not factor in the noise. She hid her scowl as she walked out of the warehouse, and over to the counter where Brian stood sipping coffee. Her eye twitched, and she fought the urge to glare. She definitely needed a jolt of caffeine.

"It's obvious where you disappeared to last night. I bet you have a helluva hangover," he said offering her a Styrofoam cup.

"Thank you for noticing." Jesse rolled her eyes. *I hate men!* She took the cup but had no clue what he was talking about or why he was there. Or why he felt the need to knock on her apartment door. After the way her night ended, she would have preferred to stay locked in her apartment all day, rather than to entertain the likes of him. She pulled off the lid and guzzled the cooled coffee, making a show of it. She was the responsible one, but for once in her life, she wanted to throw caution to the wind and tell the world to screw off. Crushing the empty cup, she tossed it over her shoulder and stepped around Brian before heading to the front of the store where Lori stood giggling.

"Ha! You snubbed him," Lori said latching onto Jesse's arm. "I tried to warn the bonehead, but he wouldn't listen. He deserves anything you throw at him."

"You really shouldn't put ideas like that in my head when I'm suffering from caffeine deficiency."

"Somebody has to keep you on your toes." Lori laughed. "I'm going on a coffee run, want one?"

"Yeah, and make sure it's hot." Jesse turned towards Megan as Lori walked out the door, expecting to see pleading eyes that said, "I'm so sorry," but instead, Megan glared.

"Were you drinking last night?" Megan whisper-hissed as she moved out from behind the display cabinet she was working on.

"Really? You, of all people, are asking me that?" Jesse scoffed. "Heaven forbid I have a pissy night." That was uncalled for, she knew, but lately, her moods were shifting so rapidly even Newton couldn't define the motion.

"Brian, Seth needs your help out back, to unload drywall," Megan said before pulling Jesse around the counter and back into the warehouse.

"Did you just lie?" Jesse asked and took a seat on a stack of pallets next to the door.

"If he's going to be here, he's going to work. I don't need him hanging around, drooling like an idiot. He did enough of that last night." Megan looked back over her shoulder. "Now tell me what's going on?"

"Oh, let's see... I was out walking in the woods... alone... at midnight... liar! You wouldn't tell me the truth about what happened to you on Hunter's Ridge, but you expect me to give you that courtesy?" Jesse cocked a brow. It was a low blow, but judging by the look on Megan's face, it served its purpose.

"I thought I was protecting you," Megan argued. Clearly, Jesse had hit a nerve.

"I don't need protecting!" Jesse hissed hearing the doorbell clang. She jumped off the pallets and hurried out of the warehouse, needing that extra kick of caffeine. Expecting to see Lori, it was Tucker standing three feet inside the door, looking just as pissy as she felt. She slid to a stop, causing Megan to plow into her backside. *Who the hell invited him?* Her heart beat erratically when his signature scent filled the room, and she swayed on her feet. But before she could reach back for Megan, fire shot through her veins, blurring her vision and she crumpled to the floor.

"Jesse!" Tucker yelled as he rushed across the room and lifted her in his arms. "She's burning up."

Jesse's mind was hazy and she whimpered as the room spun. Muddled voices ping-ponged in her head as she tried to concentrate on the words. "Help me!" She wanted to scream, but like her eyes, her mouth refused to open.

"What happened to her?"

She thought she recognized Brian's voice, but since she was stuck in a dark tunnel and couldn't see her hand in front of her face, she wasn't sure. Sweat trailed down her back as the ringing in her ears increased. And if she weren't mistaken, she would have sworn someone said, "Liquor will do it every time."

"Do you always say stupid shit, or is that reserved only for the females?" Tucker asked, holding Brian's glared. "Oh, and it was really nice of you to bring her coffee this morning. But if she needs anything else, I'll take care of it. You had your chance,"

"Aren't you supposed to be helping Seth?" Megan asked, and Brian shrugged, walking away. "Ignore him, and take her upstairs to her apartment."

Jesse couldn't make out the words, or the person Tucker was talking to, but as the vibration of his voice drifted overhead, another pain shot through her body, and her breathing grew shallow. Fighting with everything she had, against the darkness that held her down, the voices faded to nothing.

Pain intensified with each jolting step until Jesse thought it would explode in her head. It was too much! The heat radiating up from beneath her sweatshirt, stifled her breathing and her body went limp. Finally, the air shifted, and a soft rumble forced her body to calm—the heat dissipating. She inhaled the familiar woodsy scent.

"What happened?" Jack asked rushing into the bedroom behind Megan. "Is she sick?"

"She passed out," Megan said, handing a bottle of water to Tucker. Moving around to the opposite side of the bed, she knelt down. "Jesse, can you hear me?" She lifted the sheet and then looked up at Tucker. "What happened to her clothes?"

"I removed them," Tucker said as he sat on the edge of the bed and lifted Jesse's head to his lap. He opened the bottle and roused her enough to persuade her to take a sip. "Her body was overheating, and she needed to cool down." He placed the bottle on the bedside table before removing the hair clip from Jesse's hair. Laying her back on the pillow, he hurried into the bathroom. "I undressed her while she was under the sheet if that's what you're asking." Tucker walked back across the room and placed a damp washcloth on Jesse's forehead.

"Should I call her dad?" Megan asked, but before anyone could answer, Jesse blinked open her eyes.

"Megan, where am I?"

"You're in your bedroom. You passed out."

Jesse glanced around the room while pulling the sheet up to her chin. She looked back at Megan but didn't have to say a word as Megan shook her head in silent answer.

"They're here to make sure you're all right. That's all," Megan assured her. "Do you want me to call your dad?"

"No! I'm fine, just a queasy stomach." The confusion in her head hummed in her ears.

"Come on, boys, give the lady some privacy," Megan said as she ushered Jack and Tucker out of the room. "I'll keep an eye on her and if I need anything, I'll holler."

From the bedroom, Jesse scowled when Tucker said, "I want to know what's going on. Don't let her tell you she's fine; she's not!" *What the heck did he know? Jerk!*

"Just go downstairs and let me tend to her." Megan waited until the door closed behind them before going back into the bedroom. "Are you feeling better? Don't lie to me. I know something is wrong."

"So I heard. Thanks to Tucker's big mouth, everyone on the block probably heard."

"What are you talking about? There's no way you could've heard him whispering. You've been acting strange lately, so spill or I'm calling in the big guns." Megan turned as Lori rushed into the room.

"What happened? I leave for ten minutes and you pass out? Are you pregnant? Not that I'm blaming you. Hell, every time I walk pass McDreamy, my ovaries swoon." Lori set the coffee on the nightstand and then plopped down on the bed.

"Do you ever think before you open your mouth? And where the hell are my clothes?" Jesse sat up with a horrid look on her face as the wet rag dropped to her lap. How many times would she have to ask that question? The cool air that rushed through the window caused her to shiver as Lori fell over on the bed snickering. "Would you stop?" She slapped Lori with the rag and then slung it across the room.

"Your body was overheating, so we had to get them off." Megan's explanation was simple enough, but Jesse caught the offending word and glared.

"We? As in you and?"

Megan looked down, and for a moment, Jesse thought she would lie, but when she spoke it was the truth. "Tucker."

"What the hell! You did not let him see me without my clothes, did you? Megan, look at me! Did you?" Jesse's face grew hotter, and her eyes darted around the room, landing on Lori who was sitting on the edge of the bed, enjoying the drama.

"Calm down before you get yourself worked up. If you pass out again, I'm calling your dad," Megan threatened as she placed her hands on her hips and frowned.

"Stop stalling and answer the question. Did he see me naked?" Jesse hissed, and Lori grinned.

"I don't think so," Megan whispered.

"How could you do that to me?" Tears filled her eyes, and she swore at the little blonde. Had she misplaced her trust in Megan? She felt violated, ashamed, and disturbingly thrilled. "I think I'm going to be sick." Jesse covered her mouth as Lori jumped off the bed and ran into the bathroom. When she returned, she shoved a small trashcan at Jesse.

"Please don't barf all over the place or you'll make me sick." She heaved, and Jesse yanked the can out of her hand.

"Then wait in the other room," Jesse barked.

"And miss all this? Not happening, sister." Lori sat back down on the bed, despite Jesse's scowl.

"Jesse, please listen. I wasn't up here when..." Color drained from Megan's face as Jesse's head snapped around, and she hissed out another swear word aimed at the bouncy blonde.

"Tucker undressed you but he didn't do it for a cheap thrill. Your body was overheating. He was the only one up here at the time and he thought he was doing the right thing!" Megan growled in his defense.

"I'm sure he did." Jesse turned away to avoid hearing anything else Megan had to say. She was beyond pissed.

"Would you stop acting like a brat? He was only trying to help. He's worried about you; don't you get it? He's crazy about you and you can act as cold and distant as you want, but I know you're crazy about him," Megan stated.

"I am not. You don't know what you're talking about," Jesse sneered.

Megan stepped back and squared her shoulders, then glared down at her sickly friend. "Then why do you keep his picture on your corkboard?"

"You better never repeat that... to anyone. I mean it, Megan. No one knows about that picture." Jesse's fist tightened beneath the sheet, her nails digging into her skin. With her eyes closed, she fought off another bout of dizziness. Megan had done nothing wrong, she knew that, but she was still on the fence about Tucker. He had walked away from her... twice. Her chin dropped to her chest as she fought back more tears.

"I'm sorry, but I kind of let it slip." Megan looked down at the floor as Jesse fell back on the bed.

"Ain't that just frickin dandy? Not only did he ditch me on the dance floor, leaving me looking like a fool, now he thinks I'm obsessed with him! I'll never be able to face him again."

"Sure you will!" Lori snorted. "He just may not be looking at your face."

"Stop it, Lori. This is serious." Jesse glared and then turned back to Megan. "I'm not going downstairs until he's gone. I don't need his pity!" She got out of bed and pulled the sheet around her body as she walked over to the closet. With trembling hands, she grabbed the first outfit she saw and headed to the bathroom. "Yeah, the girl from Indiana hasn't a clue what it's like to hang with a player. Well, I got news for the men in backwoods country. Not only have I dated an 'actual' player'," she air quoted, "Max also taught me how to play the game."

"He's not playing you," Megan insisted as the

bathroom door slammed shut.

"Well, there's only one way to find out," Jesse yelled from behind the door.

Wearing a pair of snug-fitting blue jeans and a long-sleeved shirt that showed more cleavage than she was comfortable with, Jesse walked back into the bedroom. Ignoring Megan, she slipped on a pair of knee-high boots that added another three inches to her height and then draped a shawl around her shoulders. "May the best man win."

"This is gonna be good," Lori squeaked, following Jesse across the apartment and out the door.

Jesse drew in a deep breath to calm her nerves before walking out of the warehouse. She didn't want a repeat of the earlier episode because even though she was pissed at Tucker, a part of her desperately sought his attention. Tucker stood, and she put her hand up to stop him in his tracks.

"There's my girl. You okay?" Brian walked over and stood beside her, his eyes instantly dropping to her chest.

"I'm fine now, thanks to you." She smiled shyly when in reality, she wanted to slap the crap out of him. *Jerk!* She glanced over Brian's shoulder and glared at Tucker, who was glaring at Brian. *Serves you right, asshole!*

"You need to calm down," Jack whispered behind Tucker, and Jesse mentally rolled her eyes. Maybe there were words exchanged between Brian and Tucker before she came downstairs. Or now that Tucker's little barmaid wasn't hanging on him, maybe he was the one jealous.

Good! She turned back to Brian. "Could you give me a ride to Gramma's?"

"Sure, are you ready now?" Brian was way too eager,

nearly making her nauseous, but she swallowed the bitterness and put on her sweetest smile.

"Now would be great." She casually stumbled, her hand landing on his chest. "I know it's not that far to walk, but I'm still a bit woozy." Playing on his sympathy, Jesse smiled when Brian took hold of her elbow and led her to the door. She was determined to give Tucker a taste of his own medicine, but as soon as they arrived at her grandmother's house, Brian was history.

"Hey, wait up," Lori said, rushing across the room. "Could I hitch a ride? I need to make sure I locked the front door. You know how paranoid Mom gets."

Jesse turned but before she could say anything, Brian chimed in. "Might as well, we're going that way." His good ol' boy routine really sucked.

Nine

Tucker

"Wow, that was a fast recovery," Jack said when Brian's Jeep pulled away from the curb.

"Yeah," Tucker said, a constant rumble rattled deep in his gut. He was annoyed, and it took everything he had to keep from following Jesse out the door. Brian didn't deserve the way she was looking at him, and if Tucker had anything to say about it, it would never happen again.

"I'm sorry, Tucker, but you know she's not with him," Megan said, moving over to the counter.

"I know." Tucker rubbed the back of his neck as tension settled between his shoulders. He and Jack were standing in the warehouse, listening as Jesse threatened to give him a taste of his own medicine. She was upset about a lot of things, all of which meant she had feelings for him. But because he had walked away, her feelings were hurt. He sighed inwardly, realizing Jesse couldn't be attracted to Brian after the way she fussed about him, but his wolf wasn't as convinced. *She fussed about you too.*

"At least she's feeling better, and that's a good sign," Megan said.

"It's a front, and we both know it," Tucker groused looking back at her.

"I don't know that because she hasn't told me anything. And she would tell me," she said defensively.

"Would she?" Tucker walked over to the large window and stared out at the overcast day. Shoving his hands into his pockets, he looked over at Jack. "We need to talk."

"Could you all take this conversation to the park? I have a lot of work to do here and I'm getting a headache," Megan said, but Tucker knew she was peeved by his comment.

Jack followed Tucker out the door as Megan stood behind them, brandishing a broom. "It's about time you tell me what's going on," he whispered, with a quick glance back at Megan. "You've been acting strange lately. I mean, you've cut your hair after how many years? Not to mention Gina said you were rude when you dropped her off after the party." Jack motioned and took a seat at the first picnic table they came to.

"I wasn't rude to Gina, but she needs to mind her own business." Tucker sat down across from Jack and stared back at the store. "And stop dissin' on my hair. Jesse seems to like it." He leaned in on his elbows, prompting Jack to do the same. "What do you know about new bloods?"

"That's what you want to talk about?" Jack frowned, shaking his head. "I don't know any more than the next person, I guess. They're dangerous and unpredictable; why do you ask?"

"Well, I think anyone training to be an alpha should know the dangers of changing a human. When we grew up, it was mostly pack, but now that the pack is expanding to include humans again, an accidental nip could cost someone their life."

Jack pinched the bridge of his nose. "Dad said Dr. Stevens knows more about them than anyone. So I would suggest you talk to him." He looked back at Tucker, who was staring up at the apartment window. "Travis didn't change Jesse, if that's what you're thinking. They ran the test which is why Dr. Williams kept her in the hospital overnight. The tests are done in threes. In order to be a new blood, there has to be three positives and none were positive."

"Maybe not, but you can't tell me you haven't noticed a change in her. I just got back to town and I can see it." Tucker flipped the temporary alpha pendant between his fingers.

"I think everyone has noticed, but her test came back negative so we have to assume it's something else. Megan suggested stress or a chemical imbalance, but until Jesse admits there's a problem, there's not much we can do."

Tucker rubbed his eyes and then dropped his hand to the table. "Jesse is a wolf. I don't know what happened to her, but I've seen it in her eyes."

"There's no way. We would have known if Travis changed her," Jack insisted. "She doesn't have the scent of a wolf."

"Megan didn't either, if I'm not mistaken," Tucker said, making a point. "Look, Travis may not have changed her, but someone did. Remember Megan talking about her being in the woods and not knowing what happened to her clothes? If Jesse didn't know she was a wolf, she wouldn't know to undress. It all makes sense except, the day Megan talked to her, it wasn't after a full moon."

Jack's face conveyed his thoughts as he sorted through the details. "If that's true, then she's a danger to anyone that crosses her path. Tell me what you know. I am the alpha here."

Playing the alpha card didn't fly well with Tucker and he growled and pushed up off the bench. "All you need to know is we share a bond and I will protect her at all costs."

"But you just admitted you don't know what you're dealing with. If she's a wolf, she's dangerous." Jack stood, not backing down.

"Look, you may be the alpha, but I will leave the pack before I allow anyone to harm her. I denied our bond once. It won't happen again."

"NO! You aren't thinking straight. It's not possible." Jack paced the length of the table, his brows knitted together in thought. "The bond is hers, isn't it?" He turned and Tucker smirked.

"Well, it's not mine."

"Which is why you left the party early..." Jack shoved his hand through his hair and leaned his hip against the table.

"If I thought I could do it on my own, I would have never brought you into this, but you have to trust me. Give me a chance to bond with her wolf. Jesse's fighting it. I saw it in her eyes today before she spaced out."

"Then you have to trust me and tell me what you

know. But I will give you fair warning. If this goes bad, Dad will kick both of us out of the pack."

Tucker stared down the road, not wanting to reveal anything else, but how could he expect Jack to trust him if he didn't trust Jack? He sat back down, his finger tracing over a set of initials carved in the tabletop. "Last night, she came to me in a dream."

"That's all fine and good, except we don't share dreams. And even if we did, you haven't sealed the bond."

"I know. I don't understand that either, but she was with me last night in a dream."

"Maybe that's all it was. I mean, we all dream," Jack said dropping down on the bench.

"Normally, I would agree, but I picked out the clothes she was wearing today. I was there when Brian knocked on her door this morning, which is why I showed up when I did. I don't trust that asshole after last night. I saw the way he treated his date, and I'm not about to let him suck Jesse back into another false relationship. I stepped aside the first time; this time, he'll have to go through me to get to her."

"Well, lucky for you, she's not that stupid." Jack looked over his shoulder as Megan propped open the door. "Okay, if we're going to do this. How much time do you need?"

"Just give me until the day after the next full moon. I'll wait for her to phase and try to get close to her. If I can convince her to trust me..."

"But what if she doesn't, then what? You're dealing with something neither of us knows much about."

"She responded to me in the dream, so I'm hoping she'll trust my wolf."

"The next full moon, that's all I can promise... so long as you talk to Dr. Stevens today. I don't like this. I think Dad should know because we need to find out who changed her, and if they've changed anyone else."

"I know, but right now, I'm more concerned about Jesse and keeping her safe. So I trust you'll keep this between us."

"I'll cover for you as long as you keep me informed, but either way, Dad will be pissed. I just hope no one else gets wind of this between now and then."

"What about Megan?" Tucker asked, glancing across the street as she wiped down the large front window.

"I'll talk to her this afternoon, and if the storms hold off, we'll get together and work out some kind of plan. Mason should know also, but it will go no further than us. I hope you're wrong." Jack stood, but before he walked away, he said, "Be careful. If she is a new blood, she will be stronger than normal females and could turn on you."

"Considering we share a bond, I highly doubt her wolf will attack me. That's why I have to do this alone. Anyone else may be perceived as a threat."

Jack nodded and walked back across the street to where Megan waved from the door. Tucker waited until he was inside the store before getting up from the table. He had made a good argument as to why Jesse would trust his wolf, but what good would that do if she didn't trust him?

Thunder rolled in the distance as he walked to his car—a light drizzle coating his hair. As he opened the driver's door, the streetlights flickered overhead with the darkening sky. Storms were moving into the area and from the looks of the ominous black clouds, the next one would be a doozy. He pulled the keys out of his pocket and slid into the driver's seat. Luck was what he needed to help Jesse, and he hoped that luck could be found in Dr. Stevens.

Tucker pulled up in front of the animal shelter, relieved to see the lights were still on. Lightning streaked across the sky, and the thunder that followed rocked his car as he looked out through the windshield where large drops of rain blurred his view. He loved a good thunderstorm, and this one held promise. But even it couldn't distract him from his mission. He pushed open the door and jumped out of the car as another bolt of lightning shot across the sky. He instinctively ducked and ran up the sidewalk as the front door swung open.

"Come in, come in," Dr. Stevens said, greeting Tucker as he rushed through the door. "How's your dad?" He looked up at the sky before pulling the door shut.

"He's fine. Thanks for asking," Tucker said, moving further into the room. "I didn't mean to bother you so late, but since I'm training as an alpha, I feel it's my responsibility to learn more about new bloods. I've been thinking about it ever since Tracy brought it up at the pack meeting, and I was hoping you could help me out."

"Talk about a headache. Tracy had the whole pack whirling over that one. But I'm glad you came to me. There's a lot of misleading information floating around and I do know what I'm talking about. My great-great-grandmother was a new blood."

"So you're a new blood?" That was a surprising twist Tucker didn't see coming.

"I have the blood in my veins, but it's been diluted

over the years. My great-great-grandfather was a pure blood, and their young grew up and mated with other purebloods, so by the time I came to be, the blood had been thinned to just a trace." He motioned Tucker forward. "As you know, new bloods are humans that have been infected with the Lupine virus. It can take up to six months before any symptoms show, provided the human lives through the DNA transformation. Unfortunately, most aren't strong enough to handle it and die before the actual shift," Dr. Stevens said moving over behind the desk.

"What symptoms would they have?" Tucker leaned on the counter, his chin resting on his fist. It was intriguing and obviously, not everyone thought new bloods were monsters—but the thought of any human dying was disturbing.

"For the wolf's protection, the human will develop uncanny night vision and extreme hearing within the first thirty days. After that, they can develop flu-like symptoms or a rash. At that point, the virus has completely transformed the DNA, and the wolf is just waiting to emerge."

"Are they always sick before a phase?" Tucker thought back to Jesse that morning.

"Most likely, and they will display symptoms off and on until they accept their wolf. After which, the symptoms disappear permanently."

"Will they phase even if they haven't accepted the wolf? I mean, we saw what Megan went through."

"As soon as their DNA is transformed, they will phase whether or not they accept their wolf, but that doesn't mean they will remember it. Megan's case was different;

she was blocking her wolf. Subconsciously, she knew it was there, but refused to allow the change."

"Well, would you or I notice if someone were infected, without seeing them phase?" Tucker held his breath, hoping Dr. Stevens wouldn't read too much into the question.

"It's not likely. They have to accept their wolf before their scent changes and even then, it's gradual. Although, you might catch an eye flare if the person is angry or experiencing a strong emotion. They are also stronger than the average shifter."

"The human or the wolf?"

"The human becomes moody at times, but that's to be expected. Imagine being thrown into a world that's unknown to most. It's hard on them, and because of that, they become stronger, if only as a means of protection, you might say. But the wolf is where the real threat comes in. Protecting its human, it will stop at nothing to eliminate any perceived threat. Everything about a new blood revolves around protection. And because there are so few, most packs know nothing about them."

"So dream sharing is about protection?"

"No, that's not exclusive to new bloods. Dream sharing happens when destiny touches you twice, giving you the chance to right a wrong. Any wolves can experience dream sharing if their souls were bonded in a prior life."

"You mean like reincarnation?"

"Well, I like to think of it as old souls reuniting. It's a way to bring the pair back together, and prevent an alteration of the future. Every life is predetermined and as soon as the pair seals the bond, the dreams stop."

"What about bonding? Is that the same?"

"New bloods basically do everything we do, but what makes them different from us, other than their strength, is their wolf sight."

Tucker coughed into his fist to hide his excitement. "What is wolf sight?" Seeing Jesse's world through the eyes of her wolf, and all the new information, he struggled to keep his composure.

"Wolf sight happens when the new blood shares its sight with its mate. For instance, if your mate was a new blood, you would be able to see through her eyes and observe what was happening around her. Usually, that only happens during times of duress, confusion, fear, or injury. It's like an alarm system that keeps them safe. Again, going back to the protection theory," the doctor said.

"They are also unpredictable and have been known to turn on the wolf that changed them. And a true new blood will have a birthmark. Not like what a human would have, but a small, round mark at the bite site. Most people mistake it for a bruise, but it's actually a sign of the moon they change under. The new moon can't be seen and is considered the dark moon; they change under the dark moon."

"That sounds cool," Tucker admitted. "Do you have a birthmark?"

"No, I'm the descendant of a new blood. You only have the birthmark if you were the one bitten."

"Wow, new bloods are intriguing, and I would love to stay and talk more about them, but maybe another day." Tucker looked up at the ceiling while extending his hand. "Thank you for all the information. I do appreciate it."

Tucker walked out of the shelter, his day a lot brighter with the information he'd received. Dream sharing and wolf sight were real, which meant Jesse was with him in that moment. *She kissed me!* He wanted to call his mother and tell her the good news. She would be excited for him; hell, he was excited for him! He ducked into the car as lightening skittered across the sky.

Ten

Tucker

By the time Tucker arrived at the cabin, Jack was sitting at the kitchen table sipping coffee. He chuckled and walked over to the coffeepot, knowing Jack on caffeine couldn't be good. But if he were as antsy as Tucker felt, caffeine was the least of their worries.

After pouring his coffee, Tucker reached over the sink and pushed the curtains to the side. From that window he had a clear view of Gramma's house and keeping a close eye on Jesse was now his top priority. He turned and leaned against the counter as Jack set his cup on the table and crossed his arms over his chest.

"So are you going to tell me what you found out, or would you rather I guess?" A caffeinated Jack was a chatterbox, but toss in a bit of stress, and his smartass emerged. Tucker grinned. Jack would be his entertainment for the rest of the evening.

"Well, what exactly do you want to know?" He rolled his lip to keep from laughing at the bitter look on Jack's face.

"What the hell do you think? I haven't been sitting here all afternoon guarding your mate for nothing."

Tucker chuckled and placed his cup on the counter as he glanced out the window and the attic light at Jesse's grandmother's came on. How many nights had he stared up at that window? He moved away from the sink and took a seat across from Jack. "She's a wolf. And new bloods phase on the new moon so I'll be scoping her out sooner than we originally thought." He glanced back to the window, the light now off. At ease with Jesse spending the night with her grandmother, he turned his attention back to Jack.

"And you know that for a fact?"

"Pretty much, yeah, and we also share dreams." Tucker couldn't contain his smirk and Jack rolled his eyes.

"So Dr. Stevens confirmed it? The dream, I mean?"

"Not only the dream but also the *wolf sight*. New bloods are actually quite clever, in the way the wolf protects the human. Seeing Jesse's world through the eyes of her wolf was how I saw Brian at the apartment this morning." Tucker got up and paced the kitchen while filling Jack in on the rest of the conversation he'd had with Dr. Stevens. And by the time the sun set, he had convinced Jack that they had made the right decision in keeping quiet about Jesse.

Tucker walked over to the backdoor as a streak of lightning zipped across the sky. "The storms are predicted to be much stronger tonight. Are you staying here?" Tucker leaned against the door frame.

"Yeah, Megan's pretty upset about Jesse, and she wants to stay close. She's asleep right now, but she cried most of the day. She blames herself even though I told her it wasn't her fault." Jack placed his cup in the sink. "You can sleep on the couch if you want."

"Nah, I'm good. I think Jesse's in for the night, what with the storms and all." Tucker walked into the living room, and Jack followed. "I didn't mean to upset Megan, but I know how she feels. But why didn't Jesse tell someone? I can't imagine her going through the change alone." That brought tears to his eyes as he turned and stared out the front door. He felt guilty—somehow it had to be his fault for leaving. Maybe if he had stayed in Cloverly and hadn't denied the bond... maybe, maybe, maybe he would worry himself to death. But reminding himself that Jesse had already phased and was in no danger of dying, his wolf grew ecstatic.

"I don't know why she didn't tell anyone. None of this makes sense. If Travis didn't change her, and the test results confirm he didn't, then who did?"

"I've asked myself that a million times," Tucker said, walking out to the porch. "I'm going home to get some sleep before the next round of storms comes through. If Jesse leaves, give me a holler."

"Will do, and if you need to take shelter, come back. There's plenty of room in the cellar," Jack said from the doorway.

That night as Tucker lay in bed, sleep eluded him. He tossed and turned, and after what seemed like hours, he finally got up and went outside. To tire his body and clear his mind, he jogged down the road, hoping the storms would cease until he could get to sleep, and possibly meet with Jesse in a dream. But after four laps, Gina walked out her front door wearing a tiny pair of cut-offs and a halter shirt that was better suited for a spring day. Tucker ignored her as he continued past, heading toward Main Street.

"Hey, Tucker!" Gina yelled, catching him on his return lap. "Are you waiting for the storms?"

"Just trying to wind down." He stopped when she walked across the wet grass, a nervous smile on her face.

"I don't like storms," her voice cracked.

He ran his hand over his face to keep from rolling his eyes. He normally wouldn't take such a matter lightly, but with her fake woe-is-me act, he had no intentions of playing babysitter.

"I know that probably sounds silly but they scare me," Gina said, her arms hugging her body.

"Then why are you outside? I mean if you're afraid and all shouldn't you be at Jack's? They have a cellar." He hoped by calling her out it would shut her down, but he wouldn't hold his breath.

"I'm fine right now; you're here. I know you won't let anything happen to me." She looked up at the night sky.

"You should go to Jack's. He's your alpha," Tucker said and took a step back, his wolf grumbling low. She was up to something. He could see it in her eyes.

"I was kind of hoping I could hang out with you. It's embarrassing to admit I'm afraid of storms and I don't want anyone to make fun of me." She scuffed the toe of her sandal over the damp pavement and looked up through her sweeping lashes.

Tucker, again, fought the urge to roll his eyes. She was such a drama queen when she didn't get her way.

"Just get to Jack's before the next round of storms come through. His cabin is the only one with a cellar and you'll be safe there." He turned to leave but stopped when she placed her hand on his upper arm. *See what you started?*

"What about you?"

He scowled and shrugged her hand away. "I've got other things to do. Just don't wait until the last minute. Get over to Jack's before the storms get bad." With that, he took off down the road ending the conversation.

Glancing back to make sure he wasn't followed; he raced across the yard and continued around to the backyard of the cabin. He sat down on the damp ledge, overlooking the river. With a cold front moving into the area, the spring-like temperatures wouldn't last beyond morning. And if the rolling thunder and gusting winds were any sign of what they could expect from the storms, a run to Berkley would most definitely be out of the question. Folding his arms behind his head, he lay back and closed his eyes, waiting for sleep to consume him.

"Tucker, where are we?" Jesse asked. Wearing an old, flannel nightgown that hung down past her knees, she sat down beside him.

"We're at my cabin." He pushed up to a sitting position and looked back as if he wasn't sure.

"The storms will be bad tonight. Why aren't you inside?" She glanced skyward.

"I like watching them come in," he said, his heart racing. "Are you feeling okay?" He held his breath. Was she as eager to be with him as she was in the last dream? Or did Brian persuade her into getting back with him?

"I feel fine. I miss you though." Her forehead wrinkled

with worry.

Hearing those words, his body relaxed, and he grinned—lifting her into his lap. She didn't hesitate to join him, and his grin widened when she rested her head on his shoulder. He tightened his hold around her waist, her coconut scent delighting his wolf. "Are you cold?" he whispered against her hair when she snuggled closer.

"No."

The two sat in silence until Tucker could muster up enough courage to ask the one question that was weighing on his mind. "Jesse, are you afraid of me, my wolf?" He pressed his cheek against the top of her head, wishing it weren't a dream.

"No. I'm not afraid of you. I know what you are, and I want to be with you."

"But you know this is a dream," he said, pulling her hair over her shoulder so he could see her face. He'd always thought she was beautiful, and sitting there in his lap, it was hard not to stare. She tilted her head, exposing her neck, and he fought the urge to pepper kisses down to her shoulder.

"Yeah, that's what you said the last time, but it doesn't feel like a dream." She shifted around and looked into his eyes. "I don't want it to be a dream."

"I don't either, but until you accept..." He cut his words short and continued in a different direction. "What would you do if you woke up right this minute? Would you run?" He leaned down and kissed the tip of her nose, and when she smiled, he practically melted into a puddle.

"Maybe. I'm not sure. I don't want to run, but I am what I am, and that doesn't seem to be enough." The sadness of her words reflected in her eyes and she looked

away.

"It's always been enough for me... even before you became a wolf." He paused. A little push in the right direction couldn't hurt, could it? She looked back, and he could see her wolf stirring as she tried to make sense of what was going on in her mind.

"Am I a wolf? Is that what you see when you look at me? Is that why I'm here?" She looked confused as she wrung her hands and then buried them in the lap of her nightgown.

"I see my world when I look at you. Everything I've ever wanted is reflected in your eyes, and the reason we can share dreams is because we share a bond."

"What does that mean?"

"It means I want to spend the rest of my life with you. You're my soul mate." He twisted a strand of her hair around his finger. It may have been a dream, but the sensation of her sitting in his lap was real enough to rouse his wolf. "I know this is a lot to take in, but I need you to remember, so when you wake up you will understand what's going on. In order for you to be a wolf, you had to be bitten by a wolf. When a human is changed, they're called new bloods. Most wolves consider new bloods dangerous, but I know you aren't and I'll protect you."

"I'm not dangerous. I would never hurt anyone," she said, and he could tell the thought bothered her.

"I know you wouldn't, and I won't let anyone hurt you." His jaw clenched to stifle a growl. If he ever found the wolf that changed her, there would be one less shifter in the world. His wolf grumbled its approval.

"Do you know who bit me? Was it your girlfriend?" She blushed, apparently embarrassed by the question.

He chuckled and shook his head. "The only girlfriend I have is you," he teased, but honestly, she was his and no matter the outcome, she always would be.

"Then who was the girl at the party?"

"Gina is a member of our pack, but she's not my girlfriend. The only female I want, or have ever wanted is sitting right here in my lap." He tweaked her nose, and she scowled.

"Good, because I didn't like the way she was looking at you. She's a little handsy and doesn't seem like a very nice person."

Tucker couldn't help but laugh. "You're very perceptive." His skin prickled, and he looked back at the cabin hearing a muffled voice. "Jesse, I need you to promise you'll remember what I told you. Do not tell anyone you're a wolf. Promise me."

But before she could make that promise, the wind ripped them apart, ending the dream. Despair washed over him and he blinked his eyes open, knowing if he cut his wolf loose, even the thunder couldn't hide his pain.

"Tucker, where are you?" Gina yelled again.

He rolled over, glaring toward the cabin. "What the hell are you doing here? I told you to go to Jack's." Tucker jumped to his feet and stomped across the yard, the wind beating against his back.

"I didn't want to go alone. I would feel safer with you there." She stepped out the backdoor, her timid-as-a-mouse routine grating on his nerves. His eyes flared, and she took a step back, but the damage was already done.

Tucker took hold of her arm, lecturing her as he led her around the cabin. If she thought for one minute, he would fall for her nonsense, she was deadly mistaken.

"The next time I tell you to do something, do it." He didn't realize he was playing the alpha card, but now he understood what Jack went through with Tracy. "My cabin is off limits to you. I do not want you here."

By the time they arrived at Jack's cabin, both were completely soaked, and Tucker was furious. Not only did Gina ignore his advice, but she had also interrupted his dream—the only connection he had to Jesse. "I don't have time for this," he growled when Jack opened the front door.

"I'll take care of her; just go do what you have to." Jack turned, silently scolding Gina as Tucker ran back into the storm.

Eleven

Jesse

Curtains strained against their rods as the thrashing winds whipped chaos around the bedroom. Jolted awake, Jesse jumped out of bed and shut the window as tornado sirens wailed, disrupting the night. Disoriented by her dream-infused sleep, she staggered towards the bedroom door, tripping over her boots. "Gramma!" she yelled as she pushed up off the floor and rushed down the stairs as fast as her wobbly legs would allow. "Where are you?"

"I'm here," her grandmother called back. Fastening the housecoat around her waist, she walked out of the bedroom, carrying an old transistor radio. "We need to get a flashlight out of the pantry and then get down to the cellar."

Jesse latched onto her grandmother's arm as they descended the stairs. The old house had weathered many storms throughout the years and she didn't think this one would be any different. Rushing into the kitchen, her grandmother turned on the lights as Jesse moved over to the pantry and opened the door. "Where's Moose?" she asked, reaching into the far back corner of the cabinet to retrieve a flashlight.

"I don't know. He usually sleeps at the end of my bed, but he was gone when I got up," Gramma said. Taking the flashlight, she held it to her chest.

"He's probably hiding in a box or basket, riding out the storm. Just wait here and I'll go open the cellar," Jesse instructed, pulling a chair out from the table. She half expected her grandmother would make a trip through the downstairs rooms looking for Moose, and with the storm bearing down on them, it wasn't safe. *You are so grounded.*

Jesse yanked open the backdoor as gusting winds caught the screen door and slammed it against the house. Thunder rolled overhead, and she quickly switched on the porch light. *It's just the storm,* she told herself, glancing over at the wind chimes clanging loudly from the swaying branches of the oak tree. But nothing about their tone was comforting.

Shielding her face from the stinging rain, she raced across the porch only slowing when she neared the cellar door. Her bare feet slid across the wet wood, and she fell back, bumping her head against the house. Her eyes glazed over and she blinked away the stars that danced in her vision as she pushed up on her knees.

"Jesse!" Tucker's voice sounded in her head, and she looked up as he jumped the fence. He was crazy to be out in the storm, but he probably thought she was crazy crawling across the porch.

Using the rope handle on the cellar door, she pulled herself to a standing position and slung her wet hair over her shoulder. With all the strength she could muster, she yanked on the handle, but again, her feet slipped on the wet surface, and she landed on her rear.

"Are you okay?" She groaned when Tucker ran up on the porch and lifted her to her feet.

"I'm fine." Her face heated when Tucker caged her in his arms, her back against his chest. And for a split second, she forgot about the storm.

"Pull together," he yelled over the wind, his fingers brushing against hers when he grabbed onto the rope. With one hard tug, the door creaked open, and he grabbed her around the waist to keep her from falling down the stairs. "I'll get your grandmother. You get in the cellar." His voice was firm and demanding, and Jesse promptly did as she was told.

Relieved that she and her grandmother were not alone; she hurried down the steps and turned on the light as the storm raged overhead. "Give me the radio and grab onto the handrail," Jesse said when her grandmother started down the steps. Placing the radio on the floor, she reached for the flashlight.

Her grandmother was leery of the steep concrete steps and rarely went into the cellar after falling two years ago. But Tucker noticed her hesitation and wrapped his arm around her waist, securing her to his side. Jesse held her breath until her grandmother was safely off the steps before she allowed herself to relax. "Did you see Moose?" She knew the answer but still had to ask.

"Is this him?" Tucker pulled a large, gray fur ball out

from beneath his arm. "He's okay." He rubbed down the cat's back, and Moose nudged his hand and purred.

The gentle sound of Tucker's voice beckoned her closer. And the thought of shutting off the lights to experience that delicious rumble that was guaranteed to trigger every nerve ending in her body made her quiver to her toes. Remembering the way his body wrapped around hers, protecting her from the storm, she so wanted to purr. Then a branch snapped, and she screeched.

"You're staying, aren't you?" She wrapped her arms around her body, trying to hide how terrified she was of being trapped in the cellar. Why she felt safe with him there, she didn't know, but after the way he handled her grandmother, she had clearly misjudged him. "Please say you'll stay." Begging was not beneath her and she considered latching onto his leg if that's what it took to keep him there. Instead, he handed her the cat and reached up and pulled the cellar door shut. Looking a bit wary and rain-soaked, Jesse sensed his discomfort, but she was more than thankful he was there.

"Come over here away from the door," Gramma said. "There's another light switch on the back wall."

Jesse looked around until she found the switch and flipped it on. Three lights lit the small room, and as much as she hated being down there, it was better than being out in the rain. "I wasn't expecting the storms until morning," Jesse said setting out lawn chairs near the rear wall. "Here, Gramma, have a seat."

Her grandmother tuned in the radio as the station sent out warnings for several counties in the area. Jesse sat down next to her, scanning the darkened corners of the room. "Gramma, this is Tucker," Jesse said, glancing back at his still form, standing against the wall.

"It's nice to meet you." Gramma reached back and placed her hand on his arm. "Thank you for helping us."

"You're welcome." Tucker's hand lightly rubbed over Gramma's, and Jesse's heart melted at the comforting display.

Jesse turned back and smiled at Moose, her aggravation at him promptly forgotten. Her mind was windswept from her previous dream, just minutes before the storm hit. And if it weren't too far of a stretch, she could almost feel Tucker's arms still wrapped around her waist. *The wind howled, and he tightened his grip just as the dream ended...* Damn Sandman. It seemed lately, the dusting prankster, reveled in her misery.

When the overhead lights flickered, Jesse switched on the flashlight she was holding. She no longer feared the dark; but the thought of being trapped in the damp, musty cellar, she shivered. She glanced up as the ghastly winds beat down on the cellar door, threatening to come in. "Gramma, how are you doing?" she asked when she noticed her looking up towards the ceiling. Her grandmother smiled and turned up the volume on the radio.

"It sounds like the storm is about over." Tucker looked up as he moved over and sat down on the stairs.

Jesse smiled and rested her head on the back of the chair, closing her eyes. Something about her dream kept teasing her memory as the silent images replayed in her mind. Shocked at the sight of her sitting on Tucker's lap, and wearing a granny gown, she groaned.

"Jesse, wake up," her grandmother said, and she opened her eyes.

Jesse wasn't actually asleep, but Gramma didn't need to know she was recalling a dream where Tucker was the leading man. How embarrassing would that be? She looked over at Tucker who was grinning as if he knew exactly what she was thinking, causing her belly to flutter. Just ten feet and she could be in his lap, replaying the dream in real time. She blushed when her grandmother adjusted the radio again, saving her from making a fool of herself.

The winds had finally calmed, and the sirens were silent as they waited for confirmation that the storm had passed. Before leaving the safety of the cellar, Jesse folded up the chairs and flipped off the back switch. Once the radio gave the all clear, Tucker pushed open the cellar door. Motioning for Jesse to go first, he then helped her grandmother up the steps.

Placing Moose inside the house, Jesse was grateful to be above ground again. "Thank you," she said as Tucker lowered the cellar door. Drenched to the bone, she stood there in the clinging flannel gown, hoping he wouldn't notice her flaws. Tucker, on the other hand, looked amazing in the wet t-shirt that hugged his muscles. *You are so pathetic.* Turning away, she licked her lips.

From what she could see, the yard was a mess of scattered branches and leaves, not to mention, trash from the overturned trash bin. The damage was minor compared to what it could've been, and it surprised her to see the old, wooden shed had survived the storm.

"You're welcome," Tucker said, now standing behind her. She closed her eyes, willing him to step closer and draw her into his arms. She longed for the gentleness of his touch and opened her eyes when he placed his hands on her hips. "I've missed you." The warmth of his body against her back, and his breath brushing across her ear—she wanted more. He was there when she needed him. Would it be too much to think that maybe he had come back to Cloverly for her? Then, as Jack and Megan walked out of the cabin, followed by Gina, he took a step back. "I have to go, but if you need anything…"

I need you to pick me! She glanced over at the smirking blonde and then hurried into the house not bothering to look back.

Twelve

Jesse

It was daylight when Dr. Williams called, bringing Jesse out of her slumber. As she hung up the phone and started for the kitchen, a knock landed on the front door. She walked into the foyer and cracked open the door, not wanting the visitor to see her in her nightclothes. "What are you doing here?" she asked and opened the door wider to pull Megan inside.

"Jack's at the store and he said there was storm damage. Get dressed, and you can ride over with me," Megan said as she gently rubbed Jesse's arm.

Jesse frowned but wasted no time hurrying up the stairs to dress in the clothes she had worn the day before. She didn't plan to stay overnight at her grandmother's, but when the first round of storms passed, with more forecasted, she didn't want to leave Gramma alone.

"Gramma, I'll be back as soon as I can," Jesse said, rushing out the door.

The street was littered with debris from trash bins that flipped over during the storm, and other than a few downed branches, the damage didn't seem too bad until they turned onto Main Street. Unfortunately, the business strip of Cloverly didn't fare as well, and there were plenty of shattered windows and awnings hanging from their frames. Sheets of roofing littered the street and further down the road, a large tree was blocking one lane of traffic. Business owners were out surveying the damage while utility workers tended to the downed power lines.

"What the heck happened here?" Jesse asked as Megan steered around a branch and parked on the side street next to the store.

"We've entered the suck zone." Megan laughed, pulling the key from the ignition and opening the car door. "It has to do with the bend in the river; the winds always concentrate down Main Street."

"Great, now you tell me!" Jesse followed Megan to the front of the building as she pulled the shawl tightly around her shoulders. The temperature had dropped when the cold front moved through and the early morning chill caused her to shiver. Stepping over the shattered glass that was once their front window, they carefully made their way into the store. The window was an easy fix, but hearing voices from the warehouse, it was clear the bulk of the damage was there.

"It doesn't look so bad," Megan said and then froze at the sight of water pooling on the concrete floor.

Jesse didn't see the water when she entered the warehouse because she was too busy staring at the gaping hole in the roof. A sinking feeling overwhelmed her, and she blew out a slow breath. "Is this the worst of it?" Her eyes scanned the warehouse as water soaked through her boots. The damage to the roof was extensive, and the cost to have it repaired would be lofty. She blew into her fist to warm her hands and calm her nerves as she turned to Jack.

"The apartment is fine, but you can't stay here until the utilities are turned back on. The weatherhead was on that side of the roof, and now it's dangling off the side of the building." Jack motioned with his hand.

Jesse looked around the disaster that was now their warehouse. The merciless winds had damaged several roofs on the north side of town, and their newly rented store was one of them. "Please tell me insurance will cover this." She glanced over at Megan for confirmation.

"It's covered," Megan nodded.

Jesse spent the rest of the morning sorting through her boxes. Backed against the bedroom wall, she stared across the room as tears welled in her eyes. She'd only spent one night in the apartment, and now she would have to move back to Gramma's. *It's only temporary.*

She had no idea how long the building repairs would take, but thankfully, Seth stepped up to oversee the job.

So after gathering a week's worth of clothes, she shoved them into two boxes, and then pushed them to the door for Jack to haul downstairs. Another box held personal items, and two others held shoes, her sketch pad, and of course, her corkboard. Making one last sweep of the apartment, she jumped when Tucker cleared his throat, his hulking frame filling the doorway.

"I didn't mean to startle you," Tucker said, but his mischievous grin told a different story, and she rolled her eyes. "Do you need help?"

"No, I was just..." *He's here!* Her excitement bordered on nervousness as she looked around for a distraction. *Good grief! He's only here to help.* She cast a subtle glance his way and nearly fainted when his gorgeous face smiled back at her. She grinned down at her feet, fighting the urge to run over and jump into his arms. *Stop! He's with Gina.* She scowled and grabbed her shawl off the couch and draped it around her shoulders. "I'm perfectly capable of taking care of myself."

"You're jealous!" he said and she glared at his goofy grin.

"I am not!"

"Sure you are. You're blushing."

"You don't know me. What right do you have busting in here, assuming?"

"I didn't bust in here. But just so you know... I acted the same way when you were with Brian." His knowing grin made her nauseous.

"Ha! So you admit you're with Gina?" She had him there.

"I'm not with Gina," he growled, and in three steps he had her caged against the wall. "You're just playing hard to get. I like it."

"Dream on." She turned her head, to avoid seeing his dreamy brown eyes, and quickly pushed down the attraction she felt for him.

"I have every intention of doing just that... with you." He lifted her chin, forcing her to face him. "I bet you fantasize about me when I'm not around. Tell me your fantasies, and I'll tell you mine." Footsteps sounded on the steps, but Tucker didn't move, causing Jesse's blush to deepen.

"Are there anymore boxes?" Jack asked, coming to a stop at the door.

"No, I got it," Tucker said, but didn't take his eyes off Jesse. He smiled when Jack went back downstairs. "Now, where were we?"

"Apparently you were being a jerk and dreaming if you think I'd fantasize about you." She pushed against his chest, and he stepped back.

"We don't have to dream." A devilish grin spread across his face, and she wanted nothing more than to climb up his body and devour his lips. Or better yet, work her way up. She glanced down as he shoved his hands into his pockets and rolled her lip. *Start low, aim high.* Channeling her inner Lori, she glanced up and swore he could read her mind.

"You walked away from me," she said, changing the subject before she showed just how desperate she was for his attention.

"Not by choice. You were loyal to that ass, even though he treated you like dirt."

"And you wouldn't?" she questioned, not believing he was any different than Brian.

"No. Unlike him, I'm not stupid. I mean, look at you; you're beautiful."

"So you're only attracted to me because of my looks?" This time it was him that blushed.

"Well, there is that, but it's not the only reason I'm attracted to you. I think we have a lot more in common than you realize. Plus, you stand up for your convictions, proof you're a strong female." He reached over and tucked a loose strand of hair behind her ear. "I love the way the light sparkles in your eyes when you laugh and the way your hair sways when you walk. You have a calming nature about you, not to mention, a nice ass. Shall I go on?"

How was she supposed to respond to that? She turned away from his intense gaze; her face burning hot. "I, uh... only have one more box."

Jesse glanced back as Tucker walked to the door and lifted the box to his shoulder. She stood in awe as his long-sleeved t-shirt showcased his impressive upper body and sweet mercy—to be that box. She giggled louder than intended, and he looked back and winked before walking out the door. She pressed against her cheeks, to stop the ache.

Standing against the doorframe, she inhaled deeply, willing her body to calm. *He's here, don't blow it.* She sighed and drew in another breath. Pulling herself together, she hurried down the stairs to where Megan was waiting in the storeroom. She needed girl time. STAT!

As she entered the storeroom, she noticed Jack and Tucker were now busy boarding up the front window so she motioned Megan into the warehouse.

"I'm sorry for being such a pain lately. I wasn't feeling well, and I guess I was taking it out on everyone," she whispered.

"It's okay. We all get that way when we're under the weather," Megan said, graciously accepting the hug Jesse offered.

"Regardless, I shouldn't have yelled at you, and I know you would never do anything to hurt me. I'm so sorry."

"Stop. You have no reason to apologize. I understand... more than you know."

"Still, I shouldn't have acted like such an ass. I don't know what I'd do without you in my life."

"You would die of boredom. Because no matter how peppy Lori is, I'm still infinitely more entertaining." Megan laughed and did a little wiggle.

"Well, Miss Wiggle Britches, if I tell you something, will you promise not to repeat it?"

Megan nodded and crisscrossed her finger over her heart.

"It's going to sound totally off the wall, but I don't know what it is about Tucker. He has taken over my mind. Like right now, I feel a connection to him. It's crazy." Jesse wrung her hands. "Is there some kind of werewolf voodoo vibe that I need to know about? Because the R-rated thoughts that go through my mind, whenever I get within ten feet of him, are very distracting." She grinned when Megan fell into a fit of giggles.

"In a good way, I hope."

Thirteen

Tucker

Tucker climbed into the passenger seat of the old, blue pickup. Hoping not to appear too eager, he stared out the side window.

After volunteering to help Jesse move her things to her grandmother's house, he was thrilled when she took him up on the offer—although he tried to play it down. It was hard to hide his enthusiasm, but if hauling boxes gave him ten more minutes with her, he would haul boxes all day.

Remembering the way her eyes drifted down his body, his wolf stirred. She definitely liked what she saw, and judging by the pink tinge on her cheeks, what she thought as well. And despite her trying to keep a comfortable distance between them, he glimpsed her watching when she thought he wasn't paying attention—

her way of playing hard to get, he would accuse.

He glanced to see her blush deepen when she pulled away from the curb. Oh, yeah. She was definitely playing with his heart. He coughed against his arm and looked out the side window recalling the previous night.

Struggling with the cellar door, wearing what looked like a potato sack, Jesse was stunning. The soaked nightgown clung to her body, showcasing her glorious curves—flannel never looked so tempting. It was obvious she borrowed one of her grandmother's nightgowns, but even so, her sex appeal was undeniable.

Her coconut scent filled the cab and his thoughts drifted back to their first shared dream. He was in heaven despite his confusion over what existed between them. Just being close to her, and touching her, even if it were a dream, did his heart good. She had no clue how he felt about her, which was why he had returned to Cloverly. Now he was afraid that telling her that could actually scare her away.

The ride to her grandmother's didn't take long, and before he knew it, they were turning into the driveway. He glanced up at the familiar house. How many times had he snuck onto that porch to leave Jesse flowers? Four or five? He wasn't sure.

Tucker opened the door, and climbed out of the truck, meeting Jesse at the tailgate. "I'll get the boxes. Just show me where to put them." He pulled the boxes to the rear of the bed. Grabbing the two smallest, he followed her up to the house.

"Thank you," he said, stepping into the foyer. He stood off to the side and waited as she closed the door and then led the way up the stairs, her long hair swaying past her waist and drawing his attention. Dressed in tight jeans and an even tighter shirt, the potato sack was long forgotten. He bit his tongue to keep from saying what crossed his mind.

"Up there," Jesse pointed to a smaller staircase that continued up to the attic bedroom. Tucker grinned.

He had never been in a female's bedroom before, except for Tracy's and his sisters. But they didn't count. Climbing the last few steps, he felt like he was entering a sacred temple and the thought of removing his shoes crossed his mind. As he looked around the room, he mentally noted it was neatly kept and huge compared to the bedroom at his cabin. But the spiral staircase in the center of the room intrigued him most. "Do those stairs lead to the roof?" He knew the answer, but for whatever reason, had to ask.

"Yeah. The view is amazing under a full moon." Jesse quickly cleared her throat. "Not that I sit out there when the moon is full, but Lori and I have done so occasionally."

"If you ever get the urge to do so again, and Lori's not available, I'll gladly keep you company."

"But you're a..." Her words trailed off and she glanced down at the beige carpet to avoid his eyes.

"It's okay. I know what I am," he said, and she looked up.

"I meant, with the moon and all. I've heard you all running, I just thought..."

"We do that to exercise our wolves, to give them run time. Not because we *have* to. The human is always in control, the wolf is for protection. But allowing the wolf to run is a great way to unwind after a stressful day.

"So you don't turn just because of the moon?" She

twisted a strand of hair around her finger and leaned against the staircase—lost in thought.

Feeling the need to push her a little further, he continued. "Our human is always in control, whether or not we're in wolf form, and at no time do we *have* to change. But because we feel the pull of the moon, we often choose that night to run. And the moon makes it easier to see at night."

That got her attention, and she sat down on the edge of the bed and glanced up. "Megan said it didn't hurt. I mean, when you..."

"Shift?" he asked, moving over to take her place against the stairs. "Well, at first, it feels... awkward, but once you get used to it, it's no different from changing clothes." Tucker waited, knowing his next sentence could determine if she freaked out or not. "But we rarely phase with our clothes on."

"You mean... you hang out in the woods naked?" Her face flamed red, and she lowered her eyes.

"We usually undress under a tree... and allow the wolf to come forward. If not, our clothes rarely survive the change."

Jesse got up and walked over to the window, lost in serious thought. Tucker hoped he hadn't pushed her too far, but the sooner she dealt with her own change, the easier it would be to bring her into the pack. She pulled on her lip as she stared out through the trees.

"Jesse?" he said, and she looked over her shoulder. "I'm going down to get the other boxes. Is there anything else you need me to do while I'm downstairs?"

"Uh, no. I'm fine." She started to smile, but turned back toward the window.

Giving her a few minutes on her own, Tucker headed down the stairs, wishing he knew what was going through her mind. He walked out the front door, and slowed his steps, deliberately, to drag out their time together. As he stood behind the truck, Brian's Jeep pulled into the drive across the street, prompting a low growl that rumbled in his chest.

Brian wasn't what Tucker considered a good guy, despite what Megan thought. The way he flirted with Jesse and stalked her at the Halloween party, really ticked him off. And as much as he preferred Jesse staying with her grandmother until the new moon, part of him wanted her back at the apartment—away from Brian. He grabbed the last box from the back of the truck and slammed the tailgate drawing Brian's attention. *Yeah, it's me.* Tucker stood a little taller as he walked up to the porch.

By the time he carried the last box upstairs, Jesse had already started to unpacked. She smiled when he walked into the room. *She's at ease. That's good.* He set the box on the floor beside the bed and moved back to the door. Watching as she sorted through the items, he recognized the clothes from her closet. Feeling as if he were intruding, he cleared his throat. "I should probably go. I told Jack I'd help tarp the roof," he said as she laid the shirt she was holding on the bed. He could tell by the way she paused that she wanted to say something, or maybe she didn't want him to leave. However, she voiced neither.

"Thank you. For everything," she said as he closed the gap between them.

"Are you upset with me?" He stared into her eyes, searching for her wolf. It was there; he knew, and if he could bring it forward, it might spark her memory.

"No. Everything's just moving so fast and at times, not fast enough. I don't know what you want from me." She tried to look away, but he caught her chin with the tip of his finger.

"No more than you're willing to give. But there are things you will have to remember if this is going to work between us."

"See? When you say things like that it confuses me. I feel like I'm missing some major detail and I..." She paused and stared at the top button on his shirt. "I wish things could go back to the way they were."

"I agree, but that will never happen." Her eyes flared, and his wolf stirred—knowing her wolf was just beneath the surface. He pulled her into his arms and breathed in her soothing scent. Like her, he would have given anything if things could go back to the way they were before he walked out of the town council meeting. He would have been the one that held their bond, and he would have damn sure told her how he felt.

Her hands ran through his hair, and as he lifted her off the floor, she instantly wrapped her legs around his waist. Their first kiss was intense, explosive, and everything he needed, but then it turned soft, like butterfly wings fluttering on a light breeze, and he knew in that instant, he could never let her go.

With the bond between them intensifying, his body heated, and he had to remind himself she wasn't ready, even though she eagerly responded to his touch. He broke from the kiss, and lowered her to the floor, thankful his jacket hung down past his waist. His wolf whined, but he refused to surrender to the urge. "I'll see you later," he whispered and placed a kiss on her forehead, before walking out the door.

What were you thinking? The question bellowed in his mind as he proceeded down the street. It annoyed his wolf that he left Jesse without bonding, yet it was her bond to offer, not his. He feared if he pushed her and she broke the bond, he'd still have to live with a broken heart. *You should have stayed in Tennessee. At least there you wouldn't be screwing up her life.* He kicked a can across the street before walking into the store.

"We were wondering when you would make it back," Jack said and Megan giggled.

"Yeah, sorry it took so long." Tucker ran his fingers through his hair, visibly pissed for not showing more self-control. It was too risky with her being a new blood and not knowing how her wolf would react to him. "You ready to tarp the roof?" He needed a distraction from his current thoughts.

"We've already taken care of it," Jack said.

Tucker looked over at Megan. "Who helped you?" He looked back at Jack.

"Brian. Apparently, he saw you at Gramma's so..."

"So instead of confronting me, he ran over here, hoping Jesse was home? Chicken shit." He mumbled the last part, forgetting Megan's hearing was as good as his.

"That basically sums it up." Megan laughed. "I explained that you and Jesse were together now, so I don't think you'll have any more problems with him."

Tucker wasn't worried about Brian. He was, however, concerned that Brian was manipulating Jesse. It was easy for Megan to say he and Jesse were together, but unless Jesse thought that too, it would be a lie that Brian could twist to his own advantage. He and Megan walked out the door and waited for Jack to lock up.

When the three arrived at Jack's cabin, Gina was sitting on the porch and Whitney had just walked out the door. "There's soup on the stove and cornbread in the oven," Whitney said and stepped off the porch to meet them in the yard.

"You're not going to stay and eat with us?" Megan asked.

"I have to pick up Mason; he's with Randy. We'll be back later to help you move the rest of your things."

Tucker waited until Whitney drove away before walking into the cabin. He should've known Gina would stay behind. She had a hundred excuses for why she couldn't do anything helpful, and he couldn't wait to hear the latest.

Once they were in the kitchen, Megan grabbed a stack of bowls from the cabinet and set them on the counter. "I'm not the waitress so you'll have to fend for yourself."

Gina filled her bowl and then carried it to the table and took a seat across from Tucker. "You've been awfully quiet."

"It's nothing to concern yourself over." Tucker tried not to snap, and if he hadn't been thinking about what his mother would say, he probably would have. *Just go home.* He looked down at his bowl of soup—just her being there gave him the willies.

The meal continued with Gina being unusually quiet, which didn't bode well with Tucker. Usually, when she went into silent mode, she was up to something. He looked up through his lashes, and watched as she stirred her soup, but never took a bite.

"Wasn't Seth supposed to meet you this afternoon to fix the backdoor?" Jack directed his question to Gina.

"Oh, crap! I knew I was forgetting something. I should go." She pushed up from the table and placed her bowl in the sink. "Thanks for supper."

"Wait, I'll walk you to the door," Megan said, but Gina waved her off.

"You finish eating. I can see myself out."

Five minutes later, Tucker got up from the table and placed his bowl in the sink as Jack pulled open the refrigerator door. "So, is Jesse coming around?" Jack asked, pouring a cup of milk.

"Maybe, I don't know. We talked about wolves and she seemed interested. It depends on how much actually soaked in I guess." Tucker took a mug out of the cabinet and poured a cup of coffee. "Hopefully, by morning, she'll figure out what's going on. It was obvious it confused her the first time."

"Is there anything we can do to help?" Megan walked over to where Tucker stood looking out the window. "I'll talk to her if you want. She trusts me."

"I know she trusts you, but we don't know how her wolf will respond." Jack took a drink before setting his mug on the table. "If we're going to do this, it has to be Tucker."

"I know, but I feel helpless watching her go through it and not being there for her. She was so upset thinking she'd done something bad." Megan frowned as Jesse and Gramma walked into the house. "Maybe if you just told her everything. Explain it to her and make her understand."

"I tried," Tucker said and looked back toward the

living room.

"What is it?" Jack glanced over his shoulder, listening.

"I thought I heard something, but it was probably the wind. Anyway, I need to head home. Tell Whitney I said thanks for supper." He kissed Megan on top of her head. "Don't worry. I won't let anything happen to her." Nodding to Jack, he walked out of the room.

His wolf grumbled when he stepped out the front door, and instantly Tucker scanned the area. The hair on his neck stood from what he presumed was a threat nearby, but he noticed nothing out of the ordinary. Gina had just turned to walk into her cabin, and judging by the way Seth was glaring, she had already pissed him off. *Better you than me.* Zipping his jacket to thwart the evening chill, he headed home.

Fourteen

Jesse

"Jesse, you have a visitor," Gramma called out from the foyer, and Jesse glanced up at the clock. It was just after supper, and although she wasn't expecting company, she secretly hoped it was Tucker. She dried her hands and draped the dish towel over the side of the sink before walking out of the room. Noticing the frown on her grandmother's face, and seeing the tall blonde standing just inside the front door, her skin prickled. *Gina?*

She coughed into her fist and then grabbed her sweater off the coat rack, before meeting Gina at the door. With the rapid drop of temperature in just the past twenty-four hours, she was probably coming down with a cold... again. She pushed open the screen door and motioned Gina out to the porch. *You knew this would happen*, she thought, but she didn't expect it would happen so soon. Guys like Tucker and Brian always had flimsy chicks chasing after them, making her nothing more than a temporary distraction.

Jesse sat down on the swing and crossed her arms over her chest to ward off the night chill. Her mistrusting gaze followed Gina as she sat down in the rocking chair catty-corner from the swing. She resolved to listen to what Gina had to say and decide for herself if she were Tucker's girlfriend. "So, what can I do for you?" Jesse asked.

"I'm sorry to bother you at this late hour, but I wanted to talk to you in private. There are things going on behind your back that I think you should know. I'm not one to sugarcoat things, so please accept my apology if I seem crude," Gina said.

"I'm a big girl. I think I can handle whatever you have to say, and I can be pretty crude myself." Not offering an apology, Jesse glared, her attitude boiling to the surface. Instantly, she didn't like Gina, and although she tried to keep an open mind, she knew that wasn't possible.

"Well, obviously you know who I am, based on your attitude, which is good. So I'll cut to the chase. You're a danger to our pack," Gina said, returning the icy glare.

"Please, do tell." Jesse pursed her lips and waited.

"Look, we all know you tried to expose the pack. Humans are petty, and although we have to get along with them, we hold little stock in their opinions. You see, what you did that day only demonstrated your weakness. You couldn't handle the pressure of knowing there was something living here that was not quite like you. You did what was expected, actually."

"I know what I did, and why," Jesse cut in. "What I

don't know is why it should matter so much to you. So if you have something to say, spit it out and stop trying to attack my character."

"Tucker wants to change you. And make you one of us," Gina replied.

"That's absurd. He would never do anything like that, especially if I didn't want him to." *Are you sure about that?* Recalling the conversation she'd had with her dad, she wracked her brain, trying to remember the details of how a person could be changed, but Gina pulled her from her thoughts.

"That's why I'm telling you this. If it happens against your will, you'll become a threat to the pack, but more importantly, to Tucker."

"Can we talk crudely here for just a minute? Because that's the biggest line of bullshit I've ever heard. I think you're desperate, conniving, and just plain nasty and you'd do whatever you could to get one second of Tucker's attention. You remind me of a redhead I once knew before she grew the hell up, or maybe it was after Jack moved on... who knows?" Jesse threw her hands out, and Gina grinned.

"Like I said, we hold little stock in human opinions, but by changing you, you're not likely to buck authority. You're a very desirable female to our pack males. I know human men prefer the slim females, but for a wolf, a female such as yourself... well, you know."

"No, actually I don't, so please enlighten me." Jesse was more than pissed, and she didn't expect her mood to get any better. She fisted her hands and tucked them between her knees. The girl definitely had nerve, but that didn't mean what she said was true.

"I know you're an intelligent, young woman, so you need to think like one. Think about your body. Unlike mine, pack males find you more desirable because you are what they consider a pup pusher."

"A what?" The sound of that made Jesse gag, and she coughed into her fist. Again.

"You know, popping out one pup after another? And you're smart enough to raise them, being human and all. You see, Tucker is from a large family and he definitely wants a large family. I could never give him that, nor would I want to. I've seen how pregnancy destroys the female figure, and an alpha male deserves nothing less than perfection. But you, on the other hand, are human, and Tucker seems to think you wouldn't mind. I mean, no offense, but there is no comparison between us. Plus, human females are... um... easy."

"Honey, we saw *easy* wrapped in a barmaid costume, so don't point your finger my way! Because in case you hadn't noticed, three of them are pointing back at you. Now if you're done with the personal insults, explain how this makes me dangerous."

"Tucker doesn't have a bond with you, which means his wolf would never accept you as his mate. But if he changed you, that might be enough to bind you to him. Don't you see? It's a way of controlling you. You humans call it having-your-cake-and-eating-it, and well, Tucker loves eating cake."

"Brownies," Jesse smirked knowingly and rolled her eyes.

"Whatever. It's all the same," Gina dismissed with a wink.

"So what you're saying is Tucker's looking for a girl

that can give him everything he wants out of life, all the things that a mere wolf can't. That part I can understand." Jesse grinned, throwing out her own insult. "But that still doesn't explain how I could be dangerous." She coughed into her fist. At the rate she was going, she would probably cough up a lung by morning.

"If he changes you against your will, you could turn on him or the pack. The last time that happened, the female killed two of our males before she was killed. Is that what you want?" Gina asked, the slight sneer on her face making her every bit the smartass Jesse first thought she was.

"It's highly unlikely, don't you think?" Jesse clenched her jaw as fire swept through her veins. *Control your temper,* she mentally scolded, but since when did she have to watch her temper? She drew in a cool breath, dousing the invisible flames.

"Well, based on the conversation I overheard today, that's exactly what he plans to do. And if Jack finds out that I know, who knows what he and Megan will do?"

"Don't bring Megan into this. She's one of my best friends, and she would never do anything to hurt me." Jesse abruptly stood and walked over to the porch railing, staring across at Brian's house. His Jeep was gone, as if she really cared. She gnawed her lip while fighting the urge to toss Gina off the porch.

"She was there. The three of them were watching you and your grandmother in the backyard today. The plan is in place and based on what I overheard, Tucker has already tried to change you once. He will try to change you again."

"That's a lie!" Jesse spun around, piercing Gina with a

glare. "Megan wouldn't do that. She's like a sister." She squeezed her eyes shut as a grimacing pain shot through her head. *Calm down! She wants you to react.* Her inner voice hissed, and she opened her eyes to find Gina smirking.

"Are you sure? How nice would it be if your best friend were a member of your pack? And considering Megan is somewhat of an outsider, she needs all the friends she can get," Gina sneered and Jesse moved back to the swing. "Just watch your back. That's all I'm saying."

Jesse leaned back, her arms tightly crossing her chest. What if Gina were telling the truth? The thought of Megan being behind something so devious was devastating, which is what made it so hard to believe. "So if what you're saying is true, and I'm not convinced I believe you, what should I do?"

"You need to leave town before the next full moon, that's when he'll try to change you."

Jesse laid her head back on the swing, staring up at the ceiling.

"Look, I'm sorry. I shouldn't have told you anything. They could kill me and no one would ever know. That's what happened to the man that attacked you. Just think about what I said and do what's right for you. But just so you know, the only way to get away from him is to put distance between you, especially during the full moon when our wolves are the most active."

"And show weakness?" Jesse lifted her head, her eyes locking onto Gina. "Sorry, I didn't run from the pack the first time, and I'm not about to run because of you! So get over yourself."

"You're assuming I'm the threat, which I'm not. You

need to pay attention and actually listen to what I'm saying. You will be a danger to everyone. Stop thinking about yourself and consider others for a change. Think about your grandmother. I understand how hard it is to walk away from someone such as Tucker, but it's really for the best."

"Do you know how crazy you sound?"

"Yes. I sound crazy to myself, but I overheard their conversation, and I'm only here to inform you. What you do with the information is up to you."

Jesse glanced around the neighborhood to avoid Gina's annoying smirk. She didn't trust her, but what if she knew something that the others were holding back? "How much time do I have?"

"Three weeks."

Jesse stayed on the porch long after Gina skulked back into the woods. Why was everything bad that happened in her life always associated with those damn trees? *Yeah, blame it on the trees, because they're the problem.* She hissed a swear word and shivered as the night air settled into her bones. The darkness that surrounded her was nothing compared to the betrayal squeezing her heart. They were her friends, but could they plot something so life changing? And if so, how could they? A tear rolled down her cheek, and she angrily swiped it away. She wouldn't cry. They didn't deserve her tears.

That night, she lay in bed and stared out the front window at the orange hue of the streetlight. She wasn't an attention-seeker, and yet, there she was again centered in drama. She was level-headed, which usually meant dull and boring, and not at all like the Tracies of the world.

Maybe that was the catch. If she were in-your-face, she wouldn't be such an easy target. Her brain hurt the longer she thought about it, and she rolled over toward the nightstand and opened the drawer. She pulled out a small pocket calendar. A vacation would be nice, but did she really want to fly to D.C.?

Her mother would be more than excited to have her visit, and no one would suspect a thing, except Gina, and she wouldn't talk. *But what if she were lying?* The voice of reason sounded in her head. *But what if she were not?* It was the *not* that worried her. She flopped back on the bed and stared at the calendar. It was the holiday weekend, and the odds of getting stuck at the airport because of flight delays weren't something she wanted to risk.

She tapped her finger against her lip as her scheming mind whirled through her options. *It might work.* Grabbing her phone off the table, she called the one person she knew she could depend on. "Lori!" Jesse said, sounding winded. "I need a huge favor. I have a friend I want to visit, and I don't want to go there alone. Are you up for a road trip?"

By the time Jesse hung up the phone, she was somewhat relieved. She wasn't sure how Lori would feel about missing Thanksgiving dinner with her family and Steve, but the thought of helping others never failed to excite her. She gave Lori the dates, and now it was only a matter of talking to her friend in Alma County. But she was fairly certain he wouldn't mind their sudden visit. She tossed her phone onto the table and picked up the calendar, marking through the dates. Satisfied that her plan was coming together, she relaxed and drifted off to sleep.

"NO!" she wanted to scream, but instead, she ducked behind a tree. Her heart twisted, watching Tucker perched on the ledge, overlooking the river—no doubt waiting for her. Wake up. It's a dream. She could feel her arms thrashing in her mind, yet she remained right there next to the tree.

"Jesse?" Confused, Tucker studied her as he moved across the yard. "Why are you hiding?"

"I'm not. I was just looking at this... tree." Dang, he was good looking, and not at all like the monster Gina described but then again, he was a wolf.

"Come over here, the view is nice when it's not storming," Tucker said and grabbed her hand, leading her across the yard to the river's edge.

The thought of jumping off the ledge entered her mind as the smell of murky water wrinkled her nose. But it was a dream, so who's to say she couldn't fly away? She looked over the edge but memories of Megan at Hunter's Ridge kept her grounded. Eventually, she sat down and stared across the river and thought for a measly little river; the view was breathtaking.

"I wasn't sure you'd be here." Tucker took a seat beside her and she inched away.

"Well, it is but a dream. You've been saying that all along and you were right." Jesse cleared her throat, staring down at a piece of driftwood floating past. Wake up! Any other time the Sandman would have gladly interrupted her dreams, but nooooo, not this dream.

"Did I do something to offend you?"

Jesse wiped down the goosebumps that traveled up her arms. Not the goosebumps that sent prickly warnings to her brain, but warm fuzzies that released myriad butterflies in her belly.

"No, you're fine. It's me." She forced a smile. *You have to wake up!* She pinched the inside of her thigh.

"Is it because of yesterday? I won't lie. I've wanted to kiss you since meeting you at the theater." The way he tugged his bottom lip reminded her of the kiss and she had to look away.

No, you do not want to bite his lip! Oh, yes, she did. It was a dream after all, and in her dream she could do whatever she wanted. She blushed, her heart pounding against her ribs with all the naughty thoughts. "It was nice, but we probably shouldn't have. I mean, it's not like there's anything between us." She coughed to stifle the annoying rattle in her chest.

"What do you mean?" Tucker asked. Seeing the confusion in his eyes, she wanted to kiss his worries away, but that would just lead him on, and she needed to do the opposite.

"I'm not sure we," she motioned between them, "should be together. You're a wolf. Your world differs critically from mine and this, of course, is a dream."

"Jesse, stop! Yes, this is a dream, but you have to remember you're also a wolf." He lifted his hands and then dropped them dramatically. Apparently, she had hit a nerve by the way his jaw ticked.

She glared unable to hold her tongue. "About that. If I'm supposed to be a big, bad wolf, then why am I in so much danger? Shouldn't I have superhuman strength or some weird wolf mojo? I mean, that is one perk of being a werewolf, isn't it?"

"Yes... no. We're shifters, and our wolves are for

protection, but we don't go around terrorizing people just because we can."

She chuckled, unconvinced. "You may not now, but you did once upon a time. That I know for a fact. But if what you say is true, and the wolf is strictly for protection, then why keep it a secret? Won't my wolf protect me? You have to admit, things aren't adding up."

"That's a low blow even for you." Tucker scowled. "We're not monsters, and Travis was just one wolf. A crazed wolf, trying to take over a pack. You can't honestly hold the rest of us responsible for his actions." He shook his head, frustrated. "Your wolf will protect you, but one wolf against a pack doesn't stand a chance. You're a new blood, and the pack won't trust you. Therefore, you can't tell anyone until my wolf bonds with yours. Only then will you not be considered a threat." He exhaled loudly and then turned back to the river.

"Here's an idea. Don't change me and tell your pack I said go to hell. Threat eliminated. See how easy that was? Now skedaddle your furry butt back to your precious pack and let Gina be your pup pusher." The sneer in her words apparently caught him off guard as a crease formed between his brows.

"What are you talking about? You're already changed, and I told you before, Gina means nothing to me."

"Did you change me? I know all about the desires of pack males. You want me to be your baby mama!" Jesse glared. It may have been a dream, but that didn't mean she wasn't going to get in one last jab. That's what you do when you're lucid dreaming, right? Control the dream? Well, that might not have been exactly right, but for her, it was.

"Where did you come up with a foolish idea like that? Do you even hear what you're saying? You know I didn't change you. That's why I told you not to tell anyone you were a wolf. The wolf that changed you could come back for you, and I don't want to see you hurt. Geesh, Jesse, give me a little credit." He shoved his hands through his hair, something he did whenever he was stressed. "And what the hell is a baby mama?"

She rolled her eyes. "You think this is easy for me? I wake up in the woods not remembering anything. Then I have dreams in which you insist I'm a wolf. And I need to remember, but not tell anyone? Do you know how jacked up that is? I don't know what to believe anymore. I get two sides of the same story, and I want to believe you, but..."

"I don't want you to believe me. I want you to depend on what you know to be true. So wake up! Go back to your room and think for yourself. Stop depending on others to do it for you." He stood and offered his hand.

"So, what, you're just going to walk away again?" She jumped to her feet, smacking his hand away.

"No, this time, you are. It's my house."

"Fine, but just so you know. I don't need you or anyone else to think for me. Let's get that straight right now. As for these dreams, I think it's time to put a stop to them."

She opened her eyes to the pitch darkness of her room.

Fifteen

Tucker

The week flew by and not once did he and Jesse share a dream. It wasn't for lack of his trying, considering he went to bed early every night, hoping to meet up with her, but after repeated failed attempts, he began to worry.

Jesse said things that were out of character; and where did she get the ridiculous notion that he had changed her? It was disturbing to the point of almost being funny. He had never, nor would he ever, stoop to such a degrading act just to gain favor from a female. If the bond weren't inherently strong enough to bring them together, then they weren't meant to be.

In their case, he'd never given Jesse the chance to accept his bond. As it turned out, breaking it was the worst thing that could have happened. Not wanting to relive that nightmare, he pushed it out of his mind.

Hindsight may be twenty-twenty, but for him, it was a valuable lesson learned at a terrible cost.

"Megan," Tucker called out when she walked into the warehouse. He had just finished installing motion-sensor lights so when Jesse moved back to her apartment, she wouldn't have to walk into a dark building. "How's Jesse doing?" He stuffed his tools into the utility belt and then backed down the ladder.

"What do you mean, how's Jesse doing? I haven't talked to her. She was supposed to stop by yesterday and pick out the wall paint, but she never showed up. I figured she was preoccupied with you," Megan said, reaching to hold the ladder.

"That was the plan, but she's done nothing but avoid me for the past week, and the new moon is tomorrow. I'm worried how her wolf will respond to mine if she's angry over something I've done. I need to talk to her, today. I need her to trust me."

Megan tapped her chin, staring across the warehouse. "I don't think she's avoiding you. Maybe she's sick again. Dr. Stevens said she would be sick until she accepted her wolf."

"Maybe, but that doesn't explain why she doesn't trust me." Tucker stepped down from the last rung. "I need to prove I'm not a threat to her."

"Yeah, but what can you do?"

"I'll do what I should've done a week ago when she threatened to block the dreams." He unfastened the tool belt and handed it to Megan. "I'm going to her grandmother's house."

Five minutes later, Tucker was parked in front of Gramma's house, staring up at Jesse's window. She'd been blocking her dreams, which he thought was impossible; but if she believed that would keep him away, she was dead wrong.

He'd done nothing to warrant her attitude, and deep down, he wondered if Brian had swayed her. Would their lives together just end? Would it be the end of them for all eternity? A soul-wrenching sob climbed up his throat. He didn't like to show weakness, other than a tear or two from time to time. But being shut out, and snubbed, he longed to unleash the river that filled his heart. *You're mine, Jesse. You've always been mine.*

Pulling himself together, Tucker checked his appearance in the rearview mirror before getting out of the car. Determined to bring Jesse into his world, his days of being the nice guy were officially over. He slammed the car door, and stomped up to the house, knocking lightly on the front door. He took a step back and waited as the door slowly opened.

"Come in, Tucker," Gramma said, opening the door further. Tucker smiled, thankful that she remembered him.

"I'm sorry to bother you, but I came to see Jesse. Is she here?" He looked around the foyer, tilting his head, listening for movement upstairs. But he heard nothing.

"She's in her room. She hasn't been feeling well lately. With this crazy weather, it's a wonder we all haven't caught our death." Gramma said as she closed the door behind him. "Go on up. I'm sure she wouldn't mind the company."

Tucker walked up the two flights of stairs, stopping at the door. He tapped lightly, not wanting to wake her if she were asleep. He listened for movement and heard the muffled, "Come in." As he entered the room, flashbacks from their kiss sent a jolt of electricity to his core. *Shake it off.* "How are you feeling? Your grandmother said you were sick."

His heart crashed when he saw Jesse burrowed beneath a fuzzy blanket, the bed shaking with her shivers. "Jesse?" He hurried to her side and placed his hand on her forehead—her skin was cool and clammy. "Your fever broke," he said and looked over at the open window. "I'll be right back."

As he walked across the room, he paused at the picture of his wolf hanging on the corkboard. How she managed to take it at that angle, baffled him, but there it was. He looked over his shoulder at the fuzzy lump in the center of the bed. He may have upset her, but obviously not enough for her to take down his picture. He shook his head and continued into the bathroom.

Standing next to the tub, he pushed down the stopper and turned on the faucet. While the tub filled, he walked out of the room and closed the door. Jesse still hadn't moved, so he pulled back the blanket. "You need to get these wet clothes off and warm your body. You're chilled to the bone." Without giving her time to object, he lifted her off the bed and carried her into the bathroom, her body quivering against his. He sat her on the commode, and reached down to adjust the water, then pushed the shower curtain to the side. "Do you need help to get in?" She shook her head, and he rubbed over her hair. "Just holler if you need me."

While Jesse soaked in the warm water, Tucker went downstairs to find her grandmother. She was standing in the kitchen and he cleared his throat as he walked into the room. "Jesse's in the tub, so I thought it would be a good time to change her bedding."

"I planned to change it while she was eating her supper, but those steps are awful steep and I know what a fuss she'll make," Gramma said.

"If you don't mind, I'll do it. You have no business going up those steep steps."

"You sound just like Jesse!" She patted his arm and smiled. "You should find everything you need in the upstairs hall closet, and when you're done, come back down; I have chili simmering in the pot."

Tucker rummaged through the linen closet and carried the clean bedding up to Jesse's room. After changing the sheets, he spread a quilt and the purple, fuzzy blanket over the bed and grinned. Something about that blanket screamed Jesse. Satisfied that she would be warm as soon as she curled up under the covers, he closed the window and headed back down the stairs.

"Laundry room's through that door." Gramma pointed with a ladle. Scooping two bowls of chili, she placed them on a tray with a sleeve of crackers, and two bottles of water. When Tucker came back through the kitchen, she handed him the tray. "Do you mind?"

"Not at all. If you need me to do anything else before I leave, let me know." Tucker took the tray and walked out of the room.

By the time he got back upstairs, he could hear Jesse moving around in the bathroom, so he set the tray on the bedside table and walked over to the door. "Do you need anything?"

"I'll be out in a minute," she said.

He sat down on the edge of the bed and stared across the room at his picture. It was troubling when he thought about it. In order for her to get that picture, she had to have been in the woods at night. He moved closer to the corkboard, but it was the plaster casting that caught his eye. It was as big as his hand, and he instantly knew the print belonged to a wolf. He startled when the bathroom door rattled and nearly launched himself back to the other side of the room. "Do you feel better now?" His face flushed with guilt, but she didn't notice.

"I do. I thought I would freeze to death. Thank you." She sauntered over and sat down on the bed.

Tucker wasn't sure where she got the night clothes she was wearing, but she looked warm enough, so he pulled the blankets back and lifted her feet. As she moved up onto the bed, he covered her legs with the sheet and placed a pillow behind her back. "I brought your supper."

"You didn't have to do this," she said, pulling the warm blankets up over her body.

"Yes, I did. You were freezing." *And my wolf insists on taking care of you.* He moved the water bottles and a bowl of chili to the nightstand, and then placed the tray with her soup on her lap. "Eat."

"I've smelled chili cooking all day. I thought I'd starve before I'd get a bowl. You're a lifesaver." Jesse took a bite and closed her eyes, resting her head back against the iron headboard. Her hands were shaky, dehydrated from the fever, but at least, she wasn't ordering him out of the room.

Tucker hated that Jesse didn't understand the changes that were taking over her body. And it wasn't fair to her to be kept in the dark, but until his wolf had a chance to bond with hers, there was little he could do. However, if he had the chance to take it all away, he couldn't honestly say he would. He frowned and looked down at the floor. *Some mate you are.*

Their connection spanned for centuries, based on the information he received from Dr. Stevens. And although he couldn't remember their previous life, he prayed fate would be on his side. *She'll have nothing to do with you once she realizes someone has changed her against her will.* He tried to swallow the knot that lodged in his throat. Would she deny him because of something he had no control over? He didn't think so, yet his chest ached with the possibility.

He glanced over at Jesse, who slowly ate her soup, wishing she would say what was on her mind. Handing her the bottle of water, every few bites, she looked peaked. "Make sure you drink all the water," he said, sounding like his mother. Once she finished eating, he placed the tray on the side table, and lifted the blankets so she could slide down onto the pillow. "Is there anything else you need? I'm here to serve." He brushed the cracker crumbs off his sleeve—she didn't notice.

"I'm not totally helpless, you know, but if you could hand me that bottle of lotion, I'd appreciate it. This dry skin is itching me to death." She pointed to a tall, white bottle, hidden behind a lamp.

Tucker handed her the lotion and watched as she struggled to open the bottle. "Shouldn't you put that on before you dress?"

"It's just my hands. I must be allergic to something, but I'm not sure what."

"Here, let me do that." Tucker shook the bottle and

then squeezed the lotion into her hand, the cherry-almond scent pleasing to his nose. He watched her smear the lotion over her skin, concentrating mostly on an area between her thumb and index finger. "It doesn't seem to help," he said, noticing she rubbed it red.

"Nothing really helps unless I take an antihistamine, and the only reason that works is because it knocks me out," she admitted as he took a seat beside her and lifted her hand to his lap.

"You have pretty hands and a long lifeline." He chuckled and gently turned her hand over. He looked down to the area she repeatedly rubbed. "Is that a bruise?" He lightly rubbed over the mark, and she shuddered.

"Yeah, it's been there forever it seems. Stupid dog."

"You call your bruise a stupid dog?"

"No! I was talking about the stupid mutt that bit me. I was trying to bait it behind the shelter. You know, being the nice person that I am." She smiled weakly. "I wanted to give it a bath and brush out its matted hair, but the little ingrate bit my hand."

Tucker sucked in a breath and forced himself to stay calm. Any reaction from him could cause her to freak out and that was the last thing he needed. "Was that recent?"

"It's been about two months now. Dr. Stevens had just hired me as a paid employee, and I go and do something stupid the first day. I guess I was trying to impress him with my dog catching skills, but that rascal wasn't having any of it."

"Did you show it to Dr. Stevens?"

"Are you kidding? Do you know how embarrassing that would have been?"

"Yeah." He chuckled. "Do you know what kind of dog

it was?"

"Just a scraggly mutt, muddy brown, I think. It took off across the field. Probably someone's pet."

"Stupid dog," Tucker repeated, putting his dimples on full display. "Are you feeling better now? Seriously?"

"Just tired."

"Well, I won't keep you. I told Megan I would stop by and check on you; she was worried. I'll let her know you've already had supper." He rubbed his hand along her blanketed leg and then blushed when he realized she was talking to him. "What? I'm sorry my mind was elsewhere."

"Would you do me another favor? It's going to sound totally off the wall, but you see that paisley tablecloth over there on the shelf? Would you please deliver it to my neighbor across the street?"

"Really?" His eyes lit up. "Shall I shove it down his throat? Or wrap it around his neck?" He grinned wickedly. He knew exactly where the tablecloth came from, based on Megan's retelling of the story. The dig at Brian was him letting Jesse know he wasn't a fan.

"Neither." She giggled behind her hand. "It belongs to Mr. Tully. He lives next door to Brian, but you'll have to sneak over and leave it on his porch. He doesn't know I have it."

"You stole a tablecloth from an old man?" he feigned shocked and pulled the bundled cloth off the shelf causing it to drop open.

"I did not steal it. I borrowed it without asking, and you're returning it without telling." She tried to narrow her eyes, but her grin wouldn't allow it.

"Hmm, I don't know. I kind of like this tablecloth. The

orange brings out the color of my eyes, and the brown matches my hair."

"And the burgundy?" She pursed her lips, tilting her head to the side.

"I look hot in burgundy." He draped it over his shoulder and glanced up. "It's my color, don't you think?" He laughed when she covered her head, hiding her giggles beneath the purple blanket. "What? You don't like it?"

She peeked over the cover. "No, I like it! I've just never seen a paisley wolf." She giggled again.

Seeing her laugh, his heart soared, knowing he was the reason for her good mood. "I can imagine the pack having a field day with that one. You get some sleep and I'll see you later."

After returning the tray to the kitchen and taking out the trash, Tucker walked out the door and waited until Gramma clicked the deadbolt into place before heading down the sidewalk. He was happy to leave Jesse in a good mood even though his wolf was stewing beneath the surface. The constant grumble that rattled in his chest warned him if he turned his wolf loose, he would blaze a trail through the woods, searching for *the enemy*—a scraggly mutt.

Tucker silenced his wolf as he stepped up on Tully's front porch. He didn't think delivering a tablecloth would be a big deal, but he was wrong. He placed the cloth in the rocking chair and jumped when a little dog head-butted the front door. It sounded threatening, which made Tucker grin. *Who said I'm a nice guy?* The growl that ripped from his throat caused the dog to yelp as if he had actually reached through the mail slot and yanked its tail. Tucker ran off the porch when the porch light clicked on—silently cheering his wolf. He glanced up at the attic window as he pulled open the car door. "I owe you," he yelled as Jesse ducked out of sight.

"I'm back," Tucker yelled, walking into the store. Megan had been worried about Jesse, but when she ran out of the warehouse, to see the smile on his face, she grinned.

"Did you see her? How was she?"

"She seemed okay after her bath." Tucker tried to play it down, but when Jack walked out of the warehouse carrying a bucket of paint, he knew Jack would have something to say.

"You could charm a snake out of its skin." Jack said. "It took me a week to get Megan to share a shower." He winked over at Megan, and she blew him a kiss.

"I didn't charm her out of anything. I started the water and told her to get in the tub, or I'd put her in and bathe her myself," Tucker said, matter-of-factly.

"Yeah, right. If you'd said that, you wouldn't be walking." Megan laughed, making Tucker grin.

"Sounds like you had a good visit." Jack set the paint bucket on a tarp and turned back to the conversation.

"A lot better than I expected. Dr. Stevens said a new blood would have a bruise-colored bite mark at the bite site, and Jesse has that mark on her left hand."

"When and where did it happen? Did she say?" Jack asked, pulling Megan to his side.

"She was behind the animal shelter and the mutt, (her word, not mine), ran off across the field. She said it was muddy-brown." Tucker waited for Jack's reaction before continuing. "I know what you're thinking, but you're wrong. She would never hurt anyone. You have to trust me on this. She's like my sister, and her rough-tough exterior was only for show."

"Who's he talking about?" Megan looked up at the intense frown on Jack's face.

"Tracy."

"She wouldn't do that. I haven't been around her as much as you all have, but even I know she's not capable of doing something like that. You've seen her with Randy. She's probably one of the nicest people I've ever met. Her only fault is always trying to protect those she loves." Megan stepped away from Jack and placed her hands on her hips, "And not by biting someone. She growls a lot, but she would never stoop to that level. Plus, her wolf isn't even brown."

"A muddy-gray would look brown," Jack said, pacing the room. "And I know she wouldn't attack anyone, but that doesn't mean the pack won't accuse her. She brought something like that up at a pack meeting once."

"Well, Jesse's phase should be in the morning. Afterward, we'll have to tell Alpha Cooper. We don't have a choice," Megan said, "Especially if someone from the pack changed her."

"She's right," Jack said to Tucker.

"I know, but that doesn't mean I have to like it." Tucker turned to the door, staring at Jack and Megan's reflection on the glass. Would he and Jesse ever have that kind of relationship? One where they could comfort each other? He glanced past the streetlight, and stared up at the dark sky, remembering Jesse's giggles beneath the fuzzy blanket. *Please don't take that away from me.* As he turned back toward Megan and Jack, he sighed. "I should go get some rest before Jesse's phase. Just cross your fingers and pray everything works out."

"We've got your back if you need us, but so you know, Nigel's been roaming the woods lately. Usually it's later in the day but you never know."

"Why, he's not a member of the Cloverly Pack unless something changed since I left," Tucker said.

"No, he's still in Kinsley but he's been working at the gas station until he can find a permanent replacement for Travis. He's been after Brayden, but he won't budge. He said Nigel is bossy and needs to get laid." Jack laughed.

"That's Brayden. He calls it like he sees it." Tucker chuckled. "He will make a great beta. He reminds me of Sawyer."

"What! You can't take Brayden, he just got settled in," Megan argued and looked up at Jack with a pout.

"Unless you've got his mate in your back pocket, I don't think he will turn down the female attention he will get from the beta position." Jack shrugged.

Sixteen

Tucker

Tucker waited in Jack's kitchen as the early morning hours ticked by. It wasn't his ideal way to spend the night, and as he glanced over at the digital clock on the stovetop, he yawned. Waiting in the woods would've been the better option, but not knowing when or how Jesse would react; serving as sentry at Jack's backdoor was the only alternative that made any sense.

Seeing a shadow move across the attic window, he stepped over to the sink and peeked out from between the curtains. He didn't really expect Jesse to take an interest in the cabin, but with only one chance to rein in the new blood, he wasn't willing to risk it.

He drew in a slow breath as Jesse came out the backdoor wearing the sleep clothes she had changed into the evening before. The teal, long sleeve shirt displayed a large smiley face and matched the plaid pants she wore. He smiled. Standing on the porch, she cast a glance to the sky. Her unruly hair cascading over her shoulders, sprang out in all directions as the wind gently tugged at the curls. He froze when she looked towards the window before walking down the steps and across the yard.

Tucker moved over to the door and quietly pushed it open as Jesse disappeared beneath the oak tree. Unsure of her perception of him, he prayed it would not be as a threat and that she would not react by attacking him. He stepped out on the patio and paused, listening closely. Knowing they shared a bond, he would never harm Jesse even if it meant risking his own life, but that bit of information he kept to himself.

Once Jesse ventured past the tree line, her footsteps grew heavy, clomping over the dried leaves. It was alarming that she didn't seem aware of her surroundings, but as long as she continued along the uphill path, towards Sallee's Rock, she would be safe. Old Man Sallee's property was posted against hunting, but if Jesse ventured toward Hunter's Ridge, he would have no choice but to intervene. With deer season in full swing, and her wolf running during the daylight hours, she was a prime target for trigger-happy hunters, even if wolves were considered an endangered species in Kentucky.

Tucker jogged across the yard and ducked beneath the oak branches, bumping into a wind chime. He held his breath, waiting, but Jesse didn't seem to notice so he slowly released the breath. She shivered from time to time and looked up through the trees, and he assumed she was searching for the moon. The freezing temperature was too cold for her to be outside without a coat and barefoot, but as soon as she phased, her wolf would keep her warm.

Following Jesse deeper into the woods, she abruptly stopped—frozen in place. He stood downwind, not knowing if she had detected him there, but before he could duck behind a tree, she phased.

Her wolf was an amazing sight to see, and he stood there mesmerized by her beauty. Then without warning, she bolted up the hill, and he quickly phased, to follow.

Tucker kept a comfortable pace behind Jesse, reveling in the sweet chicory that carried on the breeze. His heart raced with the possibility that once she accepted her wolf, she might also accept him. Nearing the end of the trail, he slid to a stop just inside the tree line as the jet-black wolf scaled the boulders. She pranced across the rock with her head held high and shook out her mane—ending with a shivering butt twist.

Afraid he would spook her; Tucker slowly inched forward until he was past the trees, standing in the clearing at Sallee's Rock. It was do-or-die time, and dying wasn't an option he cared to entertain.

Jesse's wolf sat down on the boulder, looking out over the clearing—a statue in the darkness—she was flawless. Chicory and coconut floated on the breeze, tempting his wolf to step forward. Caught up in the dizzying spell, he stumbled, and she jumped to her feet. Bristling at the sight of Old Clumsy—a name he would give his wolf if they lived to see the sun—she shifted her stance.

Being a newly turned wolf, she was bold and unpredictable, and that intimidated the hell out of him. As she stalked back across the boulder, her teeth in perilous display, she bounded down the rocks and landed on the ground with a graceful thud. She flicked her ears, and her fluffy tail waved like a black flag against the early morning sky. Obedient to the control she demanded as she flaunted her authority over him, his wolf hunkered low to the ground and whimpered, waiting for her approval. Tucker loved strong females and as Jesse's power crowned around her, she wore it proudly.

He didn't mind being submissive to a female wolf; especially since she was his mate—and he would do whatever it took to gain her trust. She slowly advanced until she was standing over his wolf, at barely half the size of him. As she scented him, he remained deathly still, giving her time to assess the situation. She was cautious, but then simply turned and walked away.

Tucker stood and slowly walked over to where Jesse stopped and was staring into the trees. He never in a million years imagined his wolf would stand next to hers, yet there they were, side by side. The bond between them was overwhelmingly strong and if it weren't for his wolf, he would have sworn he was dreaming. Jesse nudged him with her nose and then took off into the woods, signaling him to follow.

The sun peeked over the horizon as the two wolves weaved between the trees, and deeper into the forest. Tucker gave her space, but never let her out of his sight as he followed her around the rocky terrain, to the lake. He stopped to catch his breath as the sun topped the trees and then gulped down the cold lake water. It was obvious the black wolf no longer considered him a threat as it quickly responded to his wolf. He pawed at the crystal clear water, offering her a drink, and she excitedly hopped and jumped, until she was nuzzled against his side. He teasingly licked over her muzzle. Now if only her human side were that easy to convince, his world would be perfect.

As Jesse continued to play at the water's edge, Tucker moved closer to the tree line. He was determined to keep her safe and far enough away from town so they wouldn't be seen. He didn't usually hang out at the lake, but if that's where Jesse was most comfortable, that's where he would stay.

While resting his wolf, Tucker kept a watchful eye, but when Jesse suddenly stumbled and fell into the water, he jumped to his feet. She was disoriented and sluggish, which, for a wolf, was very unusual. After shaking off the excess water, she staggered back in the direction towards Sallee's Rock. He quickly followed her without missing the way her wolf wobbled. Exhausted from her early morning run? Maybe. But when she unexpectedly phased and her knees buckled, sending her crashing to the ground, he knew that wasn't the case.

Old Clumsy whimpered and licked her face before running beneath a pine tree and phasing. Tucker ripped open the plastic bag that was tied to the tree trunk and sorted through the clothes. The outfits were all the same, just the sizes were different, and nothing he would ever expect to see Jesse wearing. She was all about color and designer fashions, but he had a feeling if anyone could rock a black jogging suit, she could. He rushed back to her side. *She'll be pissed!* He knew that to be true, but she was his mate, and seeing her without clothes was something she would have to get used to. *It's better than being naked beneath a tree.* His thoughts did little good at easing his mind.

Once Tucker had Jesse dressed, he glanced to the sky

and estimated the time to be around eight-thirty that morning. It was too late to take her home without questions, and he refused to leave her alone in the woods. He touched her cheek while listening. Her heartbeat was faint, and although she lay there shivering, her skin was hot to the touch.

Tucker looked back at the tree line, realizing now how Jesse had ended up beneath a tree. *She has to sleep off the fever.* The thought of her going through her first phase alone, crushed his soul. But seeing her lifeless form, and knowing she was defenseless until she awoke, scared the hell out of him.

"Sorry, beautiful, but you'll have to come home with me." He cradled her in his arms and took off through the woods as fast as his feet would carry them. It was nearly freezing, and the light November breeze only added to the chill. He looked down at Jesse; her head back, exposing the soft curve of her neck. She was his mate—his entire world revolved around her—and yet she had no clue.

Tucker glanced both ways down the road, before jumping the ditch and heading across the street to his cabin. He pushed open the door, glad the other cabins were far enough away to give him privacy, and time to figure out what to do about Jesse. Heading straight to the bedroom, she would definitely be mad when she awoke in his bed, but he had nowhere else to put her. *You can leave her on the couch,* his thoughts offered, but like his wolf, he preferred her in his bed.

The room was small compared to her bedroom, but unlike her, he had a king-sized bed. He laid her down on the comforter and plucked pine needles from her hair. Her feet and hands were ice cold, but her face was red hot. He pulled the comforter across her body and added another blanket for warmth.

Jesse instantly cocooned herself beneath the layers of royal blue, and the thought of lying down beside her, strictly to warm her, caused his wolf to stir. But he wasn't brave enough to attempt that... not yet. Then there was the issue of their clothes, and as soon as she was okay, he would go back in the woods and retrieve the scraps. Until then, he would get some sleep. Glancing down at the bed, he debated, but eventually opted for the chair in the corner. It wouldn't be nearly as comfortable as the mattress, but much better than the floor.

Staying up for more than twenty-four hours, and then running like a mad dog through the woods, his body was finally shutting down. Resting his arm on the chair, he leaned his head against his fist and closed his eyes. Within minutes, he fell asleep and memories of the black wolf played in his dreams. *His wolf towered over hers as they sat on the boulder beneath the full moon.*

He shifted in the chair to block the afternoon sun that beamed through the window and then opened his eyes and glanced at the clock. His sleep-deprived brain calculated the hour as a low growl echoed in the room. Tucker jumped from his chair and threw his hands out to ward off the wolf until he realized the sound was coming from Jesse.

A feral beauty she was, struggling to escape what she presumed was a threat as she dug her heels into the mattress and clutched the blanket to her chest. Wild and untamable, she rose higher against the headboard, practically climbing the wall.

"Shh, it's okay... You're safe," Tucker said in a low,

soothing voice.

Her predatory eyes—darker than night—scanned the unfamiliar room and then locked onto his. His skin prickled and the hair on his neck rose when she scented the air. Would she remember him? Or would she phase and attack? He swallowed down his unease and stared off to the side, not wanting to provoke her wolf, but a subtle sag in her posture gave him hope.

After the intense standoff, Jesse finally dropped to the mattress, confused. "What happened?" she asked, placing her hand to the side of her head.

"Not so fast. Your fever is back." Tucker slowly moved over to the bed, looking into her eyes for any sign of her wolf.

"What happened? And where are my clothes?" she asked again, her voice growing harsher, and more demanding.

"Jesse, nothing happened. I would never take advantage of you like that."

"Then where are my clothes?" she hissed.

"Probably in the woods where you left them," he finally said, expecting the worse.

"Seems I have a habit of doing that lately, and yet I'm wearing yours. Imagine that." The sneer on her face caused him to step back.

"You know what happened. You just refuse to accept it; and until you do, you'll have repeats. Be glad I was there, or you'd probably be waking up under a tree right now."

"So it was you! You're the reason I was under that tree!" Her narrowed glare clashed with his. "I don't remember what happened that night, and I don't think I like where this is going."

"Jesse, stop! You know what happened or you should, if you would bother to use your brain. If not, you might as well have two asses." That didn't come out the way he intended, but seeing her accusing eyes and hearing her haughty attitude, it ticked him off. She had no right to be angry when it was him that kept her safe. And despite what she believed, being at his cabin was far better than waking up under a tree.

"Whatever. I will not sit here and listen to you attack me because of something you think I should remember. You know nothing about me!" She moved sideways on the bed, refusing to look his way.

"I know enough, but if you don't trust your own memories, you're not going to trust mine." Exhausted, he turned and ran his fingers through his hair. Why couldn't she have slept just a few hours longer?

"Pffttt." She brushed him off with a flick of her wrist, and he narrowed his eyes, more than weary of her attitude. It was time she faced what she knew to be true and accept her wolf.

"Wow. I didn't realize you were such an ungrateful person."

"Oh? Well, I didn't realize I was supposed to thank you for saving my life, when you're the one that kidnapped me and brought me here. How does that work?"

"I did not kidnap you! You know that! You're just too stubborn to see what's right in front of your own eyes." He frowned when she hung her head, but not before he saw the tears in her eyes. Feeling guilty, Tucker kneeled beside the bed and lifted her chin. Being a jerk was unusual for him, but trying to get through to her was like trying to bust concrete with a rubber mallet. "I'm sorry. I want to help you, and I will. But you have to remember why you were in the woods and believe it. Until you do, this will continue to happen... you will continue waking up in unfamiliar places."

"Why can't you tell me?" she whispered blinking back tears.

"Because you feel a connection to me, but you still don't trust me."

"I do trust you." She pushed the blanket off her legs and looked down. "What? No shoes?"

"In your dreams you trust me, but here, not so much." He walked across the room and pulled open the dresser drawer. Tossing a pair of socks on the bed, he rubbed over his jaw. "At some point, you will have to accept what you are and the sooner you do that, the better."

"What do you know about my dreams?"

"I know we share them, and it's happened more than once. But what happened this morning wasn't any dream." Tucker's head jerked around when a horrid voice called to him from the front door. His jaw clenched. How many times would he have to tell Gina to stay away before she got the hint? He turned back to Jesse who was now glaring at the bedroom door.

"As if this weren't humiliating enough, now your girlfriend is here?" she whisper-hissed.

Tucker put his finger to his lips. "I'll be right back. Just stay here and be quiet."

Seventeen

Jesse

He did not just walk away! Jesse's jaw tightened as the door shut behind Tucker. Was that his way of having his cake and eating it? Maybe there was truth to what Gina had said, and he was a big two-timing jerk. What exactly did he expect from her? A booty call? That would never happen, no matter how attractive he was. It was insulting, degrading, and downright disgusting, and she would never agree to such a shallow relationship.

Shame welled in her eyes and she quietly pushed open the window. Despite what Tucker believed, she honestly trusted him until he shushed her. She closed her eyes as the cool afternoon air drifted through the screen, bringing with it, all her dreams.

Their words jumbled together as she scanned through

the memories, but at no point did she tell him she was naked beneath a tree. The one thing she did notice was how he constantly insisted it was a dream which was more proof they were sharing them. *How?* Who knew, but werewolves were real, so anything else was possible.

Her eyes opened and hot tears distorted her vision. But remembering her conversation with Gina, she slammed the window shut, and sneered at the crack spreading across the glass. *Oh, no. No, no, no.* She glared back at the bedroom door.

Conflict wasn't something she normally sought, but the urge to put Tucker and Gina in their place outweighed her better judgment. Moving over to the door, she inched it open as Tucker's voice boomed down the hall. The shadows from the late afternoon sun stretched through the doorway as she tiptoed past the kitchen only to come face to face with her worst nightmare. Tucker turned, surprised to see her there, and Gina glared down her nose.

"Don't let me interrupt. I'm just passing through," Jesse scoffed and shrugged Tucker's hand away.

Gina chuckled.

"Jesse, wait..."

She glared toward Tucker, and her eyes flared when she recalled his words. "Love me for what I am, or let me go. Funny when the shoe's on the other foot, your words no longer matter. No, don't you dare!" She lifted her hand to shut him down. "I'm not some dirty little secret you can cage in your room. You can't pretend to like me and then expect me to hide when your precious pack shows up. I will not do that for you or anyone. So if she can't give you what you want, then I suggest you look elsewhere, because I'm not interested."

Turning to address Gina, whose fake grin suddenly vanished, she glowered. "As for you... I don't know where you get off thinking you're somehow better than me, because you're not. So let me give you fair warning... I'm not the reason you can't keep your man at home, but if you come to my house again, spewing that bullshit, I will be the reason he has to scrape your sorry ass off my porch. I'm not afraid of you, and I will not be bullied. Got it?"

Jesse ducked around Tucker and stormed out the door, him pleading with her not to go. Pissed beyond reason, she had no intents of ever looking back. But as luck would have it pain shot through her head preventing her from making a hasty escape.

She stumbled across the yard and dropped to her knees, the searing pain watering her eyes. "What did I do to deserve this?" Her body stung from a thousand pinpricks and she rested her forehead against the ground. *Please, please, not here.* Fisting her hands in the grass, the pain quickly dissipated and she sucked in a deep breath.

A low growl rose from her chest and she opened her eyes. Drenched in sweat, she pushed back the urge to phase and staggered to her feet. "Do not touch me," she hissed and smacked Tucker's hand away—her own hands trembling. It didn't matter that he was sorry, or that Gina was watching the show with a stupid smirk on her face. All that mattered was she get away from them as fast as she could because like it or not, she had been changed.

She wiped the sweat from her brow as she rushed down the road, her sock feet slapping the cold blacktop. When Jack's cabin came into view, she cut sharply at the tree line, running along the edge of the woods. Ignoring

Megan when she called to her, she had to cool down before she attempted any confrontation. She loved Megan like a sister, but at the moment, she couldn't stand the sight of her. *Think for yourself.* Isn't that what Tucker suggested? As she ran up on the back porch, she realized she was still wearing the unseemly clothes. *Who wears all black?* She snarled at the thought.

Her grandmother was talking on the phone when she rushed into the kitchen. "I'll be back in a minute," she said, her voice calmer, although her body was anything but. It was a lie of course, but it would delay her grandmother from hanging up the phone.

Instead of going to her room, she veered to the foyer and grabbed the truck keys off the hall table and quietly slipped out the front door. *Think for yourself.* Tucker's words repeated in her head, and if that's what he wanted, that's exactly what he would get.

Still in her sock feet and Tucker's clothes, Jesse climbed into the truck, ignoring the waving skirt-chaser across the street. She barked the tires as she backed down the drive in her rush to get out of the neighborhood.

In her haste to find her dad, she barreled down Main Street not bothering to check her speed. She slowed and clicked on the turn signal as she steered the truck into the hospital lot. Spotting Sonya's SUV parked next to the building, she expected to find her dad still at the office, even if, unfortunately, Sonya was as well. *What did you expect? She is his wife.* Pulling into a handicapped space, she slammed the truck into park, jumped out, and ran to the door.

Jesse rushed down the hall, bypassing the desk and continued to her dad's office. She expected the usual greetings from the office staff and was a little offended when they turned and stared. Her jaw ticked. *What the hell are you looking at?* She wanted to scream. Busybodies with nothing better to do than gawk. She couldn't get to his office fast enough.

Pushing through the door without knocking, Dr. Williams looked up and frowned. Obviously, Jesse had interrupted their work schedule, but how important could filing insurance forms be? Especially when compared to what she was about to unload on him?

"Recognize anything?" Jesse asked and closed the door. "Look familiar?" She glared at Sonya, and a low rumble filled the room. "Guess where I spent the past..." Looking over at the clock on the wall, she pointed the hours out, "... nine hours?" She sneered. "I've been in the woods, running. Anyone want to guess why?" Her eyes moved past her dad and settled back on Sonya. "Do you want to tell him? Or should I?"

"Jesse, I... I'm not sure what's going on but..." Sonya's voice was barely a whisper.

"But you sense me. Tell him, Sonya."

"What are you talking about?" Dr. Williams shot up out of his chair and walked around the desk. He stood in front of Jesse and his scolding look made her insides sizzle. "Calm down and tell me why you look like... that." He put his hand to the side of her face. "You're burning up."

"Ya think? Would you like to give me the diagnosis? Or should we ask Sonya to do it?" She glared past her dad, and Sonya lowered her eyes.

"That's enough! What in the world has gotten into you?" Dr. Williams asked. His voice was demanding and hard lines appeared between his brows.

"Come on, Dad. You're the pack doctor; surely you must recognize the symptoms." She fanned her hands out. "Here's a clue. I've been changed into a damn wolf!" She glared past him to Sonya again. "You said, *don't worry, Jesse, the pack understands why you tried to expose them.* Really, Sonya? I trusted you! Is this your payback? Seems the secret of Cloverly held some truth after all."

"No, Jesse, that's not true. The pack would never do that." Sonya started to get up but stopped when Jesse's eyes flared.

Dr. Williams looked back at Sonya. "What is she talking about, *being changed?*" Anger flashed across his face, a look Jesse had never seen before.

"It's true. I can see the wolf in her eyes." Sonya's face paled beneath his gaze.

"Who did this? I want to know who did this!" he said, his voice so edgy that it cut through the room.

"I don't know. It's against pack law to change a human. It's dangerous..." Sonya's voice trailed off, and she cringed.

"It's worse than dangerous. It could have killed her!" Dr. Williams yelled and Sonya lowered her eyes—Jesse secretly enjoying her step-mother's discomfort. "This was not supposed to happen. She was safe in Indy and I brought her here. Is this the thanks I get for being the pack doctor?" He walked over to the coat rack and yanked his coat off the hook.

"Where are you going?" Sonya asked.

"I have an alpha to see. If you're coming, I suggest you grab your coat."

Jesse followed them out to the truck, bypassing the

SUV. "Get in. I'm driving," her dad ordered, nudging Jesse to the middle of the bench seat. As soon as Sonya was buckled in, and the passenger door closed, Dr. Williams backed out of the lot.

Jesse braced herself against the dashboard as they sped through town. Passing Cabin Run Road, she glanced to see Megan, Jack, and Tucker standing in front of Jack's cabin—Gina walking across the street. Her anger spiked and her lip trembled when realization set in. She wasn't like them; she didn't want to be a wolf. She wanted to be Jesse, the girl from Indiana. She squeezed her eyes shut. *What would Mom think?*

After what seemed like mere seconds, she opened her eyes when her dad pulled over and parked in front of a large two-story barn-like house. Weak and mentally drained, she asked, "Where are we?"

"The alpha house," her dad said, and jumped out of the truck, leaving her to struggle with the seatbelt.

"I want to know who changed my daughter!" Dr. Williams demanded as Sonya helped Jesse from the truck. She had never heard her dad use such an intimidating voice that even she was afraid to cross him.

"Changed your daughter? How?" Ben asked, walking across the deck.

"Look at her; she's a damn wolf! Who changed her?" His voice rose, and Jesse sunk to the ground. Rethinking her decision to tell her dad she was a wolf she wondered if it was too late to yell April Fools!? And why was she always in the middle of a pissing match when it came to the wolves? Her head throbbed, and she squeezed the bridge of her nose.

"I'm sure there's an explanation, I just..." Ben rubbed

his jaw as he approached Jesse, but when she looked up, he took a step back. "This is the first I've heard of it."

"And you call yourself an alpha?"

"David!" Sonya scolded. "The alpha had nothing to do with this and you know it."

"Was it revenge for her trying to expose the pack?"

"No. There was nothing wrong with what she did and we don't hold grudges," Ben said as he slowly stooped beside Jesse and took hold of her hand. "Jesse, I'm sorry this happened to you, and as the Regional Alpha, I will get to the bottom of it. But first, I need you to tell me everything you know."

Jesse's face heated beneath the alpha's stare, but she wanted answers as well, so she quickly filled him in on everything that had taken place over the past month. From waking under a tree, to Gina's warning, to that morning at Tucker's cabin... she left out the bed part, intentionally. "I didn't want this. I never wanted to be a wolf."

"I know," the alpha said in a soothing voice as he briefly looked over at Dr. Williams. "There's nothing I can do to change this, but I can promise you I will find out who changed you and deliver a harsh punishment to whoever it was. They had to know the risk, and that is unacceptable."

"You're damn right it is." David pushed away from the truck and paced back and forth, listening as Alpha Cooper continued questioning Jesse.

"You need to calm down. Your ranting is only making this worse on Jesse. She needs your support, and you're making her feel like she's a monster," Sonya scolded again.

Jesse glanced over her shoulder, glad she wasn't the one standing next to her dad. His eyes were full of rage, and at that point, she feared him more than the wolves.

"I will always support her, but that doesn't mean I have to like what happened." Dr. Williams stomped over and pulled Jesse off the ground. Wrapping her in his arms, he couldn't hold back the tears that filled his eyes. "I never meant for this to happen, but know I love you no matter what you are." Jesse tucked her head into his chest and cried. "We can leave Cloverly, and you'll never have to see the pack again," he said, and his voice was much softer and understanding, in stark contrast to the glare he aimed towards the alpha.

"You can't do that. She has to have a pack," Ben insisted, moving over to where they were standing. "It will be dangerous for her without a pack."

"He's right, David. You need to think this through before you do anything," Sonya added, but he shrugged her away.

"I was supposed to protect her. I'm her father! I came here for you, not for the pack to change her."

Sonya wrapped her arms around him and Jesse. "I know, and I'm sorry. This shouldn't have happened, but we have to find out who changed her before we can decide if it was intentional."

"She told you who changed her. Did you not listen?" David pulled Jesse around to his side as if he were trying to shield her.

"Dad?" Jesse tugged on his shirt to get his attention. "Don't do this. I don't want to leave Cloverly. I don't want to leave Gramma."

"I have to make sure you're safe. And if that means

taking you away from here, I will."

"At least give me enough time to find out what happened. I promise I'll have all the answers before the sun sets," Alpha Cooper said. "Just take Jesse home and monitor her. I think the worst is over, but just in case, I'll send Dr. Stevens to your house. He can answer any questions you have about new bloods."

Dr. Williams looked down at Jesse. "Are you good with that?" His face was a mixture of anger and confusion, but Jesse knew it wasn't directed toward her. He loved her and he would protect her against the pack if he felt it necessary.

She nodded.

Eighteen

Megan

Megan stared out the window, her mind scanning over the details Tucker shared about Jesse's change earlier that morning. It was something they had discussed for a week, but she truly never believed it would happen. Jesse was moody, agitated even, but at no point could she ever imagine her friend as a wolf. Megan rubbed her forehead. How could she face her knowing a wolf had changed her? It was one thing being born a wolf, but being changed against her will was quite another. *What if she weren't changed against her will?* That question also entered her mind, but she knew Jesse, and that was something she would never agree to. *Was Tucker the one behind the change?* Another absurd thought she quickly pushed out of her head. Tucker would do nothing of the sort, and why should he? He and Jesse already had a bond; plus, he was out of town for the past couple of months.

Megan closed her eyes and leaned her head against the windowpane. Visualizing how well the Regional Alpha would take the news, as the alpha female of the Cloverly Pack, she was sure to have a front-row seat to his eruption. She opened her eyes and gasped when Alpha Cooper's large, black truck slid to a stop in front of the cabin. His angry jaw tick was the first sign they were in for trouble; the second was the scowl he aim towards Tucker's cabin. "Jack, you need to get in here. Now!" The softness of her voice couldn't disguise the panic she felt. Alpha female or not, she had no intentions of facing an enraged alpha male on her own.

"Right here." Jack walked into the room, followed by Tucker, as a knock landed on the door. "Dad, I can explain," Jack said as the door swung open.

"You can explain why an angry father just confronted me at my house, demanding to know who changed his daughter. A new blood with the potential to turn on anyone she deems a threat?" The alpha scanned the room, stopping at Tucker, who stood in the kitchen doorway. "You." He pointed.

"Dad, Tucker didn't change Jesse. He's the first one that noticed her wolf. They have a bond; it's hers."

"Then why would Gina tell Jesse that Tucker planned to change her?" Alpha Cooper's gaze slowly moved between the three.

"The same reason Tracy chased after Jack," Megan offered, walking over to stand beside Tucker. "She wants to be mated with an alpha. She's obsessed with the idea."

"So that's what she meant by... it all makes sense

now," Tucker said.

"Well, I'm glad it makes sense to you; do you mind explaining it to me?" The alpha walked over to stand nose to chin with Tucker. "I really would like to know what the hell is going on."

Megan stepped to the side as Jack tensed up.

"I have a bond with Jesse and I was trying to get her to accept her wolf. We've shared dreams and wolf sight. She was bitten by a stray behind the shelter. She said it was a brown mutt," Tucker said, but nothing in his voice sounded threatening.

"Exactly how long have you known this?" The alpha narrowed his eyes and Megan shifted on her feet.

"Since Halloween, or that's when I suspected it. That was the first night we shared a dream," Tucker said.

"And what about you?" The alpha turned to Jack.

"Right after."

"And you didn't think I should be informed?"

"Yes, I did, but this is my pack; and when Tucker came to me, I agreed to give him until the new moon. He thought if he could bond with Jesse's wolf, she wouldn't be a threat, and the pack wouldn't feel threatened by her. I thought it was a brilliant idea." Jack stood his ground. He was a true alpha, standing up for his pack. Megan winked when he looked her way.

"So what went wrong? Obviously, that plan didn't work out so well, or I wouldn't be here now." Alpha Cooper turned back to Tucker.

"Nothing went wrong. Don't you see? She remembers her wolf, which means she remembers mine. She may not be happy about the change, but she bonded with my wolf, and she trusts my wolf."

Megan tried to keep the grin off her face as Tucker's enthusiasm filled the room. It was true. His plan worked for Jesse's wolf, but as for Jesse? Not so much. That was bound to take time and knowing that Gina filled her head with lies, Megan wondered if her friend would ever speak to her after everything that happened.

Listening as the alpha grumbled and ranted about being left in the dark, it didn't help matters when Mason and Whitney walked through the door expecting a showdown.

"Am I the only one here that didn't know what was going on?" The alpha looked around the room and Megan gave a one-shouldered shrug. "Has anyone seen Gina?"

"She's at home. Would you like me to fetch her?" Whitney asked, sounding more eager than she should have.

"Yes, if you don't mind," Alpha Cooper said.

"Alpha Cooper, I understand you think what we did was wrong, but it wasn't. I may have been a member of this pack all my life, but this pack hasn't always been my family. I've lived with humans for the past fifteen years and Jesse has been like a sister to me for eight of those years. Family protects family, and I will protect her at all costs. We were waiting to see how things went with Tucker, and from what she told you, his plan worked."

What started out as an optimistic day faltered when Jesse raced across the yard that afternoon. And knowing Gina deliberately spread lies to get Jesse out of the picture irritated Megan to no end. She tried being nice to the newest pack member but seeing the way she chased after Tucker was off-putting. She hadn't known it at the time when Gina moved to the cabin, but after talking with

Tracy, she found out Gina even tried to capture Jack's attention. *Funny that, huh?*

Listening as the crap-fest wound down, Megan glanced over at Gina and observed her pouty face. After putting Jesse in danger the way she did, Alpha Cooper insisted she return to the pack grounds that evening. A part of her was relieved that Gina would no longer be a member of the Cloverly Pack, but another part wanted to snatch her from her seat and beat the wolf out of her.

"As soon as you get settled in the alpha house, Seth will take your cabin, and I'm giving Gina's to Brayden," the alpha informed Jack, and it relieved Megan. She was friends with both of the males after they guarded her while she was still recovering from Travis's attack a few months back.

"But..." Gina objected.

"Gina, you have to prove you are ready to live among humans, and clearly, you're not. We don't have a problem with them knowing we're here, but at no time can you ever tell someone to leave town at the risk of being changed. That was a threat to get rid of Jesse and you know it. She could have easily considered you a threat and had she; we wouldn't be having this conversation right now. Consider yourself lucky. It was dangerous not only for you but for her and the entire pack. What you did is inexcusable and I will not tolerate it," Alpha Cooper said as he crossed his arms over his chest. Megan knew that stance, and if Gina were smart, she'd keep her mouth shut.

"But I only repeated what I heard. It was a mistake, I admit," Gina protested. Megan bit her lip and glanced over at Jack. The girl definitely needed a muzzle.

"You intentionally eavesdropped on a conversation that was none of your business and then used the information to get rid of Jesse. I don't care why you did it, but I guarantee it's a mistake you won't ever make again. Now go pack whatever you need and I'll stop by and pick you up on my way back to the house," Alpha Cooper said, dismissing her promptly. Megan held her chuckle in as Gina walked out the door and the alpha turned back to the group. "Now about this brown mutt."

"It's not what you think. Tracy didn't change Jesse," Tucker insisted.

Megan was glad to see Gina go, but confronting Tracy just because she lived with Randy on a farm, and his land was behind the shelter was not good. She would defend Jesse no matter what, but since her memories returned, Tracy had proven herself to be a good friend.

Unease upset her stomach as they followed Alpha Cooper to Tracy's house. Staring out the passenger side window as the sun hung low in the sky; her mind was going in ten different directions, although none resulted in the outcome she hoped for.

As they turned onto the gravel drive, a trail of dust in their wake, Tracy waved from the side yard. She was comfortable being there with Randy and it showed in her smile. She was relaxed, at ease with her life, and happy. Tracy rushed across the yard and waited on the porch, but as the alpha got out of his truck and stalked toward her, her smile faded.

"Alpha Cooper, is something wrong?" she asked, looking past the alpha to the rest of the pack. "Come in and have a seat." She pushed open the door and led them into the living room.

Everyone took a seat except for Megan who casually paced the room. She wasn't comfortable being there. She suspected when Alpha Cooper questioned Tracy, she would probably take it the wrong way. Tracy wasn't as tight with the pack, as most wolves were, because of how she'd been raised. It was sad, but Megan understood her situation. And being the alpha female of the Cloverly Pack, she would not let Tracy be the fall guy.

Megan stood beside the back window and noticed Randy near the barn, looking up at the house. She pushed the curtain over to draw his attention, making a slicing gesture across her neck and motioning for him to hurry. She glanced over her shoulder as he ran into the barn.

Tucker tried to explain to Tracy that Jesse had been bitten behind the shelter, without making it sound like she was being accused. When the backdoor opened, Megan glanced into the mudroom as Randy put his finger to his lips and she smiled, relieved that Tracy's backup had just arrived.

"You think because the mutt was brown and I live here on the farm, I was the one that bit Jesse? Why the hell would I do that? Jesse is my friend." Tears swam in her eyes, and she fell back against the sofa.

"We don't think you did anything, but you once suggested it during a pack meeting, so the pack will automatically point their fingers at you," Alpha Cooper said.

"Well, excuse me! I didn't realize at the time that you were talking about Jesse. If I remember correctly, you didn't mention a name. It was a suggestion, and that was before I found out what a new blood was. I didn't do it," Tracy said.

"I hate to break up the tea party, Alice, but I don't think I like where this conversation is going," Randy's voice thundered, drawing everyone's attention to the backdoor. "Get over here, Tracy."

"What are you doing?" Tracy jumped up from the sofa. Seeing Randy standing in the doorway, a shotgun aimed in their direction, she lifted her hands to shield the pack. "It's okay; it's not what you think."

He looked from face to face and then over to Megan and winked. "I may not be a wolf, but that doesn't mean I can't protect my family. You are welcome at my house, but at no time will I ever stand back and watch Tracy getting cornered or blamed for something I know she would never do. So unless you've got proof, I suggest you apologize to her and then maybe we can sit down and talk."

"I agree. We all know Tracy had nothing to do with changing Jesse, and we will not accuse her," Megan said, walking over to join the others. "Tracy, have you seen any wolves running around this area? Perhaps one that was brown, smallish, and matted? Jesse thought it was a stray."

"I've seen nothing. I swear."

"We know you had nothing to do with Jesse being bitten, but we had to ask because there are pack members that might think otherwise," Alpha Cooper said to Tracy.

"Well, you send anyone who thinks otherwise, my way, and I'll gladly change their mind," Randy smirked, still holding the gun.

Megan chuckled.

"That won't be necessary. If the person who bit Jesse is a member of the pack, we don't want to tip them off. I don't think this conversation should leave this room," Jack said, walking over to Tracy. "I'm sorry if you thought we were accusing you. We weren't."

"I didn't really think you were, but I'm still in shock. I can't believe Jesse's a new blood. Is she okay? Has she phased?" Tracy chewed her nails and dropped back down on the sofa.

"She's fine. Pissed off and with good reason. But she likes my wolf." Tucker grinned, which made Megan laugh. Tucker had a way of easing the tension in a room, and based on the smile on Tracy's face, it was working. Maybe Jesse would eventually come to terms with her wolf and give Tucker a chance. Out of every male in the pack, he was the most compassionate, and he truly cared about her.

"What makes you think she likes your wolf?" Tracy squinted curiously.

"My wolf spent most of the morning with hers. We share a bond," Tucker braggingly said.

"What?" Tracy jumped up off the sofa, practically landing in his lap. "Randy, did you hear that?" She hugged Tucker and wiped the tears from her eyes. "How? I thought you denied the bond."

"I did. The bond is hers." Tucker beamed, finally able to tell everyone he shared a bond with Jesse. He was proud, and if Jesse ever spoke to Megan again, she would be sure to tell her how special Tucker truly was.

"Congratulations," Randy said, placing the gun in the mudroom before he walked over and shook Tucker's hand. "Sorry about the gun."

"Hey, I'm just glad you had the balls to defend our girl." Tucker winked at Tracy and she poked him in the ribs.

"Just trying to even the odds. That's all." Randy laughed.

"By the way, Randy, where's your dog?" Whitney asked. "I'm surprised it didn't meet us at the door."

"I don't have a dog."

"I saw a dog the other day when I came here to pick up Mason. It was in the backfield."

Megan walked back over to the window and stared across the field. That proved to her that it wasn't Tracy that changed Jesse, and although she should have felt relieved, she wasn't. Memories of Travis attacking her flashed before her eyes. He was dead, but his mate wasn't. *Maybe she's out for revenge.* She turned from the window. "What color is Vivian's wolf?"

Nineteen

Jesse

Eager to get away from all the drama in Cloverly, visiting Jago seemed like Jesse's best option. He was a friend when she attended Franklin Academy and although she hadn't seen him in nearly two years; she didn't expect there would be a big change. He was nearly perfect in her opinion: the athletic type, tall with dark brown hair, dark eyes, super cute and loaded. Most of the students that attended the Academy came from money, but she, unlike most, was just a day student. She smiled when the *Welcome to Alma County* sign came into view.

Jesse had considered canceling the trip to Jago's, but Dr. Stevens assured her she no longer posed a threat since her wolf had bonded with Tucker's. And because someone had changed her against her will, putting distance between her and what would soon be her pack, if only for a few days, would do her good.

She turned off the highway and reminded herself she was doing the right thing—if only to distract her mind. Tucker had taken over her thoughts—*his beautiful dimples and comforting eyes.* Her heart ached to be near him, but seeing him brought back memories she desperately wanted to forget. As if that could actually happen.

"So are you going to tell me what this is about? I mean, I'm surprised you didn't want to stay home with the family. It's your dad and Sonya's first Thanksgiving after all," Lori said, bobbing her head to the beat on the radio.

"I needed a little breather is all." Jesse shrugged. After showing herself, and witnessing her dad's subsequent fit, the Regional Alpha was determined to find the wolf that bit her, but unfortunately the scent trail had faded. But how hard could it be to track down the mangy mutt, considering wolves were supposed to be such magnificent creatures with an amazing sense of smell and vision that could see to the moon.

Pushing all thoughts of wolves out of her mind, she turned right onto the narrow county road that led to Jago's house. She was there primarily to relax and escape the screwed-up world she found herself stuck in, not to dwell on snarling, hairy beast.

"If you say so." Lori looked up when Jesse steered the truck between twin wrought-iron gates. "Is this where we're staying?"

"I hope so, if not, we'll probably be arrested for trespassing." Jesse laughed and continued up the drive to the front of the three-story mansion. Putting the truck in park, she looked up as Jago and an elderly man walked out onto the porch. "Looks like we're at the right place."

"I think I'm in love," Lori said, smiling up at the two men. "Looks and money. I need to get out of Cloverly more often."

"Do not embarrass me. I'll tie you up and lock you in a closet if you do," Jesse warned and pushed open the driver's door.

"Can it be a closet for two?" Lori chuckled but her eyes never left Jago as he walked around to the driver's side of the truck.

"Hey, Jesse. I was just talking about you the other day. I'm glad you called," Jago said, pulling her into a hug. "You haven't changed a bit."

"Well, maybe just a little," she said and closed the truck door. "I haven't seen anyone since I left Indy. I've missed you guys, and thanks for letting us crash your Thanksgiving." She followed Jago around the truck to the passenger side.

"You're more than welcome to crash anytime you want. We can always use extra hands at Alma's House this time of year." Jago opened the passenger door. "So who's your buddy?"

"This is my best friend, Lori."

"It's nice to meet you. Are you all hungry? We just finished supper, but there are plenty of leftovers," Jago said but Lori just stared.

"She's shy, but she'll come around." Jesse laughed. "Lori, are you hungry?"

"No. I'm good."

It's official. The world is ending. Jesse turned away and chuckled.

"Come on in. I'll get your bags later." Jago led them up the steps to where his grandfather was waiting. "Pappy, this is Jesse, a good friend of mine from the Academy, and her friend, Lori."

"It's nice to meet you gals. Come in out of the cold and make yourself at home," Pappy said while holding open the door.

It surprised Jesse at how big the house was when they walked into the foyer. She knew Jago came from a family that had old money, she just didn't realize how much. Looking over at Lori, she shrugged as they followed Jago into the kitchen. He was sweet to look at also; too bad she dated his best friend back in high school, and not him.

"Have a seat and I'll fix you up," Jago said, motioning them to the bar. Walking over to the oven, he pulled out the leftover deep pan pizza and placed it on the table along with a stack of napkins. Then grabbing two sodas from the fridge, he took a seat across from them.

"Is this homemade? It looks delicious," Jesse said, taking a slice out of the pan.

"Gram makes the best pizza in town when she has the time," he said before pushing the pan towards Lori.

Hesitantly, Lori pulled a slice of pizza from the pan and placed it on a napkin. *Now she has manners?* Jesse looked over at Jago, who was grinning at Lori. She took a bite of pizza to keep from laughing. It wouldn't surprise her if Lori bit her tongue, the way she drooled over Jago. She grinned when Lori licked her lips.

"This is delicious. A lot better than beef jerky," Lori said, wiping her mouth with her hand.

"That's what we packed for the trip," Jesse said. "But Lori is a meat and potatoes girl."

"Finally, a girl that's not afraid to eat decent portions. Help yourself. There's plenty."

Jesse popped a pepperoni in her mouth, again, trying to keep from laughing. True friendship blossomed before her eyes, knowing Lori loved to eat and Jago was offering her food. "So how have you been? Is there a girlfriend in the picture now?" Jesse asked, trying to ignore the pizza hog sitting beside her.

"Everything's good here, and yeah, I have a girlfriend. She wanted to come over tonight, but she couldn't make it. She's excited to meet you though."

"A day late and a dollar short," Lori mumbled and Jesse covered her mouth to keep from spewing her drink. "Just sayin'." Lori grinned and Jesse groaned.

"And this is the not-so-shy Lori. She says things with no forethought, but you can't help but love her." Jesse wiped the soda off her chin.

"Then she and Wesley will get along great. He's my best friend."

"Is your friend as hot as you are?"

"Lori, have you no filter?" Jesse palmed her forehead. She was joking about tying Lori up in a closet, but now she was seriously considering it.

"What? It was just a question." Lori winked and Jago snickered behind his hand. Jesse rolled her eyes. The two thought they were funny and now that Lori had relaxed, it was obvious they would get along just fine.

Once they had finished eating, Jago unloaded their bags while his grandparents visited with them before heading up to bed. Afterward, they helped Jago clean up the kitchen, and then he showed them to their room.

"Can I live here forever?" Lori asked, looking around

the lovely guestroom.

"Forget you. I want to live here." Opening the bathroom door, Jesse walked into the room. It was huge compared to her measly eight-by-ten, and she turned as Lori's jaw practically hit the floor. The room was the size of her apartment bedroom, with a large, walk-in shower, Jacuzzi tub, and a glass bowl sink. "Have you ever seen anything like this?"

"No, but I could grow to love it." Lori thought a moment and then added. "Why didn't you tell me you had hot, rich guy friends?"

"Because this is not the Jago I knew; plus, I used to date his best friend," Jesse said. After taking her sleep aid, she walked out of the bathroom and sat down on the edge of the bed. The room was large and comfortable, with two picture windows and a walk-in closet that was bigger than her apartment bathroom.

"Is his friend single?" Lori steepled her hands in front of her face.

"Knowing Max, probably. He's a chick magnet, or at least that's what Jago used to call him. He had wild, blonde hair, a deep California tan, and the brightest smile," Jesse said, remembering him fondly.

"So what happened?"

"He was a player that loved the waves more than me." Jesse chuckled. "He's a good guy though. We had fun together, but it wasn't true love. More like a passing fancy."

"Well, Alma County is looking better and better," Lori said as she leaned in and looked around the bathroom once more. "I sure could get used to this lifestyle."

"No, you couldn't. You would have to leave Cloverly,

and we both know that will never happen."

"One can always dream." Lori walked over to the door. "If you need me, I'll be dreaming in my room."

Jesse watched the door close behind Lori and then lay back on the bed, exhausted from the drive. As tired as she was, there probably wasn't any need for the sleep aid, but it was a precautionary measure to keep Tucker out of her dreams. She quickly changed into her bedclothes, and then stretched out beneath the covers and drifted off to sleep.

The following morning Jesse awoke feeling rested and more than a little excited to be helping at Alma's House. Having heard Jago talking about the shelter when they attended the academy, she wondered why she waited so long to volunteer. Dressed in dark jeans, and a soft sienna sweater, Jesse slipped on a pair of comfortable loafers and headed down to the kitchen for a quick breakfast of orange muffins and coffee—eager to start the day.

By the time they arrived at the shelter, the coffee had kicked in and Jesse and Lori were raring to go. After meeting Margo, they spent most of the morning helping her peel potatoes and bake cookies for the kids. "I love this. It's wonderful what you're doing here," Jesse said when Margo stopped to take a five-minute break.

"It keeps us busy, but I would be lost without it," Margo said. "By the way, thank you both for volunteering. This is our busiest day of the year."

"We're glad to be here." Jesse grinned as Jago walked through the backdoor. The tall redhead that was holding his hand reminded her of Tracy, but with softer features and a pile of curls that made her own hair look like a ratty mess.

"Jesse, Lori, this is Aggie," Jago announced ushering her over to the stainless steel table.

"It's nice to meet you," Jesse said, getting up from her stool, she glanced up at Aggie's smile.

"It's nice to meet you, too. I'm sorry I wasn't here last night. Are you staying for supper?" Aggie looked over at Jago. "They are staying, aren't they?"

"I hope so. Gram was excited to know we'd have company this year. It's been quiet for far too long." Jago looked over at Jesse and Lori. "You are staying, aren't you?"

"Well, if you're sure we're not imposing..." Jesse looked over at Lori and she nodded, eagerly.

"Not at all. We would love to spend Thanksgiving with you," Aggie said.

"Everyone, take your places," Margo yelled, ending their conversation.

As the workers gathered along the serving line, Jesse's heart went out for the people that arrived at the shelter. Some were homeless, others didn't have families and preferred not to spend the holiday alone, but what touched her heart the most was the way the volunteers interacted with each person as they came through the line. They were treated as family, and it didn't take Jesse long to settle into her role—offering a warm smile, and a kind word. Scooping the mashed potatoes and gravy onto the trays, she spoke to everyone—Mr. Johnson being her favorite.

Once the meal was served, Jesse and Lori were taking a break when she noticed Jago pushing a stainless steel cart out to the floor. Going from table to table, he made small talk with everyone and even handed out candy to the kids. She looked over at Lori. "No reason why they should have all the fun." She nodded as Aggie pushed another cart to the opposite side of the room.

"You can take mine," Margo said, adding three pies to her cart. "It'll give me a few minutes to rest my aching feet."

"Quick, grab the cart before she changes her mind," Jesse said, jumping to her feet.

Following Lori out to the floor, they moved from table to table, refilling coffee, and serving extra pie to anyone wanting seconds. They laughed and listened to shared stories of past Thanksgivings, and Jesse was utterly amazed at the abundance of love that filled the room. It was an eye-opening experience for her, and one she would never forget.

As the day wound down and the kitchen finally cleaned, everyone piled into the van and headed back to Jago's house.

Jesse felt bad for leaving her dad and Sonya, knowing it was their first Thanksgiving as a married couple. But wanting to escape her own problems, she lashed out at anyone trying to help her, including Tucker and Megan. They were her family. How could she be so selfish when there were plenty of people that had no one? Her heart ached with guilt.

That night, Jesse lay in bed, her thoughts drifting back to the little town she loved and her family there. She was thankful for each of them, and as much as she wanted to be mad at Sonya, she couldn't. She went out of her way to help Jesse as much as possible and deep down, Jesse respected her for that. Pulling her phone out of her purse, she dialed her dad's number.

"Dad, I love you, and I'm sorry if I ruined your and Sonya's Thanksgiving." Tears rolled down her cheeks as she waited for him to say something. Anything.

"You didn't ruin Thanksgiving, sweetie. We love you no matter what." After that, the conversation came easy as Jesse talked about Alma's House. Her dad listened; interrupting from time to time to ask questions, which she thought was sweet. They talked for an hour before she promised to be home on Saturday, and when the bedroom door opened, she ended the call.

"Now are you going to tell me what all this is about?" Lori shut the door and walked over to the bed. "Megan was tight-lipped when I talked to her last week, so it's time to 'fess up."

Twenty

Jesse

Jesse wasn't sure where to start, much less, how Lori would react, but they were both due for some good, old-fashioned girl talk, and there was just as good a place for it as any. Of course with Lori, there was nothing old-fashioned about it. She would say whatever popped into her head, with no regard or care about who might over hear. Which was why they had to keep it down; but since Pappy and Gram turned in hours ago, and it was safe to assume they were asleep. However, to err on the side of caution, Jesse did close the bathroom door.

Settling on the bed, Jesse turned to Lori, who had just popped a piece of peppermint candy into her mouth. "Do you remember the day I showed you the bruise on my hand from the dog that bit me behind the shelter?"

"Vaguely, but yeah." Lori fluffed a pillow and stretched out on the bed.

"Well, apparently, that mutt wasn't a dog, and I should've known better than try to wrangle it. I told myself it wasn't a wolf because they didn't run during daylight hours, but it turns out I was wrong. It was an actual wolf."

"But you said it didn't break the skin, so what does that matter?" Lori asked as she closed her eyes.

"That's the part I don't understand. Apparently, it was a puncture wound, and it healed super-fast. Something a shifter does, if you remember what Megan told us. But because it was in wolf form, I got infected and the virus spread through my bloodstream, which is the reason I've been so sick," Jesse said before getting up off the bed and locking the bedroom door. She looked back across the room to see Lori connecting the dots.

"You have rabies?" she blurted out a little louder than necessary.

"Would you keep it down?" Jesse hissed, crawling across the bed. "You've read the stories, and that's your first conclusion?"

Lori's eyes widened and she rolled back, not paying attention to how close she was to the edge of the mattress. Falling to the floor she landed with a soft thud, her fall muffled by the plush blue carpet. "You're a wolf? Get the hell out!" Jesse chuckled and looked down at Lori, who was rubbing the back of her head. "Who do I need to take out?" Lori pushed up on her elbows and scowled.

When pissed, Lori could run a good bluff, or at least, Jesse hoped that's what it was. And being a little hell-cat, which Lori definitely was, anything was possible.

"That's just it. No one knows who bit me."

"Okay, now that worries me. If you were bitten by a wolf, and..." She dropped back to the floor and stared up at the ceiling. "How come they can't track it?"

"Because I didn't tell them when it happened, and now the scent trail is gone. Or at least, that's what the alpha told us, and I have no reason to believe he would lie."

"You talked to the alpha? An actual alpha!? Was he hot? I mean, in the books, the alphas are like these hunky, gorgeous, hot guys that bark orders and everyone bows down to lick their feet—among other things." Lori sighed.

"You are so twisted. We're talking about Jack's dad here, so could you be serious?" Jesse rolled back on the bed, her stomach bouncing with silent laughter.

"I remember him; he's the hottie that was sitting with your dad at the council meeting. Or at least for an old guy, he was hot."

"Yeah, actually he is, but that's beside the point. We're talking about me, not the alpha."

"Well, I have to admit the story sounds crazy, especially coming from you." Lori pulled herself up on the side of the bed, and Jesse slapped her over the head with a pillow.

"I'm telling the truth and you know it."

"I know nothing of the sort. It could all be fabricated to freak me out. But, I'd be more inclined to believe you if you would show me your wolf." Lori winked, making a clicking sound.

"You know I can't do that. Megan said they weren't allowed to show their wolves just because." Jesse groaned when Lori nudged her over on the bed.

"Yeah, but I know about them so I don't see why it would matter. As for you, I was just teasing. I know you're a wolf." Lori took hold of her hand. "I've seen it in your eyes."

"When?" Jesse asked and rolled over, grabbing Lori's waist to keep her from falling off the bed again.

"At the Halloween party, you had the same look Tucker and Jack had. I've seen their eyes too. Tucker's eyes lit up a bronze color when you left with Brian that day at the store, and at Sallee's Rock, when Jack confronted Randy, his eyes were a bright blue. You have that flare. Only, your eyes are so dark, they flare red. It's kind of wicked-cool, actually."

"To you maybe, but I promise it's not."

"Whatever, chicka. It's cool as hell and you know it. And now that the damage is done, I can honestly say my best friend is a wolf."

"Oh, no you can't. You know it's not safe."

"Sorry, sister, but you're like a celebrity now."

"No, I'm like a dangerous wolf that can't be trusted." Jesse moved over and sat up on the bed.

"Why? You're no different from the others." Lori sat up beside her and grinned. "So Tucker knows you're a wolf, and Megan?"

"Yeah, apparently Tucker was the one who noticed first. At the Halloween party."

"Of course he did. I told you, he's always eyeballing you," Lori said, stifling a yawn.

"Don't even start with that. You're always making a big deal out of nothing." Jesse pulled down the blanket and lay back on the pillow.

"Come on, give the guy a chance. He's fu..."

Jesse slapped her hand over Lori's mouth. "Language."

"But he's hot, like... frickin sweltering. And if he looked at me the way he looks at you, shoot! I'd be climbing that mountain every chance I got, because that man is definitely packing."

"You did not go there." Jesse turned to face the door, intense heat radiating up her neck. She knew exactly what Lori was talking about, but to admit it would only spur her best friend's dirty imagination, and anyway, she didn't need the reminder.

"Aww, man, do you have to suck the fun out of frickin everything?"

"I'm not. You're just being foul-mouthed."

"It's called a dirty mind, and you just wish you had the balls to talk smutty about Tucker. Speaking of which... I noticed those tight slacks he wore to the dance. They hugged him in all the right places, kinda like a glove." She lifted her hand in the air. "A really large glove." Lori snickered when Jesse giggled and swatted back at her. "Seriously, though, you have a guy that looks at you like you're his whole world. I'd give anything to find a guy that looked at me like that."

"What about Steve? He loves you."

"Yeah, he does." Lori smiled and moved to the bottom of the bed. "What does it feel like? Being a wolf, I mean? Do you go out with the pack and howl at the moon?"

Jesse rolled over and looked down at Lori. She was honestly asking the question and not joking around. "I've never actually howled, or been with the pack in the woods, well, Tucker... once. But my wolf phases under the dark moon; theirs doesn't. Which is kind of crappy."

"You can call me, I'll go with you."

"I know you would, but I'm not sure I have that kind of control over my wolf, not yet."

"So now you're saying you might eat me?" And there Lori went; right back to her old self.

"I'm not going to eat you, but that doesn't mean my wolf would trust you. From what I've been told, my wolf will protect me at all costs."

"Then you should let me go with you. I think me and your wolf would hit it off just fine because I'll protect you at all costs as well," Lori said matter-of-factly.

"Maybe one day when I have things better under control, but first, I have to fit in with the pack, because without them, my wolf will become dangerous."

Thirty minutes later, Lori was asleep and because Jesse didn't want to be alone, she covered her with the blanket. As she reached down to push the hair off Lori's face, she noticed a single tear resting on the side of her nose. She couldn't remember ever seeing Lori cry, but maybe telling her about the wolf upset her. She frowned and adjusted her pillow. She was tired, but there was one more person she had to apologize to, and she hoped he was still waiting for her. Staring up at the ceiling, she slowly drifted off to sleep.

Jesse walked across the boulder as Tucker turned her way.

"Where are you?"

"I'm right here." She smiled and took a seat next to him. Glancing around the clearing, she often wondered what it would be like to sit on the boulder beneath the full moon. It was spectacular.

"I'm not talking about this dream. Where are you?"

Tucker demanded.

"Whoa, bushy butt. No need to cop an attitude." She smirked at his frown.

He growled.

"That sounds like a nasty cold you got there. Are you sure you should be out in the chilly night air?" The moonlight highlighted his features… gosh, she missed him. And although she was supposed to be mad, it was hard to be when she was with him in her dreams. "I'm surprised you didn't track me down using your wolf mojo." She grinned when his eyes flashed her way.

"It doesn't work like that."

"Sure it does. Jack used the bond to find Megan." Bam! She had him there. Again, she grinned.

"Yeah, but it was his bond. Normally, the male holds the bond, but with you nothing is normal."

"Oh, so what you're saying is you can't track me, but I can track you. I think I like this bond thing." She laughed when he rolled his eyes. "So where's the pack?"

"Probably at Jack's."

"Then why aren't you with them? Old Clumsy needs his pack."

"Old Clumsy needs you too, and if I were with them, I wouldn't be able to sleep, which means we couldn't be having this conversation." He grunted and shoved his hands through his hair, and she fought the urge to do the same.

"I remembered him, after well, you know." She lowered her eyes.

"I figured as much when the alpha paid us a not-so-nice visit. You should have told me. I would have told you everything, but I couldn't until you admitted you remembered your wolf. It was too dangerous." Tucker trained his eyes on her, and she gave him a side glance to see the frown still on his face.

"I'm sorry. I was scared and confused, and then Gina showed up. I just didn't want to be around that kind of drama. I'm not the kind of girl to just hook up for a thrilling night. I expect more, and I demand it from a relationship."

"So do I," he muttered under his breath as he looked out into the trees. His face hid no emotions, and it was obvious he wasn't pleased with her comment.

"We were out here. It wasn't a full moon, so I thought it was a dream." She looked up through her lashes and a sad smile appeared on his face.

"That, Jesse," he said, pointing at her hand. "That so-called bruise is the moon in which you phase under. That's why there wasn't a full moon. You're a new blood and you change under the dark moon."

"I know. Dr. Stevens explained everything to me. He also said the dreams would stop once we sealed the bond." She sighed. "I'm not sure I'm ready for that kind of commitment. It's all happening so fast, and like I said, it seems like I'm living in a dream world where anything is possible, but nothing makes any sense."

"Well, it wasn't a dream, and here are your clothes to prove it." He pulled the scrap material from beneath his leg. "You really should undress before you let your wolf come forward. It would prevent me from having to follow you and gather up all the rags." He chuckled and nudged her with his shoulder.

"You saw me naked?" It wasn't as much a question as a statement and she pinched her eyes shut.

"We leave nothing to the imagination. But you'll get used to it." He flicked his brows when she opened her eyes.

"That's comforting to know." She wasn't that modest around other girls, but Tucker and the guys? Not happening.

"Jesse, please trust me. I love you and I would never do anything to harm you."

Her heart swelled, and she drew in a hesitant breath. "I do trust you. I'm just scared about what all this means. Dad was extremely pissed when I told him I was a wolf. Of course, acting like a raging lunatic didn't help my cause too much." She looked down at her lap, slightly embarrassed by the way she had handled the situation. "How will he react when I tell him about our bond?" A tear slipped down her cheek and she brushed it away. "And you said I was dangerous. What if the pack doesn't want me?"

Tucker pulled her into his lap, the warmth of his body soothing her. "That's why I was out here with you during your last phase. If our wolves bonded, you would trust me, and in turn, you'd trust them as part of my pack. As for your dad, he was livid with good reason. You could have died during the transformation. It scared him, which is why he won't betray your trust and tell me where you are right now. He loves you."

"I know, but I need time to work this out in my head. Can you give me that?"

"I'll give you whatever you want, just come home. I can't stand knowing you left Cloverly because of me." He rested his chin on top of her head and when she looked up, he turned away.

"I didn't leave Cloverly because of you." She reached up with her finger to catch the tear at the corner of his eye. "Well, in the beginning, I tried to escape so you wouldn't change me." She chuckled low. "But once I accepted the truth, it was too late to back out, and being here has done my heart so much good. I needed this, it was all for me, and I'm glad I came."

Tucker kissed the top of her head and then hugged her tightly against his chest. His sadness engulfed her, nearly crushing her soul. So vulnerable, she thought, inhaling his earthy scent. The connection between them was rock solid and for a split second, she swore she could hear his every thought.

"I have to know you're safe. You need this pack; your wolf needs the pack more now than ever before. Please come home. I can go back to the mountains and you won't have to see me again. Just come home."

"You would do that for me?" She pushed back and stared into his eyes. Seeing the pain there, and knowing she was the cause of it, shattered her heart.

"There's nothing I wouldn't do for you."

"Then don't leave! Give me more time to get settled into this life. This comes easy for you, but I need to know what's between us isn't just because of the wolf." She kissed his chin. "I'll be home this weekend, but I need time."

Jesse opened her eyes, ending the dream.

Twenty-One

Megan

Megan made one last walk through of the apartment before shutting off the lights. Tucker was spending most of his days in Berkley, but his nights were spent right there at the apartment. He was getting it ready for when Jesse moved back and the apartment looked awesome. Too bad Jesse didn't know the hoops he jumped through for her. But Megan was sworn to silence and had no intentions of spilling the beans. She loved Jesse like a sister, but why couldn't she see what was right in front of her eyes? As she walked down the stairs, the security lights clicked on, lighting the entire warehouse. Another thoughtful thing Tucker did, but of course, Jesse had no clue.

Nearly three weeks had passed since Megan talked to

Jesse, and the only way she knew what was going on came through Lori. It seems she was still pissed at the pack, but Megan didn't understand why. It wasn't a pack member that changed her, so it wasn't fair to punish them all. Megan swallowed hard. She missed hanging out with Jesse at the store, but ever since the storm, things had changed between them.

Jesse asked Tucker to give her more time, so maybe that was what she needed from Megan. Still, she wondered if Jesse's silence had anything to do with Gina's lies.

She looked around the warehouse, knowing she needed to stock the shelves, but without her partner, it wasn't the same. "Give her a few more days," she told herself, but they were running out of time. The plan was to open the boutique by Christmas, and with less than a month to go, she wasn't sure it would happen.

Megan shut off the lights and walked out the side door as headlights streamed in front of the store. It was just after dark, and most of Cloverly was shutting down for the night, and she was more than ready to call it a day. But hearing a car door slam, she walked down to the corner, surprised to see Jesse walking to the back of her dad's pickup.

"Do you need help with anything?" Megan asked, coming to a stop when Jesse glanced to the corner. She crossed her fingers.

"Actually," Jesse paused before smiling, "I could use help to get these boxes inside."

Megan grinned and bounced over to the truck with no attempt to hide her excitement. If Jesse were smiling, it had to be a good sign, and she would take what she could get. "What are these?" She looked over at Jesse, her smile still in place.

"Some boxes are inventory, and some are my personal things. There's more at the house," Jesse said over her shoulder.

"Does that mean you're moving back to the apartment?" Megan asked, surprised, but thrilled.

"Yeah, I think it's about time" Jesse used the box she was holding to prop open the door.

After three trips in, and three trips out, the boxes were unloaded and Jesse was on her way to pick up a second load. Megan stood inside the door watching the truck pull away from the curb. She took in a deep breath before pulling her phone from her pocket and calling Jack. Squealing into the phone when he answered, Jack laughed as Megan shared her good news.

"I don't know when I'll be home. I'm going to stay here with her as long as I can. Maybe make a night of it. I need to make sure we're okay," she said, hearing Mason and Whitney in the background. "I'll let you go now. I don't want to hold up supper." She ended the call and pushed the phone back into her pocket and smiled, knowing Jack was as excited as she was.

Megan rushed over to the cafe to grab a bite to eat, and since Jesse was moving her things back to the store, she naturally assumed Jesse would also be hungry. "Hey, Ester," she said as she walked through the door and made a beeline to the kitchen. Juggling her time between the farm, and preparing for the boutique's grand opening just around the corner; Megan had to give up her job at the diner.

"How's the store coming?" Ester asked, moving

around the counter.

"It's been iffy, but things are finally turning around. It looks like we'll meet our opening deadline after all." The smile on Megan's face felt pleasantly familiar, and she was glad Jesse was the reason for it. "Can I get two meals to go?" she asked, her stress instantly dissolving.

"You and Jack keeping late hours again?"

"No, this time it's me and Jesse! She's finally moving back to her apartment, so I thought I'd surprise her with supper."

"Well then, let's get you fixed up." Within minutes, Ester had filled the order and handed Megan the takeout bag. "Tell Jesse I said hi."

"I will and thank you." Megan waved as she walked out the door and hurried back to the store. Placing the bag on the counter, she sat down on a stool and waited for Jesse to return. Her knee bounced and she chewed her nails, something she hadn't done in years. Headlights cut across the sidewalk when the truck pulled over to the curb and Megan hurried out the door.

"This is the last," Jesse said, grabbing two boxes at once.

"What about Moose?"

"He's on Gramma's lap. It looks like we'll be sharing custody."

"I bet Gramma loves that. The last time I was there, they were watching the news together," Megan said. She pulled two boxes to the edge of the truck bed as Jesse walked into the store. Jesse lifted her nose, and Megan grinned, knowing she smelled the aromatic food. It wasn't anything fancy, but country fried steak was a specialty at the cafe and most of the customers loved it. She carried the boxes inside and placed them on the floor.

"You brought food?" Jesse looked over at the takeout bag.

"Yeah, I hope you're hungry because I'm starved and I haven't had supper," Megan said, following Jesse back out to the truck.

"I'm starved too. I've been so busy packing boxes today, I missed lunch."

"That's probably a good thing. Ester piled enough food on the trays to feed an army." Megan laughed as they carried the remaining boxes inside.

Sitting down with their food trays, the two settled into a light conversation—talking about everything from stocking shelves, to what needed to be done before the grand opening. After a few minutes of pushing her green beans around the plate, Megan finally glanced up. "I'm so sorry about everything. At the time, I noticed changes in you but... you were sick a lot and I thought it was a bad cold. That's no excuse or anything, but I honestly didn't know."

"I know you didn't. I blame myself, not you. The rapid changes confused me, and I don't know, it's just been a chaotic couple of months." Jesse reached over and took hold of Megan's hand. "We're good."

Megan smiled and blinked the moisture from her eyes. "I'm glad because life without you sucks."

"How's Tucker?" Jesse asked as she pulled her hand away and picked up her fork. "I haven't seen him since I've been home."

The question surprised Megan after Tucker told her about their latest dream. Jesse wanted time, which he was giving her and the primary reason he kept a low profile. "He's doing okay, considering everything that happened. He's been spending more time in Berkley, getting ready for his pack and all. But you know, he never meant to hurt you, and Gina? He was never with her. He misses you, if that's what you're asking." What else could she throw in there without sounding like she was pushing him on her?

Jesse nodded. "Don't tell him I asked. I'm not ready to go down that road just yet, but I wanted to make sure he was all right."

"I won't say anything you don't want me to, but you know how he feels about you. It's just as hard on him."

"Maybe, but right now is not the time. I'm still coming to terms with everything, and I'm trying to make the best of a bad situation without blaming anyone. I know that sounds selfish, but I have to figure this out on my own. Tucker helped me a lot, and I know what he did for me; I remember everything. But enough about me," Jesse said, eager to change the subject. "I want to know about you and Jack. How's life after the bonding ceremony?"

Megan's face split with a grin. "The dress was beautiful and everyone loved it; there are several girls that want you to design dresses for their bonding ceremonies."

"And... the lacy underwear?" Jesse's brow arched in question.

Megan chuckled. "They were a hit with Jack for sure."

"Good. Lori thought long and hard about what you should wear under that dress." Jesse nearly fell off her stool laughing, which caused Megan to blush and roll her eyes.

"We both know what Lori thought long and hard

about, and it wasn't my underwear. By the way, where is she tonight?"

"At the front door. I called her on my way back. Girls' night!"

With Lori in attendance, their circle was complete, and they moved away from the counter to the small sitting area in the middle of the store. The sofas were more comfortable, and the large, rectangular table was perfect to lounge around and rest their feet on. There were plenty of magazines and books, and a few potted plants on the small side tables.

Megan grinned as she looked across the table at Jesse and Lori. "So would you like to hear the details?" she asked, knowing it was out of character for her to kiss and tell, but she wasn't ashamed. It was a memory she would never forget, and one she often thought about.

Lori's jaw dropped when Megan mentioned the riverbank. "If that's what happens when you wear lacy drawers, I'm updating my undies," Lori said and they both laughed.

"So you were out there in the open, and the pack was... where?" Jesse asked, her elbows resting on her knees. *She was most definitely taking notes*, Megan thought, but never commented.

"To be honest, time stood still once I straddled his lap." Megan laughed and fell over on the sofa, her face a deep crimson red. Jesse and Lori jumped across the table, joining her.

"That sounds so... I can't believe you did that!" Jesse gushed.

"Me neither, but it was amazing." Megan practically swooned with the memory.

After all the questions were asked, and answered, they sat back on the sofa, all three in a row. Lori was the first to speak. "I didn't understand the need for this sitting area, but now I'm glad you created it. We should have a girls' night more often."

"Would you settle for a girls' afternoon, or evening?" Megan asked, and they chuckled.

"Yeah, we wouldn't want to put a crimp on your love life," Jesse winked at Lori.

"Oh, I have a surprise for Lori. Well, it's more like a suggestion. Come on." Megan got up, and they followed her around the sofa.

"I'm in," Lori said.

"You don't even know what it is." Jesse laughed, nudging Lori's shoulder.

"I don't care. After what she just told us, I might get lucky."

"Well, since you provided the lacy underwear for my bonding ceremony, I thought you might want to sell them, which is why I left this space empty," Megan said, fanning her hand out, and directing their attention to the area opposite the sofas.

"I think it's a great idea," Jesse offered, glancing at Lori who was scanning the small space as if mapping out the display area in her mind.

"And who better than Lori to tend to it. Megan giggled at Lori's goofy grin. And just like that, everything was right in Cloverly.

The three worked late into the night, stocking the shelves with everything from bath beads, to lotion, and of course, Fortuity, Megan's favorite perfume. It was well after midnight when they shut off the lights and headed upstairs to Jesse's apartment. Walking through the warehouse, the security lights came on and Jesse looked up. "Wow, that's nice," she said as she continued toward the stairs.

Megan had totally forgotten about the lights and she grinned at the surprised expression on Jesse's face. Following Lori and Jesse up the stairs, she didn't miss the gasp coming from Jesse when she opened the apartment door.

"When did you do this?" Jesse asked, looking down the steps at Megan.

"It's been a work in progress for a little while now. I hope you like it."

"I absolutely *love* it!" Jesse pushed the door open and walked further into the apartment.

Lori flopped down on the sofa and pulled a brightly colored throw blanket over her body, motioning for them to go on without her.

The freshly painted walls in shades that matched Jesse's colorful personality were Tucker's idea, but that was a detail Megan kept to herself. He said nothing bland would do, and he made sure the apartment suited Jesse to a tee. Paintings by local artists hung on the walls, along with other craft items, which he said would inspire Jesse's designs, and he was right.

Megan walked into the bedroom where Jesse was staring at a large painting hanging on the wall. The paisley wolf, in rich colors of orange, brown and burgundy matched the paisley theme of the room. "You don't like it?" Megan asked, coming over to stand beside her.

Brushing away a tear, Jesse trailed her fingers over the canvas, as if absorbing the essence of the painting and smiled. "It's perfect. Thank you."

"That's a gift from Randy."

"Are those paintings downstairs Randy's?" Jesse looked over at Megan and she nodded.

"Mostly. I thought it would bring more color to the boutique, and maybe he could sell a few."

"I'm stunned. I don't know what to say other than I'm sorry I wasn't here to help you." A frown contorted her face, and Megan pulled her into a hug.

"I wish you could have been here too, but considering what you were going through, I understand. Don't worry though; I didn't do all of this on my own. There were plenty of volunteers."

By the time they made it to bed, there was no more talk of Jack or bonding, and although from time to time, Lori would throw in a reference to Tucker, all things wolf were forgotten.

Fluffing her pillow, Megan hid her grin when Jesse moved the nightlight from one wall to the other, casting a soft glow over the wolf painting. Seeing Jesse so relaxed, Megan knew she would eventually come out of her shell, and when she did, the pack would be waiting for her with open arms. "I'm glad you're home."

"I'm glad you were here waiting for me," Jesse replied.

Twenty-Two

Jesse

"Thanks for the ride," Jesse said and waved when Megan pulled away from the curb. Moving back into her apartment, and having her two best friends stay the night was exactly what she needed. But now it was back to the grind, and she was looking forward to getting her hands dirty. Clutching her purse to her side, she turned toward the animal shelter.

Hair rose on her nape as she scanned the farmland to the left of the building, unable to shake the feeling of being watched. She crossed her arms over her chest and hurried up the sidewalk as an icy chill inched up her spine. *Stop being paranoid.* She shivered and opened the door.

"How was your Thanksgiving?" Dr. Stevens asked as Jesse walked further into the room. Business was usually slow that time of the year, and being the cool boss that Dr. Stevens was, he gave her a whole two weeks off for the holiday.

"It was great. I had a wonderful time," Jesse said and tucked her purse beneath the counter and then pulled off her jean jacket. "How's everything here? Any new bundles of joy?" She smiled at the grin on Dr. Stevens' face.

"Well, we had a few cats come in last week, but nothing for the past few days," he said and flipped through the surgery schedule, pretending to ignore her.

"That is not what I meant." She grinned, and he chuckled.

"No, the little bundle is being stubborn, but I guess when it's ready, it will make its grand entrance." He pushed the chair back and walked out from behind the counter.

"Do you have a name picked out?"

"We've narrowed it down, but we're waiting until the baby is born. We want to make sure the name fits, instead of naming it something it has to grow into," Dr. Stevens said. "So how are you feeling? Is there anything you have questions about? I'm a good listener."

"I'm fine, thank you. I've come to terms with what happened, and I'm trying to make the best of it. I'm sure things will work out. Not that there's anything wrong with being a wolf, I'm not saying that. It's just…" She hung her jacket on the coat rack and then turned back to Dr. Stevens.

"You don't have to explain. I know you probably still

have doubts about the pack, but we're lucky to have such a strong female join us. If there is anything I can do to make things easier for you, I'm here."

"Thanks, I'm fine really, and Megan has been a great help. I don't know what I'd do without her."

"Well, since you mentioned her, maybe I should revise my earlier statement. We're lucky to have *two* strong females join our pack." He squeezed her shoulder as he walked past to his office.

At ease, Jesse grabbed a smock off the coat rack and walked down the hall. Entering the kennel area, the first thing she noticed was the little dog sleeping in the corner of a large run. She walked over to the cage and read the index card that was attached to the wire. "Hello, Bones. How are you doing today?" She smiled when the little pug stretched before approaching her. "You remember me, boy?" Jesse placed her hand against the wire cage, and he licked her fingers. "Aren't you a little sweetheart? Don't worry; your daddy will be here to get you in a few days." She poked a small treat through the fence and then headed over to the feeding room.

Once all the animals were fed, she started at the front of the room and began cleaning cages. She kept busy for most of the morning, moving cats from one cage to another, and paused when her phone vibrated in her pocket. She answered the phone and smiled upon hearing her grandmother's voice. "I'll stop by this afternoon. I have a bag of cat food and some vitamins for Moose." Hanging up the phone, her stomach rumbled. In her excitement to get to work, she forgot to eat breakfast but thankfully it looked to be a short day.

Jesse had just twisted up the last trash bag and moved

it over near the backdoor when Dr. Stevens stuck his head into the room. "Jesse, do you mind locking up when you leave? I'm heading over to the hospital," he said, his grin wider than normal.

"I will, and congratulations!" Jesse grinned back.

Thinking about the new baby as she carried the trash bags out the door, she dismissed the strong odor in the air as manure from the nearby farm. Scanning the farmland again, the icy chill had returned, accompanied by the feeling of being watched. Hair stood on her neck, and she spun around, dropping one of the trash bags to the ground. It was the exact same location where the straggly mutt had bit her, and probably why her wolf was so uptight. "There's nothing here," she whispered although she wasn't totally convinced.

Jesse exhaled as she picked up the bag, and wondered if she would ever go a day without feeling paranoid. But Dr. Stevens had said her wolf was all about protecting its human, so probably not. It sounded crazy in her head, and she could imagine how it would sound if she said it out loud. She was still trying to absorb the changes in her life, but her wolf seemed comfortable with its new position as her protector. She rolled her eyes, prompting her wolf to grumble.

After placing the bags on the ground next to the trash bins, Jesse removed the cinderblocks, and her wolf stirred. Tension moved through her body and a low grumble worked up her throat—her wolf on full alert. *It's just your imagination,* she told herself, and then picked up the trash bags as a sharp pain spread across her back—the crack sounding in her ears. She cried out—the red-hot sting taking her breath as she dropped to her knees. Balanced between the two trash bags, she struggled to catch her breath as a second and then third blow landed across her shoulders—knocking her to the ground. Her eyes glazed over. The intense pain burned through her body, setting every nerve ending on fire. She pinched her eyes shut. *What the hell!?*

"I expected you to be dead," the female voice hissed, and Jesse rolled over and opened her eyes, squinting against the noonday sun.

"I don't understand."

"You pretend to be innocent and act like you're somehow entitled, but you're nothing more than a stupid human."

The harsh words caused Jesse to panic, and she kicked back with her legs to put distance between her and her attacker. Again, there she was in the center of drama, which she had done nothing to warrant.

"I know you. You're that woman that was at my house," she said, realizing the girl standing over her was Travis's mate.

"Aren't you the clever one?" Vivian sneered as she slowly circled around. "I thought the bite would have killed you by now, yet here you are. I must be losing my touch."

Jesse's eyes widened with Vivian's confession. Had she actually killed someone before? A slow tremble worked through her bones, and she said, "You're the one that bit me." She wasn't sure what she had done to provoke the loathing that flashed in Vivian's eyes, but she assumed she was about to find out. She pushed further away and glanced around, looking for an escape.

"Well, obviously I didn't break the skin, because

you're still breathing. But I am here to finish what I started. The pack killed Travis because of your big mouth! Not to mention that half-wit he called a niece," Vivian spat. "And although it was a toss-up between the two of you, unfortunately, you drew the wrong straw."

Jesse braced herself, knowing she couldn't get inside or call for help. And like it or not, it was her against Vivian. "You are no longer a member of the pack, if I remember correctly. And if they find you here... You don't want to do this," she warned but Vivian only laughed and moved closer.

"Travis deserved what he got after what he did to Megan. He tried to kill her, and like you, he failed." Now Jesse was pissed, but as her wolf recoiled, she wondered if she would be able to phase. Her eyes flared as a slow rumble rose in her chest.

"You're a wolf? That can't be." Surprised, Vivian narrowed her eyes but was still unconvinced. "You don't have the scent of a wolf."

"You mean, unlike you? I thought that was cow shit the farmer spread over his field," Jesse jeered and pushed up on her knees. Her irritation with Vivian was evident, and wolf or not, she refused to go down without a fight.

"Shut up! I don't know how you did it, but you are not a wolf." Vivian glanced across the field and then back at Jesse. The sneer that spread on her face should've been warning enough, but Jesse didn't think the snarling she-wolf would be ballsy enough to phase right there behind the shelter.

"I wouldn't advise you to test that theory," Jesse said, but when Vivian's clothes rained down on her, her eyes rounded with fear. "Stay away from me!" Her scream was muffled by the blow to her chest, and she threw her hands up to protect her face as the brown wolf bit down on her shoulder—provoking her own wolf to come forward.

The snarling growl was proof Vivian was out for blood, but when Jesse's wolf bared its teeth and homed in on the threat, Vivian turned and raced across the farmland, prompting her to follow. Jesse wasn't sure where the rogue wolf was leading her, but she also wasn't willing to give up the chase.

It was the middle of the day, a dangerous time for any wolf to be running, but Jesse shrugged it off. She raced along the tree line, snapping at Vivian's heels in her attempt to bring down the wolf. The longer she chased, the angrier she became, until her wolf reeled forward, causing Vivian to yelp. The frustrated brown wolf darted into the trees, and Jesse slid sideways, following suit.

The woods were dense, more so than at Hunter's Ridge and the first thing Jesse noticed when she glanced up was a deer stand high in a tree. Her heart thumped hard in her chest, but her wolf was determined to destroy the threat. And the further into the woods they ran, the narrower the trail became.

Kicking off one tree and then another, it wasn't until after Jesse cleared a small stream that the path widened out. It was well-traveled by hunters, she assumed, and that's when a sense of foreboding slammed her in the gut.

Crossing into the neighboring county as the trees thinned, and farmland came into view, she barked out a series of yelps. Allowing Vivian to stoke her anger, and then following her to an unfamiliar area, had only put them both in more danger. She yelped again, a warning for the brown wolf to not cross the field, but Vivian refused to listen.

You stupid wolf! Clearly, Vivian was enjoying the chase, or maybe it was her plan all along—to lure Jesse to an area that could result in her downfall. Then a shot rang out, and Jesse dived under a thick layer of brush, her black fur blending with the shadows. Peeking out from her hiding spot at the wolf lying lifeless on the ground, she whimpered.

One shot was all it took to take down the brown wolf, and if Jesse hadn't taken cover at the edge of the tree line, she would have suffered the same fate. She was in unfamiliar territory, with gunfire, and although a new blood, even she couldn't survive a well-aimed bullet. Her ears flicked as voices came nearer and she slowly inched further back into the brush. Out of sight of the hunters, she watched as they celebrated their kill.

Jesse lay still as death and waited until the hunters were near Vivian before bolting back into the woods. Clearing the stream, she launched herself off the side of a tree as another shot rang out, and a heavyweight slammed into her, pushing her to the ground. She struggled, but with little effect, and fearful she would attract the hunters, all she could do was growl a warning. But the growl that returned, and the nip at the back of her neck, quieted her wolf.

The weight of Old Clumsy held her in place, his great size shielding her body. And as he rested his head against hers, she closed her eyes. Her heart thundered against her ribs and she could imagine the indention she was making on the ground.

Tucker stayed with her for hours in wolf form, and from time to time he would lick the tears that trickled from her eyes. Being a wolf was new to her, not to mention the dangers they all faced. It would have been better for her had she just called for help, but Vivian didn't give her that option when she hit her across the back with a board. She opened her eyes to the large, brown paw that rested near her face. How many times would Tucker have to save her ass? She didn't deserve his loyalty. She hadn't earned it. And if it were possible, she would have sunk into the earth to hide her shame.

When the sun set, Tucker led her back through the woods, but even in wolf form, her body trembled. He was cautious and kept her at his side until they walked past the tree line and the shelter came into view. He nudged her wolf into a sprint, and followed her across the field.

Seeing Megan motioning them to the open door, Jesse knew if she could get inside, she would be safe. She could breathe again.

Relief washed over her, stealing her breath as she followed Megan into an exam room. Once the door closed behind her, she phased and took the clothes Megan offered.

"Lie down. We need to clean your shoulder," Megan said as Tucker entered the room, followed by Jack and the Regional Alpha.

Jesse closed her eyes, her teeth a constant chatter as someone carefully lifted the smock away from her shoulder. She bit her lip as a warm cloth pressed against her skin, and a tear rolled down her cheek. As she listened to Tucker fill the alpha in on the events of the day, her body relaxed. Hearing his version, she had temporarily forgotten about wolf sight, but now she was grateful for it.

Megan squeezed her hand as the bandage was

applied, and she cracked open her eyes. But if Megan was on her right, who was on her left? She looked down toward the end of the table where Jack and his dad stood, and heat filled her face.

"It looks good and should be completely healed in a few hours," Tucker said as he helped her to a sitting position. Jesse glanced over her shoulder when he tossed the blood-covered towel into the wastebasket and walked out the door.

"Come on, we'll take you home," Megan said.

Lori stayed with Jesse the rest of the night, but no matter how good her intentions were, Jesse still felt something missing. She lay in bed, staring up at the paisley wolf painting, and sometime after eleven, finally drifted off to sleep.

"What are we doing here?" Tucker asked. He glanced over at the animal shelter before sitting down beside her.

Jesse leaned against a trash bin, staring out across the field. It was a dark, cold night, but in her dreams that didn't matter. She pulled her knees to her chest as her flannel gown stretched over her legs—she tucked it beneath her feet. She didn't say a word and the rest of the dream was spent in silence as she struggled with Vivian's death.

If it hadn't been for her wolf's quick reflexes, she would have been in the field, mere seconds behind Vivian. And if it hadn't been for Tucker, there was no doubt she would have been shot trying to get away. Now she understood the dangers of exposing the pack, and why they didn't run freely during the daylight hours—another danger facing a new blood.

Then she wondered how many wolves were killed by hunters every year, and how many people that went missing in the United States every year were actually wolves.

No matter how much she disliked Vivian, it was sad to think she died in that field. And except for the pack, no one would ever know she was gone. Jesse rested her head back against the bin and glanced at Tucker. He never said a word but stayed at her side, proving his loyalty. Then a shot rang out, and Tucker slumped over on the ground.

She screamed.

Sweat beaded on her forehead as she bolted upright in the bed. "It was a dream," she told herself, but that couldn't stop the pounding in her ears. She reached over and turned on the bedside lamp.

"Do you want to talk about it?" Lori asked from the doorway. "I heard you scream. A nightmare, I assume."

"You know how I am. Anything that freaks me out, I dream about," Jesse said and drew in a breath. "I didn't mean to wake you."

"I was just dozing. That couch isn't very comfortable."

"There's plenty of room in here." Jesse patted the bed and Lori walked over and lay down beside her.

"Are you sure you don't want to talk about it?" Lori asked through a yawn.

"No. Get some sleep. Morning will come early."

Twenty-Three

Tucker

Tucker's eyes opened and his heart raced for the third time in less than twenty-four hours. Jesse hadn't been sharing her dreams lately, so when he dozed off, he didn't expect to be sitting with her behind the animal shelter, but the bullet to his chest felt real enough.

He sat there on the deck, unable to calm the tremor that pulsated through his body. His wolf was wired, and he was feeling the effects, kind of like Jack got on caffeine. He glanced over at his cousin, who was sitting on the opposite side of the deck, looking out over the river. "Thanks for being at the shelter," he said, raking his fingers through his unruly hair.

"No need to thank me. I'm just glad you got to Jesse when you did. Everyone knows that was private property, and it's probably why Vivian led her in that direction," Jack said, taking a drink of the water Megan handed him.

"I can't believe Vivian came back. What was she thinking?" Tucker released a heavy breath that vibrated his lips.

"Apparently, she was out for revenge and had she not been shot, she would have eventually tracked Megan and Tracy down as well. We dodged a bullet in more ways than one tonight."

"Yeah," Tucker said, resting his head back on the seat. "That was not the way I planned to spend my afternoon. My heart is still racing. My wolf is stoked."

"I'm sorry. I know that had to be hard on you, seeing it through wolf sight. I'm just glad you got to her in time," Megan added as she sat down and lay back against Jack's chest, a glassy sheen in her eyes. "And I'm glad you sent Lori to stay with her. She and Lori are really close, and sometimes you just need that one person who won't judge you, but is always there."

Tucker nodded and closed his eyes as images of Jesse's wolf, looking terrified and running for her life, flashed before them. He had to do something to get her to accept the bond, because his wolf was adamant it was his place to protect her at all cost.

She was new to their world, and his heart ached at the thought of losing her. A tear rolled down his cheek, and he quickly swiped it away. He said he would give her time, and had by keeping busy and out of sight, but now, he was determined to change things; he just wasn't exactly sure how.

Waiting until Jack and Megan turned in for the night; he called the one person he knew would always be there for him. The conversation lasted five minutes, and during four of those minutes, Hayden was on the road heading towards Kentucky. That was the great thing about having a brother who was also his best friend. No matter when he called, Hayden would stop what he was doing if Tucker needed him. Tucker yawned as he backed out of Jack's drive.

Three hours later, Tucker pulled off at a rest stop at the halfway point between the mountains and Cloverly. He parked beside Hayden's truck, but before he could pull the keys from the ignition, Hayden was opening the passenger door.

"What's up?" Hayden asked, his face filled with concern as he climbed into the cab. "You don't look so good."

"Thanks, I really needed you to tell me how crappy I look." Tucker chuckled and pocketed his keys. "Promise this won't go any further than us."

"I won't tell a soul, you know that. Not even Mom, although she questioned my need to meet you so early in the morning."

"What did you tell her?" Tucker ran his hand over his face, and yawned, again.

"I told her you were having withdraws and needed some brotherly love." Hayden grinned.

"Well, you're not totally wrong. I need someone I can talk to. Someone that understands me." He looked over at Hayden's nod. "I have a bond, but this can't go any further than us because I don't want Mom getting her hopes up."

"No way! That makes two for you, and I haven't even had one shot at a mate." Hayden pretended to be pissed and narrowed his eyes.

"It's the same female, just a different bond. I know what you're thinking because I thought the same thing, and I'll explain it later if she actually accepts it. But for now, I just need to talk." Tucker swallowed down his rising emotions and continued. "Yesterday, I thought I lost her."

"Why? Did she threaten to deny the bond?" Hayden's voice shifted and his big brother emerged, which was what Tucker expected.

"No. She was out... running... and crossed the county line into an area frequented by hunters. One wolf was killed, but she was about five seconds behind and managed to hide. But when she ran back into the woods, they fired off another shot, hitting the tree beside her. If I hadn't shown up when I did, she would be dead." Tucker exhaled as tears welled in his eyes. "I pinned her down and kept her from moving until they left the area. They were within seventy feet, I guess, I could smell the alcohol they'd been drinking. I can literally say my life flashed before my eyes. It scared the hell out of me, but training as an alpha, I couldn't show that weakness." Tucker dropped his head to the steering wheel as the tension seeped from his body. "My wolf would have killed them if they had shot her," he whispered.

"And if it didn't, I would have taken you down," Hayden said, and although Tucker knew he was trying to lighten the mood, he hoped it was the truth. "Look, just because you're an alpha, doesn't mean you can't show your emotions. If I were you, I would have bawled like a baby. Especially if I thought I'd lost my female."

"No, you wouldn't. You're ten times the alpha I'll ever

be." Tucker wiped his eyes and rested his head against the rear window. "I don't know what to do."

"How about not trying to meet anyone else's standard of what they think you should be? Be yourself. That's what's required to be a great alpha. Ben picked you for a reason. You have a caring heart, and there are times I wish I could be more like you. So don't underestimate yourself. You have what it takes, and as for this female, just give her time. She will not walk away from you again," Hayden said as he opened the large, black bag that lay in the backseat. "What is this?"

"I wasn't sure if I was going back or not," Tucker admitted.

"Oh, you are going back. You have a bond. You have the chance to have a mate, and a family. To be happy." Hayden stuffed the bag in the back floorboard.

"Yeah, because those are the things you want out of life. I remember the lectures. How we would run the pack, the two of us. Bachelors to the end." Tucker lifted a brow.

"Hey, I have a reputation. But between us, sometimes I stand on that damn mountain and I know there is someone out there for me. I would give anything to find her." Hayden looked out the window to avoid Tucker's gaze. "I envy you. Twice! I want what you have. I want a female that will be mine for the rest of my life. I want a family. I just don't think that will ever happen on the mountain, though."

"That sucks. I never thought about it that way," Tucker said, knowing if he hadn't left the mountains, he might not have met Jesse. "Maybe you need to get away. Take a vacation, visit Cloverly or Kinsley. You might get lucky."

"Maybe when you become an alpha, I can visit you for a week or so," Hayden said, lost in thought.

"I'm up for that. Relive old times." Tucker laughed but noticed the strange look on Hayden's face. "Did I say something wrong?"

"No, actually, I think you might be on to something. It's a good idea. I'll have to see when I can get away from the pack." Hayden grinned and fist bumped Tucker.

Hours later, Tucker awoke and glanced around until recognition settled in his mind. "How long have I been asleep?" he asked, rubbing his eyes.

"Four hours, but you needed the sleep before heading home," Hayden said, pushing a bag of fast food his way. "Breakfast for the road."

"Thanks, I appreciate it."

"I'm a phone call away," Hayden said getting out of the truck. "Call me later so I know you made it home."

"I will. And Hayden?"

"Yeah?"

"Thanks," Tucker said, and Hayden nodded, climbing into his truck.

Waiting until his brother pulled out of the parking spot, Tucker backed out behind him. Seeing the turn signal, blinking toward the mountain, a part of him wanted to follow. But his heart was in Cloverly and no matter how much he missed his family, Jesse had to come first. He beeped as he turned, heading in the opposite direction and pulling a breakfast sandwich out of the bag. Glancing up at the rearview mirror, he watched until Hayden disappeared out of sight.

Twenty-Four

Jesse

More than a week had passed since Jesse moved back to her apartment, and one week since Vivian's death. Jesse tried to push the details of that day from her mind, but once the story broke that was all the locals talked about. It was a big to-do since the last time someone sighted a wolf in Kentucky was well over one hundred years ago.

If they only knew.

And other than the pack, no one knew the dead wolf was a shifter, not even the hunters who claimed it was an accidental shooting. But Jesse knew the truth, witnessed it, and if it wasn't for Tucker, she wouldn't be alive to tell about the ordeal. So, distracting her mind, she stayed busy creating new designs and setting up her area at the back of the store—preparing for opening day.

Nearly every female in the county attended the Grand Opening of the Lucky Leaf Boutique. It was overwhelming at times, but exciting nonetheless, as the Christmas crowd eagerly sorted through various items such as dresses, perfume, and body lotion—and as Megan predicted— lingerie. Sales were expected to be good, and by noon they had exceeded their expectations.

Jesse paused near the dividing wall when Jack entered the store, carrying an armload of pizza boxes. Her stomach rumbled in anticipation until she glimpsed Tucker standing on the sidewalk. She had been so busy preparing for their opening; she didn't stop to think how that might look to Tucker.

However, it was confusing how fast life had changed as she struggled to keep up with the everyday grind. *Only losers make excuses.* Guilt consumed her, and she rushed into the bathroom to catch her breath. When had she become so cruel and hateful that she had completely disregarded his feelings? He'd only tried to help, and this was the way she thanked him? He was right; she was ungrateful.

She looked in the mirror, not recognizing her hateful self. *Who are you?* Splashing cold water over her face, she then patted her skin dry.

"Are you all right?" Megan asked, coming to stand beside her when she walked out of the restroom.

"No, but I will be." Jesse smiled at the customers browsing the store.

As the day wound down and the customers thinned out, Jesse stepped out of the changing rooms as Tucker walked into the boutique accompanied by a pretty brunette. She was tall and thin, and her chestnut-brown hair was pulled up into a ponytail that hung halfway down her back. Wiping his feet at the door, he smiled as the young woman strolled about the store and sampled a few of Megan's beauty supplies.

Jesse grabbed a stack of dresses that had been tried on throughout the day and hung them back on their hangers, avoiding the customers at the front of the store. Her jaw ached from constantly grinding her teeth, and the thoughts that crossed her mind were anything but nice. She honestly tried not to glance at the couple as they moved over to Lori's Lingerie. But hearing the girl's laughter, she did the unthinkable.

Tucker grinned and shook his head at the skimpy panty set his date held up. Just knowing she was asking his opinion caused Jesse's eyes to flare and she quickly ducked beneath a dress rack. *Just like Brian.* She swallowed her tears and tucked her knees against her chest, but hearing the doorbell chime she parted the skirts as the girl walked out the door, leaving Tucker behind.

Megan handed Tucker a small bag, and he laughed as he stuffed it into his pocket. Jesse frowned and crawled out from beneath the dress rack and hurried into the dressing room not wanting to see him leave. She told Tucker she needed time, but from the looks of it, her time had run out. *What did you expect?*

Ten minutes later, when Jesse was certain Tucker had gone; she walked out of the dressing room. Not seeing him, her foul mood melted away, and she instantly felt alone. She glanced up at the overhead clock. In less than an hour they would lockdown the store, and then she could go upstairs and take her frustration out on a large tub of chocolate-chip ice cream. But until then, to keep from falling apart right there in the middle of the store, she turned for the warehouse and bumped into a solid mass of muscle.

"Excuse me," Jesse said, but as she side-stepped around the customer, she inhaled that wonderful woodsy scent. *Damn him!* She looked up, and Tucker winked. "Can I help you?" She would treat him like the customer he was, and nothing more.

"You most definitely can." Of course, he would find her reaction amusing, and the smirk on his face caused her to bristle as he delicately sorted through the dresses she had designed. Wanting to slap the silly smirk off his face and kiss his dimples, she clenched her jaw instead.

"Well, unless you give me a size, there's not much I can do." Her voice was gruff, and she glared.

"Don't be so modest. There's plenty you could do if you wanted." The overhead lights sparkled in his eyes and his dark brown hair, longer now and with more curls, looked like strands of silk against his dark complexion. She mentally slapped herself for the R-rated thoughts that filled her head.

"Look, if all you want is a one nigh—"

"That's not all I want." He cut her off before she could start her rant. Stepping into her personal space, he twisted a strand of her hair around his finger, and then placed it over her shoulder.

"Really? Then exactly what do you want? A dinner date, maybe a movie? Take me to meet your parents, brother, or sister? Or would you rather make me the trophy that sits on your mantel?" By now, Jesse was pissed, and she took three steps back, eager to get away from the big lug.

Megan and Lori ducked into the warehouse and she swore she heard a giggle. Tucker turned to look out the window, and Jesse glared, waiting for his answer.

"Dinner and a movie would be a good start, but I prefer dancing. Meeting the family could be arranged if you're willing to travel. As for the trophy, I can think of plenty of places for you to sit, but the mantel isn't one." Tucker turned, and her face flushed with his words. "So if you're interested, this lace on that dress will do," he said pointing out two different dresses.

Jesse looked between the lime green dress and the white lace. "High, low, short, long?" She returned his smirk, expecting to throw him off his game.

"Easy access is not what I'm looking for. Long."

Soft lime green and delicate lace; it would be beautiful. Still, in her smart ass mood, she lifted a brow. "Would you like pearls with that, or do you prefer diamonds?"

The corner of his mouth twitched. "Just you and a pair of three-inch heels."

She stood speechless, unable to stop him as he turned and walked to the door. Staring at his rearview, she wanted to stomp her foot, have a conniption—her grandmother would call it. *How dare he walk away!*

"Excuse me. I need a time," she yelled across the store, drawing the attention of the remaining customers, as her wolf urged her on.

"Five," he said without stopping.

"That's a little early for a date, don't you think?"

He paused at the door but never looked back. "It will be a long night."

"Day?"

"Your choice."

"Tomorrow night," Jesse blurted.

"I'll be here." The overhead bell rang as the door shut behind him, and again, Jesse stood and watched him walk past the window, confusion etched on her face.

"What did I just do?"

"You just captured the heart of an alpha," Megan whispered and then hurried to the front of the store.

"What?"

"You'll figure it out," Megan yelled, walking in behind the counter as Lori giggled from somewhere beyond the dividing wall.

Jesse looked at Megan and then back at the door. "Oh, crap! I've got a dress to make."

"Then I suggest you get busy." Megan grinned as Jesse gathered the dresses and rushed into the warehouse.

"How did I get myself in this mess?" The panicked question echoed through the building, and laughter filled the store. It was only then that she realized even the customers thought her predicament was hilarious. "You all could help you know." Jesse chuckled as more laughter wafted through the warehouse doors, and she looked up at the large overhead clock and groaned. With the store's Grand Opening and the long hours, she couldn't believe she had agreed to a date with Tucker.

Removing the lime green dress off the hanger, Tucker's scent filled her nose, and she sighed. What was it about him that was so irresistible? You share a bond, remember? She did remember, but after slipping into the last horrid dream and avoiding him for so long, she forgot what it felt like.

Jesse worked late into the night determined to finish the dress before her date. Not that she was excited about it, she wasn't. LIAR! Truth be told, it thrilled her but she would never admit that to Tucker. Still unsure he truly had feelings for her, she would do what was needed to shield her heart.

The following evening, while Lori watched the store, Megan assisted Jesse with her hair. "I think I have a new favorite color. I like," Megan said, referring to the dress Jesse wore.

"How often do you see someone wearing lime-green at this time of year?" Jesse asked as she looked into the mirror. The lime green skirt touched the floor, and she turned from side to side. The white lace, which looked great over the lime green bodice, trailed up over her shoulder and framed her back, meeting at the waist. Definitely a dangerous dress by Lori's standard, but anytime she went braless, Lori deemed it dangerous. She smiled at her reflection.

"I hope you plan to wear something over the top because they're calling for snow," Megan said, staring at her through the mirror.

"I have this." Jesse picked up the waist-length, faux fur off the arm of the sofa. "What do you think?"

"That's beautiful. Do you know where you're going?" Megan moved over beside Jesse to clip her hair back, leaving two strands to frame her face.

"I don't know, but with the weather, I hope it's only to dinner. I don't want to get stranded on the road."

"Well, before you leave, can I ask you something?"

"Sure," Jesse said. She sat down to slip on her heels as

Megan moved around to the sofa.

"Why have you been so hard on Tucker?"

"I'm not trying to be, but I was so humiliated when Gina showed up at his cabin. She told me things about him and even though he said she was nothing to him, I find it odd she would just drop by that very morning. I don't want to fall into the same mess I found myself in with Brian. I want a man that knows the value of a relationship and will put me above all else, and I'm not sure Tucker can do that."

"Oh, Jesse. You can't judge all males based on Brian. He's one of my best friends, but he's an ass."

"That's the point. He is one of your best friends and you didn't see him as a player. So what makes you think Tucker will be any different?"

"Tucker isn't afraid of strong females. He prefers them over the clingy types. There was never anything between him and Gina. He took her to the party, but only as friends. He was uncomfortable with the way she kept hanging on him, but he honestly thought you and Brian had gotten back together, which was why he ignored you for most of the night. And since he and Tracy are best friends, he caught on quickly to what Gina was doing."

"But she's part of the pack."

"Not the Cloverly Pack. Alpha Cooper sent her back to Kinsley and I could be wrong, but I think he's going to place her with the Danbury Pack as soon as they get an alpha in place."

"And the girl he was with yesterday? Was she Gina's replacement? They seemed to hit it off if I remember correctly."

"Of course they did. That was his sister, Alyssa. She

wanted to meet the pack because she's planning to move here."

"Please tell me you're kidding. You knew this and still allowed me to make an idiot of myself? I can't believe I was jealous of his sister," Jesse confessed, falling back on the couch.

"Yeah, that was funny, but it only proves how much you like him. You really should stop being so headstrong and give him a chance." Megan laughed. "There's nothing he wouldn't do for you. I've seen it with my own eyes."

"Exactly what have you seen?" Jesse's grin widened with the flick of her brow.

"You tell me. You're the one going on the date."

Twenty-Five

Tucker

Tucker twirled a single white rose between his fingers as he stood inside the front door of the Lucky Leaf Boutique. Hoping his instincts were correct, and if he knew Jesse, she would wear the dress he'd suggested. That is unless she figured out what he was doing; in which case, he'd be lucky if she wore a potato sack. He blushed when Lori looked up and narrowed her eyes.

Jesse asked for time, so he purposely avoided her until he had a plan in place to sweep her off her feet. She assumed his absence was because of her request, but she couldn't have been more wrong. Keeping his distance by working on the cabin in Berkley, she never noticed when he was nearby. Like the night in her apartment, while sketching her latest design. The old building noises were terrifying until she realized it was the heating unit kicking on. Fiercely wielding a wooden baseball bat when all she had to do was call on her wolf was adorable. Still, he waited across the street at the park until she had calmed down. His wolf loved defending its mate and showed up anytime Jesse shared a vision. It was fortunate for him that after her blocking her dreams, she had forgotten about her wolf sight. But he wasn't going to be the one that reminded her, that was until the *stupid dog* returned.

It was dangerous for his wolf to be seen running across town in broad daylight. But protecting Jesse was his highest priority; and come hell or high water, he would be there for his mate.

He had just crawled out from beneath his car and was wiping his hands when the vision hit. Frozen in place, he watched as Jesse fell to the ground, experiencing her pain. He didn't understand what was happening to her until she rolled over and looked up at Vivian. And seeing the rogue wolf was all it took to spur him into action, and after shouting instructions to Brayden, he phased.

Afterward, he thanked the stars that everything had worked out, but the fear that gripped his heart at that moment was a little more than he could handle. So setting his plan into motion—a week later—brought him to the boutique that night.

Alyssa had driven to Cloverly with his mother, to meet with Alpha Cooper and discuss her moving to Berkley the next year. But Jesse had no clue she was his sister, so when he accompanied her to the store, it set Jesse on edge. As she hid in the dressing room, he dashed to the back of the store while visions flashed in his mind. Her heart ached thinking he had moved on without her, but deep down, she never thought he cared. But little did

she know, he would prove how wrong she was and
subsequently steal her heart.

Tucker lifted his nose as chicory and coconut mingled with the lavender fragrance of the room. He turned, and his breath caught as Jesse glided toward him, her long gown flowing with each step. He longed to touch the soft, white lace peeking out from beneath the white fur-coat she wore. And her hair, pulled back on the sides—lovely.

"You're beautiful," he finally said when she joined him at the door.

"Thanks to my designer." She looked up through thick, black lashes that framed her ebony eyes, and smiled.

Captivated by her gentle nature, he stared for a moment longer—glimpsing her wolf—before handing her the rose, and then offered her his arm.

As he escorted Jesse out to the waiting car, she lightly squeezed his elbow, sending a jolt of electricity to his heart. He drew in a sharp breath to douse the fire that raged in his soul. It was painful to have her so close since they had yet to seal their bond. *Soon.* His wolf perked up.

The date started out better than Tucker expected, and he was more than eager to get her alone. And after securing the seatbelt at her waist, he hurried around to the driver's side and got into the car. The pine scent from the air freshener hanging on the rearview mirror couldn't mask the sweet smell that wafted around Jesse. It was like a drug that drew him in, and he looked forward to the addiction.

"Is something wrong?" he asked when he noticed she was staring.

"I wasn't expecting this." She motioned with her hand to the tuxedo he wore.

"What? This old thing?" He rolled his eyes, and pulled away from the curb. Jesse had no idea he would also be dressed for the occasion, which was why he was relieved to see her in the gown he chose.

Living in a small town, there weren't any formal dress shops that rented tuxedos, so he settled for the next best thing. After calling his brother, Hayden met him at the Tennessee border late last night. Like shady drug dealers in the dark, Tucker handed him the cash to pay for the package.

It was the second time he had met Hayden to pick up a tux, but this time, before Hayden gave him the package, he made him promise to come home for the annual Christmas party. A full moon meant the whole pack would be there, and it wouldn't be the same if all the Wilson clan wasn't gathered there for the midnight run.

He glanced over at Jesse who was listening to the music playing low on the radio. Humming softly, she lifted the rose to her nose and closed her eyes... breathtaking

The twenty-mile drive was somewhat awkward, but before Tucker knew it; he was escorting Jesse into the restaurant where more soft music played in the background. Greeting the waitress, she smiled and graciously ushered them to a private table in the far corner of the room.

Jesse couldn't hold her smile when she noticed two white tapered candles and a single red rose displayed in the center of the table. She looked up at Tucker, and he winked.

"I was told you liked flowers." It wasn't a lie. Seems Lori had picked up on his feelings for Jesse, and since she didn't want to see her best friend with Brian, she was quick to offer advice.

"Anyone I know?" Jesse eyed him suspiciously as he pulled out her chair.

"Sorry, I've been sworn to secrecy. Scouts' honor." He grinned as he moved around to the opposite side of the table.

She tilted her head and bunched her lips to the side. He would kiss those lips before the night was over. "I'm not sure I can picture you as a Boy Scout." She worked her bottom lip as if mulling the idea over.

"I'm a scout for the pack. It's not the same." He looked up when the waitress approached the table.

"Welcome! I'm Andria, and I'll be your waitress for the evening." She gave a slight nod. "Are you ready to order or would you like a few more minutes?" She smiled and readied her pen.

"Thanks, Andria, but I've already placed the order," Tucker said, and the waitress excused herself and walked away. "I hope you don't mind." He took the rose from the vase and offered it to Jesse.

"I don't mind at all. Thank you." Jesse blushed, but there was no way she could contain her smile. She looked down at the rose before sniffing. "I can't believe you did all this for me." She met his eyes when he took hold of her hand.

"Only you."

It elated Tucker to be sitting across the table from Jesse, and after the initial breaking-of-the-ice, which amounted to him handing Jesse the red rose, they laughed and talked for hours—while enjoying their meal.

It was weird, but once they were away from the pack,

the conversation came easily, and he realized, not only him but Jesse had relaxed. "We should probably get going or Megan will think I've kidnapped you," Tucker joked, but little did Jesse know, their date was far from over. He stood and nodded to the waitress.

"Let me guess, you've already paid." Jesse chuckled as he led her out of the restaurant, only this time her hand wasn't wrapped around his arm. Instead, his arm was wrapped around her waist—as it should be.

The ride back to Cloverly didn't take as long, and Tucker was glad Jesse had finally warmed to him. Listening to her singing along with the radio, even if it was off key, it sounded amazing. "You make it really hard to concentrate on driving, you know." He glanced over as she swayed in the seat, her shoulders bouncing with the beat.

"What can I say? I love to dance, and this is better than nothing." She flashed a goofy grin and winked.

Tucker knew Jesse loved dancing as much as him, but to wink? Yeah, she had definitely warmed to him, and he liked it. He held his breath as he pulled over on the side of the road, next to the park. "I have a surprise," he said and opened the driver's door. He grinned through the windshield as he rounded the car, and opened her door. Waiting until she had unfastened her belt, he then ushered her into the park.

"Wow!" Jesse said as tiny, white Christmas lights—decorating the gazebo—blinked with the rhythm of the music playing. "This is wonderful." Her smile turned to a grin when they walked into the gazebo, and she noticed the small table that held two wine glasses and a bundle of daisies. "I don't know what to say. I never expected this."

"Well, I know you love music and dancing, so... to our first date." Tucker handed her a glass of grape juice. It was just the two of them, and part of his plan to win her over. He tipped his glass and smiled when she sniffed her drink before taking a sip.

"For a minute there, I thought you were trying to get me sloshed." She giggled and set the glass back on the table, the festive lights sparkling in her eyes.

Following her lead, Tucker placed his glass on the table, and with a slight bow, held out his hand. "Would you honor me with a dance?"

"I would be delighted." Jesse curtsied, causing his grin to widen, and then stepped into his arms.

With her head resting against his shoulder, he closed his eyes and lightly kissed her hair. She was his world; why couldn't she see what she meant to him? Lost in the feel of her body moving to the beat of his heart, or the music, depending on how he would eventually spin the story, he sighed.

"You do realize it's freezing out here," Jesse said, and he tightened his grip, making her laugh. "Did you do all this? The lights?"

"No. I just took advantage of it."

"And the music?"

"Um... that was Megan." His eyes remained closed.

"And the grape juice?" She glanced up.

"That was me, and also the daisies."

"And... the snow?"

Tucker opened his eyes and looked out over the park as heavy flakes fell silently to the ground. "Not me, but I wish I'd thought of it. I've always wanted to dance in the rain." He pulled her out into the snow, his laughter filling the air.

"This isn't rain," Jesse squealed, looking up at the flakes.

"It would be if it weren't so cold," he said and spun her around before bringing her back into his arms. Holding her close as the snow melted in their hair, he dipped her low. *I love you.* Remembering the first time he whispered those three little words, they were true then and even truer now.

Two dances later and a dusting of snow, Tucker led Jesse back to the car. "Would you like some coffee to warm you?"

She nodded.

As Tucker steered the car away from the curb, Jesse held her hands in front of the heater vent. "What were we thinking?" she asked through chattering teeth.

"I wanted to give you a night you wouldn't forget," he said and clicked on the turn signal. *So far, so good.* Taking her back to his cabin was risky, but where else could they get coffee at the late hour? Again, another part of the plan to win her over, he just hoped she wouldn't be upset. His breath caught as he turned into the driveway, noticing her smile had disappeared. But when he parked and turned in the seat, she had already gotten out of the car.

"So this is your idea of coffee," she said, grinning at him, overtop of the Camaro.

"Not only coffee. I also have homemade brownies." She snorted, making him laugh, and he hurried around and took hold of her arm, both of them slipping on the freshly fallen snow.

Helping Jesse to the porch, the warmth of the

fireplace greeted them when they entered the cabin. Tucker took her coat and hung it on a hook, next to the door, before reaching over and flicking the porch light on and off—his signal to thank Seth for the fire. "Make yourself at home, and I'll get the coffee."

Carrying the tray of coffee and brownies into the living room, Tucker paused in the doorway. Seeing Jesse sitting on the floor in front of the sofa, he hurried into the room. With her shoes off and her toes stretching toward the fire, he couldn't wait to remove *his* shoes. He placed the tray on the hearth and sat down beside her on the rug.

It was cozy, sipping coffee there in front of the fire, more so than at the restaurant. He nodded, listening as Jesse talked about her family, her friends, and her future. She was fascinating, brilliant actually, and he wanted to learn everything he could about her.

Jesse had always wanted to live in Cloverly, and she loved working at the animal shelter. The boutique was a dream she and Megan shared, even though her mother wanted her to move to D.C.

Tucker memorized every small detail like the way her lips pressed into a straight line, right before she said something snarky. The pink nail polish that matched her toenails and somehow worked with the lime-green dress she wore. And the way she blinked lazily when she was flirting—he liked that a lot. But the most amazing thing he noted was the way her eyes sparkled when she talked about serving Thanksgiving dinner at Alma's House. He wanted to be that sparkle.

Then out of the blue, Jesse changed the subject, and before long, they were both talking about Old Clumsy. Tucker rolled over onto a large throw pillow, his whole body vibrating from laughter.

"Aww, look, you're blushing," Jesse teased.

"What did you expect? You had him shaking in his boots." Tucker sat up and inhaled a much-needed breath.

"I'm sorry, Clumsy, I didn't mean to scare you," she cooed, and they both broke into laughter again.

Tucker squeezed his jaws to relieve the ache. He couldn't remember a time when he had laughed so hard, and that was saying a lot considering he was usually the source of everyone's entertainment. "Jesse, as much as I hate for this night to end, it's getting late and the road is now covered with snow." He ran his thumb over her bottom lip, and she bit his finger.

"Well, since we've nowhere else to go, how about you walking me home instead? I'm staying with Gramma tonight."

Tucker grinned. *More time to win her over.*

As Jesse slipped on her shoes, Tucker pulled on his coat and then held out hers. "Are you sure you want to walk? You're not exactly dressed for the weather."

"I'm always up for a challenge." Jesse fastened up her coat and then opened the front door

Trudging through two inches of snow was not how Tucker expected their date would end. And by the time they had reached Seth's cabin, Jesse was reconsidering her suggestion of him walking her home. But being the gentleman he was, he lifted Jesse into his arms and cut across Seth's yard. She claimed he was cheating by taking the short-cut; he claimed it was to keep her from freezing to death. In all honesty, he just wanted to hold her close. As he followed the tree line alongside Gramma's house, Jesse hid her face against his neck. Her squeaks and squeals, every time he adjusted his hold, made him chuckle. "Safe and sound," Tucker announced, placing her on her feet at the front door.

"Why thank you, sir," she said, smoothing down her dress.

"No need to thank me. I'm the reason you're out in this mess." Tucker smiled, but what he really wanted to do was kiss her. Would she kiss him in return? His eyes closed fleetingly, and then opened when Jesse pressed her lips to his. *Holy Mother of Luna!* He wasn't expecting Jesse to make the first move, but since she had, there was no sense in wasting the opportunity. Backing her against the house, he fisted his hands in her hair and deepened the kiss. His whole body trembled with her nearness, her scent making him dizzy. "Wow, you've got talent," he said when he broke from the kiss. "I think my toes are tingling." He grinned when she giggled.

"I think you're the talented one, and the tingling is from the cold," she countered, wrapping her arms around his neck. "Actually, I'm quite sure of it." She kicked one foot out, her wet shoe dangling from her toes.

"Yeah, you're probably right." He peppered kisses along her jaw, stopping at the corner of her mouth. "Goodnight, Jesse." Pressing one last kiss to her lips, he then backed away.

"Night." Jesse opened the screen door as he descended the steps. "Do you have to leave right away?"

"Well, I had planned to give Old Clumsy a bath, but it can wait." He bounded up the steps to stand in front of her.

Jesse laughed and pulled him into the foyer where Gramma was waiting. "Gramma, you remember Tucker, don't you?"

"Of course I do," Gramma said with a smile. "What's the occasion?"

"Tucker took me out to dinner and dancing, and then we had coffee."

"Well, you look nice. And it's refreshing to see a young man wearing something besides jeans all the time." Gramma patted Tucker's arm. "You, young man, are a keeper."

"Gramma!" Jesse blushed. "Do you mind if Tucker visits with me for a while?"

"Lord, no, make yourself comfortable. I just turned off the pot, but the coffee is still hot, and there's lemon cake on the table."

Tucker grinned when Gramma headed upstairs to her room. "I think I'm in love."

"Yeah, she seemed pretty taken by you as well."

Tucker followed Jesse into the kitchen and wondered how many times he had been in that very room? Only once that Jesse knew of. He took the cup of coffee she offered and then glanced up at the daisy-clock hanging on the wall. "Are you sure you don't want to call it a night? It's getting pretty late."

"Not a chance. I told you everything about me, so now it's your turn."

"There's not much to tell."

"Yeah, well, humor me," she said, and he shook his head, his dimples winking with his grin.

Over coffee and cake, Tucker talked about his family, and what it was like growing up in Tennessee. What he missed the most, and why he moved to Cloverly? He took a sip of coffee as Jesse patiently waited. She was a good listener, and from time to time, she grinned. Tucker placed his mug on the table and continued answering all her questions, even the embarrassing ones about the pack females that chased after him and Hayden. But it wasn't until he told her about Hayden delivering the tuxedo to the border, twice, that she laughed.

It was midnight by the time Tucker left Jesse's, and just his luck, the walk home had turned treacherous. Wearing slick-soled shoes didn't gain him any traction, and he imagined if he fell he'd just leave a snow angel in her yard.

Plodding across the backyard, Tucker turned as the porch light came on and Jesse opened the backdoor. "Be careful," she called out at the same time a snowball slammed into the side of his head. He jerked around as Seth's backdoor slammed shut, followed by Jesse's—and then the light went out.

Dusting the snow out of his hair, Tucker laughed visualizing Jesse behind the closed door doing the same thing.

Twenty-Six

Jesse

Jesse kicked off her blanket and groaned. Getting up at five in the morning didn't sound so great to her drowsy mind. She stretched as visions of Tucker flashed behind her eyes. Not only was he the greatest guy she'd ever gone out with, but he was also big, buff, and despite what he thought, beautiful. Just picturing him, her skin sizzled—he was that hot.

She cracked a sleepy grin and pried her eyes open.

Glimpsing at the glowing numbers on the alarm clock, she yawned and sat up on the side of the bed. She would have preferred to crawl back under the covers and dream about Tucker, instead of running through the woods in the blue cold. But Jesse was fully prepared to allow her wolf one day—each month—to run. It just sucked that she would be running alone. The pack was everything, or so she was told, but as far as Jesse was concerned, she didn't have a pack. Unlike normal wolves, if werewolves could be thought of as normal, she phased with the new moon.

Jesse pulled back the curtain and glanced down at the thick blanket of snow covering the ground. She wasn't a fan of winter, but her wolf was more than excited to leave tracks in the snow. She chuckled as her chest softly rumbled. For months, she thought the rumble was indigestion, but now knowing it was her wolf, she could stop chewing antacids. Funny how something so simple could confuse a person, but she still had a lot to learn about being a wolf.

With Tucker still on her mind, she bounded out of bed and hurried over to the closet. She wasn't sure if he would remember her phase that morning, but she wanted to look nice if he did. Sorting through her clothes, she snickered knowing Lori would suggest her birthday suit, but she opted for the wretched jogging pants instead.

After using the bathroom and washing her face, she studied her image in the mirror. Frumpily clad in navy blue sweats and a pair of brown hiking boots, she was definitely not dressed to impress. She sighed and hurried downstairs, hoping she wouldn't wake the others.

The smell of sausage drifted to her nose, and her stomach rumbled when she neared the bottom step. The kitchen light illuminated the foyer, and she smiled at hearing her grandmother moving about the room. As she walked into the kitchen, she inhaled deeply. *Caffeine.* She loved the smell of coffee brewing in the morning. "Gramma, what are you doing up so early?"

"I wanted to make sure you had a good warm breakfast to start your day."

"That's not necessary," Jesse said as Gramma rolled down a large paper bag. Jesse assumed breakfast would be leftover pizza, but she wouldn't turn down sausage and biscuits.

"It's something quick to eat on your way to Sallee's."

Jesse had no intention of walking to Sallee's Rock, just to phase, but her grandmother was acting strange, so she would go with it. "Thank you. I'm sure it will be delicious." She hugged her grandmother and looked down at the bag. "You packed enough food for an army."

"Well, you never know," Gramma said and then quickly changed the subject. "It's blustery out this morning so make sure to keep your feet warm." She pushed the bag into Jesse's hands and then ushered her out the door.

"These boots are rated for the cold, so I think I'm good." If Jesse hadn't known any better, she would have thought Gramma was trying to get rid of her. She glanced back as the door shut and the kitchen light went out.

Dumbfounded, Jesse shrugged and turned toward the woods, the hair on her neck standing on end. She lifted her nose, deciphering the various smells in the air. Woods, pine, moss, and vanilla? Then she realized she wasn't alone. She scanned the yard, and other than Tucker's footprints from the night before, the snow was undisturbed. She chuckled remembering the snowball that hit Tucker up-side the head as she trudged through the deep snow. Lost in thought, it wasn't until she looked up that she noticed Tucker's silhouette leaning against the oak tree.

"You remembered." Her stomach filled with soft flutters as Tucker pushed away from the tree, his eyes locked onto hers.

"You didn't honestly think I would let you run alone, did you?" Entranced by the deep, soothing voice she had grown to love, she shuddered.

"I guess I didn't know for sure." She rapidly blinked the moisture from her eyes, and he lifted her chin. *Some strong female you turned out to be.*

"Jesse, the pack is everything, and we'll be here for you no matter what." Tucker's words comforted her as the fear of waking under a random tree vanished from her mind.

"Would you like some more company?" Jesse startled when Megan popped out from behind a tree wearing a black jogging suit that matched Tucker's.

"Oh my gosh! I can't believe you're here," she squeaked and shoved the bag of biscuits into Tucker's arms and then pulled Megan into a tight hug. ·

"And miss the opportunity to run with your wolf? Fat chance," Megan said, taking hold of Jesse's hand, leading her up the trail.

The further into the woods they walked the more aware Jesse became, and when she looked over her shoulder it was Jack who winked. She squeezed Megan's hand. "You did this?"

"I wish I'd thought of it."

Jesse looked back at Tucker, and he smiled, causing her face to heat. It was amazing having them there, and for once she felt like she belonged with the pack. "This is just what I needed."

"No, what you need is a hug from your best bud."

Jesse squealed when Seth stepped out on the path and pulled her into a hug. "So what's with the bag?" he asked, glancing over her shoulder at Tucker.

"It's breakfast," Jesse said pulling out of the hug. Now she knew why her grandmother was so quick to push her out the door and she assumed at some point she must have talked to Tucker.

"And she brings food. Again, why couldn't I have met you first?" Seth asked, and Tucker looked away.

"That's sweet of you to say, but it wouldn't have mattered. I fell for those dimples the first day I saw them." That wasn't a lie, and Jesse winked when Tucker glanced back. Staring a minute longer than necessary, to see his dimples, oh, what she wouldn't do! "You're amazing," she mouthed causing him to smile.

Jack cleared his throat of a snicker, but it wasn't until Jesse looked around that she realized everyone was grinning at her.

She moved over beside Tucker, trying to hide her grin. *Damn. Caught ogling a guy again.* Her belly bounced with silent laughter, and she buried her face against his chest. She inhaled his woodsy scent as he wrapped his thick arms around her, planting a kiss on top of her head. The pull to him was hard to deny, and if she looked into his eyes, she suspected she would see his wolf there. Her breath hitched when he leaned down and whispered, "I like you checking me out."

Kill me now!

Trying to distract herself from the wicked thoughts that raced through her mind, she swallowed hard and changed the subject. "Anyone hungry?" Tucker growled, and she added, "For breakfast." Her face flushed with the naughty notion, and as if the others could read her mind, they grinned.

Tucker handed out the breakfast biscuits as they continued up the trail to where Mason, Whitney, and Tracy were waiting just around the bend. It was the best morning ever, as far as Jesse was concerned, and proof the Cloverly Pack had accepted her as their newest member. Tucker passed the bag to Mason and then pulled Jesse to his side. She instantly froze.

"What is it?" Tucker asked, scanning the darkest areas of the woods.

"I don't know. It smells like... rain."

Everyone turned when the youngest of the scouts busted through the trees. "Sorry I'm late," Brayden said, yanking off his wet coat. "I fell in the ditch."

That had them all rolling with laughter as they continued up the trail. And paying attention to how the pack communicated, Jesse understood the bond between them wasn't the same as the bond she shared with Tucker, yet it was equally important.

As Jesse's thoughts drifted, Tucker draped his arm over her shoulders, shielding her from the early morning chill. *Her mother wanted her to move to D.C. but the draw to Cloverly, couldn't be denied. Visiting the small town each summer, it had captured her heart and also set the course for her future.*

The first time she saw Tucker, there was an instant attraction and she didn't understand the reason why. Maybe because she was young and awkward—an early bloomer—and shied away from boys.

"I remember you," Jesse said when Tucker reached over and tucked a strand of hair behind her ear.

"I'm glad. I tried really hard to impress you."

She rolled her eyes. He had no clue what she was talking about.

It was Jesse's first summer, spent in Cloverly, and the year she, Lori, and Megan became best friends. And attending her first-ever county fair, with Lori, was exciting.

Riding the double Ferris wheel tickled her tummy, making her squeal and squeeze her eyes shut. But on the downward turn, she opened her eyes as Lori laughed and snapped a photo of the crowd below. Then her breath caught in her belly as her eyes locked onto a young boy handing a white teddy bear to a little, brown-haired girl. She remembered wishing she were that little girl. Then the boy turned and smiled, staring straight into her eyes.

It was funny how fate had a way of bringing two people together, and in this case, it was her and Tucker. He was her world, and there was no denying their lives were meant to be shared.

As they walked into the clearing at Sallee's Rock Tucker turned to Jesse and said, "Your wolf knows what to do, the worst is over."

Jesse looked around as the others ducked beneath random trees and nodded. "I hope you're right because I don't remember any of it."

"Just take your time. There's no hurry. Picture your wolf and bring it forward." Tucker ran his hand over her hair, and she leaned into his touch.

"Okay, I can do this," she said as if trying to convince herself. She looked past Tucker as a black wolf darted across the clearing, followed by a smaller silvery wolf. "Which tree is mine?"

"Just pick one, it's that easy."

Ducking beneath the first tree she came to, Jesse paused when Tucker yanked his shirt over his head. Enjoying the view, she eagerly kicked off her boots. It would be a great run, and for the first time, she would be running with her pack.

She quickly phased and followed Tucker to the top of Sallee's Rock where she stared out over the clearing. Remembering them sitting there in her dream, she nuzzled against Old Clumsy as the sun broke the horizon, bathing their wolves in a warm glow. He nudged her shoulder and then licked kisses over her ear. It was perfect, and her wolf was content to call the pack family.

Twenty-Seven

Jesse

Two wonderful weeks had passed since Jesse's date with Tucker. And as she stared up at the star on top of the Christmas tree, it was hard to believe she was spending the holiday with him. But there he sat across from Gramma, on the sofa, talking with her dad. She smiled and made a wish upon the star, and then grinned when Tucker laughed, drawing her attention back to him.

It was a small gathering with plenty of food and more presents than necessary, but being the first Christmas for Sonya and her dad, it would be a holiday to remember.

"Anyone want dessert?" Sonya asked as she walked across the living room, to the kitchen.

Jesse looked over at Tucker and said, "I'll be right back." Following Sonya into the kitchen, she paused at the door as she sliced up a pie. It was weird to think Sonya was her step-mother, but her dad was happy and that was all that mattered to Jesse. She cleared her throat.

"Oh, I'm almost finished," Sonya said, slicing through the remaining pumpkin pie.

"I'm not in a hurry. Actually, I was hoping I could talk to you for a minute," Jesse said.

"Sure." Sonya motioned her over to the counter as she pulled dessert plates from the cabinet and placed a slice of pie on each. Wiping her hands on the dish towel, she turned when Jesse joined her at the counter.

"Thank you for sticking by me after all the hateful things I said to you. I didn't mean to accuse you or insinuate that you were a horrible monster because I know better. I was having a major meltdown and didn't know how to handle it." Jesse looked down at the pie, still feeling guilty for lashing out at Sonya, after finding out she had been changed.

"I understand. Your dad understands. He doesn't like it, but he's dealing with it. I'm just glad we know who changed you and that she's no longer a threat. She was a very troubled female and would have done anything to get what she wanted. But never mind about her. All is forgiven, we're family now, and I'll always be here for you." Sonya smiled as Jesse looked back over her shoulder.

"Can I ask you something private?" Jesse whispered, and motioned Sonya into the laundry room. "I know how I feel about Tucker, but I don't know how he is with the pack when I'm not around. Is he the gentle giant I see, or is that an act?"

Sonya grinned. "Your dad told me you two share a bond, and I'll tell you what I told him. Tucker is everything you think he is and probably much more. He's from a big family, and everything he does centers on protecting and nurturing the people he loves. He's one of a kind. You'll never regret bonding with him... if that's what you're asking."

"That's a relief to know. I've been confused about everything lately and being with him feels like the only stable part of my life."

"That's how I feel about your dad. My life could never be complete without him."

Jesse bit her lip and chuckled. "I can't believe we're hiding in the laundry room, having this conversation.

"I know, right?" Sonya teased. "I feel as giddy as a school girl."

"Well, with your looks, you could definitely pass for one." Jesse snickered and bumped against Sonya.

"You're just saying that because I'm the evil stepmother." Sonya bumped back.

"No, you're the best," Jesse said, opening the door and following Sonya into the kitchen. "Guess we should feed them." She picked up two plates and turned toward the living room, waiting at the door for Sonya. She had been an idiot for listening to Gina trash talk Tucker, when she should've trusted her own gut instinct. And looking back, she could blame her actions on a lot of things, but mostly her own insecurities.

It was a great Christmas, Jesse thought watching Gramma feed cat treats to Moose. Sonya and her dad were busy, reading instructions on how to hook the new Blu-ray player, to the big-screen, and Tucker was trying to get her attention by flicking paper footballs in her direction. Finally, after the third football hit her in the back of the head, she looked over her shoulder to see him mouthing from the foyer, "Let's go for a walk."

Jesse grinned knowing their walk would end up with them at his cabin, and since she still had one more gift to give, it would be the perfect place for privacy. "We'll be back shortly," she said and hurried into the foyer. No one seemed to notice so she slipped on her coat and met Tucker at the door.

Fastening her coat as they walked around the house, the snow had melted, but still she shivered from the brisk wind cutting across the river. She hastened her steps, nearly running the short distance between her grandmother's and Tucker's cabin. "Geesh, it's freezing out here," she said, and ran up on the porch, the smoke from the chimney drifting to her nose.

"Don't worry, it's warm inside." Tucker pushed open the front door.

Jesse hung her coat next to the door, and then hurried across the room to kick off her shoes. Standing on the hearth, allowing the heat from the bricks to soak through her socks, she sniffed the air. Pine, smoke, and cinnamon—all reminders of the holiday season. "Your cabin smells better than the boutique."

"Oh yeah? Maybe you should bottle it..." He waggled his brows and walked over to the small spruce that stood in the corner of the room. Everything about the tree screamed Tucker, from the white Christmas lights that cast a soft glow around the room, and highlighted the popcorn and cranberry garland, to the red ribbons tied at the tips of the branches. It was simple, yet fit the cabin perfectly.

Tucker pulled a shiny, foil-wrapped package from between the branches, and handed the gift to Jesse. "For you."

"You don't think I opened enough gifts at home?" she asked, but quickly took the shiny red box, and sat down on the sofa.

"Well, it's not much, but I think you'll like it."

Jesse loved knowing she was the reason for the gleam in his eyes, and she suspected her eyes reflected the same.

"This is proof you were the one sending me flowers." She smirked and pulled the handmade name tag off the package and fanned it in the air.

"How do you figure?" He arched a brow.

"Well, your penmanship is beautiful, and you spelled my name wrong." She laughed when he yanked the card out of her hand.

"I didn't spell your name wrong, what are you talking about?" He flicked the card back at her.

"You did so. I think I would know how to spell my own name." She plucked the ribbon off the package.

"J E S S I E spells Jessie." He was confident he knew how to spell her name based off the smirk spreading on his face.

"True, but my name is not spelled with an I. My mom wanted a boy when I was born."

"Well, I'm glad your mom didn't get what she wanted." He sat down beside her as she ripped off the paper, exposing a white cardboard box. Nuzzling her neck, she shivered and shrugged him away. "I don't care how you spell your name, either way, it means *mine.*" He tweaked her nose, and she slapped his hand away.

Her jaw dropped when she opened the box and saw the rose-gold locket in the shape of a heart. She looked over at Tucker. "I thought you said... this isn't handmade. This must have cost a fortune. You shouldn't have." She placed her hand on her chest and blew out a breath. It was the nicest gift she'd ever received.

"I should have, and normally I would have made you a gift, but I wanted this gift to last a lifetime. You'll see why when you open the locket." He watched excitedly as she snapped open the little heart.

"Is this... us? Me?" She moved closer to the end table and clicked on the lamp. Staring at the small picture of a large, brown wolf standing watch over a smaller black wolf, she recognized Sallee's Rock. "This is us, isn't it?" She looked back, hoping he would say yes.

"It is."

She closed her eyes and held the locket to her chest. "I finally accepted what I am, but I could never picture myself as a wolf. This means more than you will ever know. Not only because it's my wolf, but because you're standing with me. This is the best gift ever. Thank you so much." Her hands trembled as she looked back at the picture.

"Let me put it on you," Tucker said, and she lifted her hair. After fastening the necklace, he leaned down and kissed the back of her neck. "I'm glad you like it. I was hoping it would impress you."

"I'm very impressed. You did good. Now, I have something to show you." He looked surprised, and she grinned, knowing the picture would blow his mind. "I remember my first vacation in Cloverly. That weekend Dad took us to the county fair." She walked over to her coat, hanging beside the front door.

"We used to go to the fair every summer. It was a blast," he said, watching as she dug into the pocket.

"Yeah, I assumed as much." She handed him the photo and stood back to watch his reaction.

"That's me and Jaylee. And Hayden in the background." He looked up, not understanding. "How old was I in this picture?"

"Well, I was ten." She watched him calculate the numbers in his head.

"Fourteen." He looked back at the picture. "But where are you?"

"I'm sitting beside the photographer. I don't know why Lori took the picture, but I remember you. And that day."

As he placed her, his eyes widened, and she laughed. "That was you? The girl with a gazillion braids? I dreamed about you for years, but I thought you were older." His brow furrowed.

"I was an early bloomer, and most people thought I was thirteen."

"I told Hayden that night that you were my mate. He thought I was attracted to you because well... you looked like you were thirteen."

"I thought you were older as well, and if it makes you feel any better, that was the day I fell in love with your dimples. I've also dreamed about you; and at the theater, I knew you were familiar, but your dreads threw me off."

"This is amazing; I can't wait to tell Hayden."

Jesse and Tucker spent the better part of an hour, lying on the rug in front of the fireplace. Propped up on his elbow, Tucker played with Jesse's hair as she stared into the roaring blaze. Thinking about the locket and the picture it held, Jesse felt a stronger connection to her wolf. And it comforted her. She looked up at Tucker. "Why did you deny your bond?"

He rolled over onto his back and stared up at the ceiling. Unsure of what he would say, she rested her chin on his chest as he caressed the back of her head. After a few minutes, he looked into her eyes.

"I wanted to meet you the first time I saw you on the sidewalk in front of the flower shop. And at the theater when the bond appeared, I wasn't expecting it." His lips pressed tightly together and he inhaled through his nose. "

Seeing you with your boyfriend, and laughing with your friends, what chance did I have? I couldn't very well throw you over my shoulder, without taking Brian out of the picture. I did consider it though." He smiled, remembering. "I decided to wait it out because you seemed so happy. I tried not to interfere even though I did send the flowers." He grunted when she poked his stomach.

"And at the dance, that was probably the hardest day for me. I wanted to steal you away, but you left the party and that asshole didn't go after you. He didn't deserve you." Tucker rolled over, pushing her onto her back. His finger traced over her lips, and she bit down, causing him to smile. "I decided that night to tell you what I was, but I didn't see you again until the council meeting. You were scared of us; we were monsters. I couldn't put you through that so I denied the bond and went home." He looked over at the fire, his emotions swimming in his eyes.

"That was probably the worst day of my life. When you walked away, it was like my world stopped spinning. I didn't know about the bond, but I felt the loss as soon as the door shut behind you. I'm sorry if I made you feel like a monster. I never thought of you that way." Jesse reached up and turned his face toward hers. "I dreamed about you."

"Please tell me it was a good dream and not about monsters."

"I wouldn't necessarily call it *good*." She paused as the smile slipped off his face. "It was like an out-of-body experience where everything felt real, and the heat that consumed my body had me panting, unable to douse the fire." She grinned.

"Wow, that sounds hot."

"Sweat-drenching hot." She giggled and wrapped her arms around his neck. His scent mingling with hers was blissfully pleasant, and giving him a light kiss, she whispered across his lips. "Tucker, do you accept me as your bond mate?"

He jerked back; surprised by the question as he stared down at her like she lost her mind. "Do you know what the bond means?" His large hand cupped her cheek as his thumb brushed over her lip.

"I know exactly what it means. I've been talking to Megan for a month now. I know that it's forever and forever is what I'm looking for. I love you." His eyes flared with her confession.

"I never thought I'd ever hear you say that. I love you, too," he said as she turned into his palm and kissed his hand.

"Is that all? I mean, you can't steal my heart and then

expect me to walk away." She blinked up.

"No, we can't have that. I accept you as my bond mate." He chuckled and kissed her with a softness she'd never experienced before. Feather light, and breathlessly delicious, she tugged him closer, deepening the kiss. "Now that was hot," he said when he pulled back and drew in a deep breath. "But do you accept me as your mate?" He arched a brow.

"I always have. I was just too confused at the time to admit it." Tears filled his eyes, and she kissed them away. Snuggling closer to him, she relaxed in his arms as she thought about their future together. "Tucker, when are you leaving for Tennessee?"

"I planned to leave after I took you home tonight, but now I don't want to go." He rested his cheek against her hair.

"If you'll wait until morning, I'll go with you."

"You want to go to Tennessee?"

"Of course I do. I'd love to meet your family, and what better time? Just because I phase under the dark moon doesn't mean I can't run with you under the full moon, and anyway, it's Christmas," she argued with a teasing tone.

"What about your dad?"

"Well, we did spend most of the day with them, and it's still early. We could go back to Gramma's and spend the rest of the night there and leave really early tomorrow morning. Then Dad can't say we weren't there Christmas Eve and Christmas Day... for a little while at least."

"Then what are we waiting for? We need to go if we're going to butter him up before you break the news." Tucker jumped up off the floor and raced around the room, gathering their shoes and coats.

"Slow down, Hoss, there's plenty of time." She grinned as he dropped her coat down on top of her. And when he kneeled down and shoved her boot onto her foot, she rolled with laughter. "Okay, I get it. You're in a hurry."

Taking the shortcut back to her grandmother's, they walked hand in hand. Not knowing how her dad would feel about her going off to Tennessee on such a short notice, she hoped he would understand. If not, she would enlist Sonya to act as her go-between. Because her dad didn't stand a chance against Sonya.

As they walked in the backdoor, Jesse yelled through the house. "Where is everybody?"

"What's all the yelling about? You're as feisty as a June bug in May," Gramma replied, walking into the kitchen.

"Gramma, look what Tucker gave me for Christmas," Jesse said, holding up the pink locket. Popping it open, she didn't want to give away the surprise, so she waited for her grandmother's reaction. She never told her grandmother what happened to her, but she knew her dad and Sonya had explained the change. She moved her left hand behind her back and crossed her fingers.

"Oh, my word. Is that…" Her grandmother reached into her apron pocket and pulled out a pair of reading glasses. She lifted the locket to the light.

"It's me, Gramma."

Her grandmother looked up at Tucker. "And you?" He nodded. She looked back down at the picture and smiled. "You sure are a pretty thing, but then again, you always were."

"I love you, Gramma." Jesse sniffled and wiped her nose. "Thank you."

"No need to thank me. I had help dealing with your change, and he's standing right behind you," Gramma said and squeezed Tucker's arm. Jesse's brow crinkled as she looked back at Tucker when her grandmother walked out of the room.

"You weren't the only one that struggled through your change," he said and pulled her into his arms. "I had to do what I had to do. She's my homie."

"You did not just call Gramma your homie."

"Yes, I did, and you're jealous. We're best buds, peas in a pod." He beamed, and she looked back toward the doorway.

"Well, thank you for helping her." Jesse planted a quick kiss to his cheek.

"I didn't help her, she helped me," he whispered across her ear.

"Hurry up, love bugs, it's dirty bingo time," Sonya said, passing through the kitchen.

"What do you mean, she helped you?"

"Just what I said. If it weren't for her, I would have gone crazy from rejection, but she said you'd come around. I just needed to chill." He laughed when she poked him in the ribs.

"And I thought she was on my side."

"She's definitely on your side. Did you know she has a nice collection of iron skillets? She showed them to me."

Twenty-Eight

Tucker

The six-hour drive home would've been boring had Tucker been alone. But with Jesse riding shotgun, he would have driven to the moon with no complaints. Crossing into Tennessee, Tucker glanced over as Jesse stared out the side window. It was surreal, dreamlike, and he feared he would wake up and poof! She would be gone. He breathed in through his nose, enjoying her chicory scent.

He had never taken a female to meet his family, so introducing them to his bond mate would surely rock the house. And not wanting to spoil the surprise, when he called his mother that morning, he offered very few details about his companion. Lucia was sharp though, so he suspected she probably had a good idea who was coming with him, considering Jesse was the reason he had gone back to Cloverly. He hid his grin, imagining Hayden and Sawyer's face the first time they saw Jesse.

Hayden loved brunettes, and Sawyer leaned more towards the blonde spectrum, but both were red-blooded males that never missed an opportunity to check out a gorgeous female.

"This is so beautiful. Why would you ever want to leave?" Jesse asked as they continued up the mountain road.

"Because you're not here." Tucker squeezed her hand, and she blushed. "Just up ahead. You'll see the roof line as soon as we make the turn."

"I hope they like me." Jesse wrung her hands. Why was that always the first thing people said when meeting parents? Tucker had actually said the same thing to her.

"They'll love you. Wait and see." He turned into the drive that snaked around to the back of his family's large, two-story cabin. After parking the car, he hurried around to the passenger side, as the backdoor of the cabin flew open. Hearing his name, it was hard to hide his excitement.

Obviously, his mother had relayed their conversation, and everyone was eager to see who was joining them for Christmas dinner. The grin on Tucker's face as he looked over the top of the car kept them in suspense as they whispered amongst themselves, and for once, the Wilson household went quiet.

"Are you ready to do this?" he asked, putting his hand out to Jesse. Wearing a pair of designer jeans tucked into suede hiking boots and a cranberry sweater beneath a russet-brown leather jacket, Jesse came well-prepared for the snowy weather and looked sexy as hell. She smiled nervously, and he could tell she was anxious when she got out of the car. The gusting wind lifted her hair, and he could have sworn he heard a pin drop.

Seeing all the stunned faces at the backdoor, you would think his family had never seen a female before, but that wasn't the case. They had just never seen one with Tucker before, and he found their expressions somewhat amusing. He kissed the top of her head, but it was more for show than necessary. She was his mate, so why not flaunt it? He wrapped his arm around her waist and they started toward the house. "It's okay, breathe. They'll love you."

Tucker chuckled when Jesse looked up through her hair, trying to get a take on the family before she got to the door. But they didn't give her time, and instead, raced off the porch and met them in the yard. Then, hearing the smallest voice of them all, he dropped his arm from Jesse's waist and stooped down as Lily Rose crashed into him. He lifted her in his arms.

"I missed you," Lily said, hugging him around his neck.

"I missed you too, peanut." He hugged her tightly until she giggled and then he glanced down at the smile on Jesse's face. "Lily Rose, I'd like you to meet Jesse."

Lily looked down, her bashful smile lifting her shoulder to her cheek. "Is this your friend?" she whispered in his ear.

"It is," he whispered back and tickled her ribs.

Lily squirmed, and he placed her on the ground. It was unusual for her to push away from him so soon after he arrived, but apparently she wanted to make a good impression. Adjusting her dark green dress over the red tights she wore, Lily looked up. Standing in front of Jesse, she leaned her head slightly to the left and curtsied. "It's nice to meet you." She smiled as a rosy sheen covered her cheeks.

Tucker grinned when Jesse curtsied back, knowing that was all it would take to win Lily's heart. She stooped down and lifted the red ribbon that was tied around Lily's waist. "It's nice to meet you, Lily Rose. Your dress is lovely."

When Jesse stood, Lily latched onto her hand and pulled her through the crowd of siblings. Tucker followed behind them, elbowing Hayden and Sawyer who were arching their eyebrows waggishly. His sisters snickered when Jesse glanced over her shoulder, catching the brothers in the act. They both quickly looked away.

"Mom," Lily said as they walked into the cabin. "I'd like you to meet my new friend, Jesse." Lily's face beamed as her parents walked across the large family kitchen. Filling in around them, the brothers and sisters took their seats at the bar.

"It's nice to meet you, Jesse," Lucia said. She took Jesse's coat and handed it to Jaylee to hang on the coat rack next to the backdoor. "I'm sorry about Lily; she gets carried away when company stops by. She thinks everyone comes here just for her." Lucia cleared her throat and looked down at Lily.

Tucker stood behind Jesse, lightly kneading her shoulders until her body relaxed. His family, being large, could intimidate, but Jesse didn't really seem to mind.

"No, Mom, she's my friend. Ask Tucker. She loves me because I don't have my wolf yet," Lily retorted, and her mother looked over at Tucker. "What is she talking about?"

"She's human," Lily said as she moved over and stood in front of Jesse. Crossing her arms over her chest, it was her way of protecting her new friend, which made Tucker smile even more.

"Lily, sweetie, she's not human." Lucia looked confused as she glanced between the three.

Tucker looked down at Jesse and winked. "Lily, Jesse's a wolf," he said, and her smile faded.

"But you said she would love me because she was a human." Lily pouted, her lower lip trembling with the devastating news.

"I did, but now that she's a wolf, she'll love you twice as much." His voice rose with excitement, and Lily arched her brows.

"Twice as much because you are now my new best friend," Jesse said, pushing Lily's hair over her shoulder as Lily flashed a toothy smile.

"Lily Rose, you young'uns go wash up so we can have dinner and then we'll open gifts," the alpha said taking a seat at the bar and motioning for Jesse and Tucker to do the same. Waiting until the youngest four left the room, Alpha Wilson looked back across the bar. "Jesse, welcome to the pack. I'm Samuel Wilson, but you can call me Sam."

"It's nice to meet you," Jesse said. Glancing around the table as the older siblings introduced themselves, she smiled when Alyssa spoke.

"I have to ask this question because I'm not sure I heard you right, but did you say 'now that she's a wolf'?" Alpha Wilson glanced between them, and Jesse squeezed

Tucker's hand beneath the table.

"Yes, sir, Jesse is a new blood." Tucker pulled Jesse's barstool next to him and wrapped his arm around her protectively. "She was changed about four or five months ago, right?" He looked over at Jesse and she nodded, looking down at her hands.

"So is she or isn't she the girl you broke the bond with?" Lucia leaned against the bar.

"She is. I broke the bond I had with her, and while I was here, a rogue wolf bit her. To make a long story short, when I returned to Cloverly, we met at a Halloween party and the bond was back, but this time, it was hers." Tucker chuckled as his siblings' mouths hung open for a second time, in less than fifteen minutes.

"That's interesting and practically unheard of. I've never actually met a new blood," Sam said. "Most humans aren't strong enough to handle the transition."

"Oh, hogwash! It's just fate correcting a wrong." Lucia looked over at Tucker. "I hope you know that." She pursed her lips.

"Whoa! No need for a lecture. We've righted the wrong and are now happily bonded."

Lucia's hand slapped against her chest, startling Jesse. "Thank the moon. This is such great news."

Jesse looked up at Tucker and he smirked. "I told you they would love you."

"Dude, no way. I'm related to a new blood? Those are bragging rights right there. I don't know anyone that even knows a new blood, much less, being related to one." Sawyer fist bumped Tucker from across the table.

"Welcome to the family," Lucia said as Sam reached across the table and shook Tucker's hand. "Have you decided when or where you're having your bonding ceremony?"

"Slow down, Ma. We just sealed the bond last night so Jesse may need to get her thoughts together before we start down that road. Her parents are human, and although her dad is bonded with Sonya from the Cloverly Pack, her mother hasn't a clue we exist," Tucker said, side glancing to Jesse when she squeezed his hand.

"No, it's fine," Jesse insisted. "Actually, I'm glad you brought it up. Alpha Wilson, could you perform the ceremony if we wanted to have it here?" She looked over at Tucker and then back to the alpha. "I mean, tonight?"

"Are you sure? You haven't even talked to your dad about this," Tucker said. It was hard to hide his excitement when he had sisters sitting across the bar from him silently clapping. He rolled his eyes.

"Would you excuse me for a minute?" Jesse got up from the table and grabbed her coat off the hook and walked out onto the back deck.

Tucker stood nervously by the door, unsure of what she was up to, but willing to let her make her own decision. With her face tilted to the sky, she leaned against the deck rail and closed her eyes, soaking up the noonday sun. His heart swelled when she lifted the phone to her ear. *She really wants to do this!* Anticipation loomed in the air, and he pinched his arm to make sure he wasn't dreaming.

"Does she have a sister?" Hayden asked, standing beside Tucker at the door.

"No. Sorry." Tucker reached over and squeezed the back of Hayden's neck. "Have faith. I have a feeling she's closer than you realize." As he turned back to the window, his stomach dropped when Jesse looked his way with a frown on her face. That had to mean someone wasn't happy with her decision, and he didn't like to see her frown. He paced the room, and his siblings remained quiet as they all waited for Jesse to come back inside. When the door finally opened, she smiled.

"What happened? Did you talk to your dad?" Tucker couldn't help but ask, even though he knew he was putting her on the spot in front of his family.

"Dad is fine with the bonding ceremony as long as we have another when we get back to Cloverly."

"But…"

"Mom wasn't as thrilled with us eloping. She was hoping I would move to D.C. and go to college before I settled down." His smile slipped and she squeezed his hand. "But after I told her about the boutique it eased her mind, although it wasn't the career path she would have chosen for me. I also told her we would visit D.C. next summer. She was pleased about that." Jesse chuckled.

"So does that mean you want the ceremony to take place tonight?" Sam asked.

"Could we?" Jesse looked up at Tucker. "They're my family too, right?" She glanced around the table, flipping her hand for their support.

"Yeah, she's our family now. We should be able to run with you on your bond night," Alyssa said, and once she did, everyone joined in.

"Fine, we'll have the ceremony tonight," Tucker agreed as ear-splitting squeals ricocheted around the kitchen. And for a split second, he wanted to squeal himself. Well, maybe half a second, being a red-blooded male and all. He laughed and bounced his brows, making

Jesse laugh.

"Go now, we have things to talk about that you need not hear," Alyssa said as she and Jaylee pulled Jesse over to the bar.

Mimicking Alyssa's words, he followed his dad into the family room, while listening to Jesse argue the point she wasn't company and wanted to help with the family meal. Lucia tried to run them out of the kitchen, but Tucker knew his mother had met her match. Oh, how he loved strong females.

Sitting with Lily on his knee, he looked up at the massive Christmas tree in the corner of the room. He was still in shock at the turn of events, and if he weren't dreaming, he would be the happiest male on the planet by morning.

"Come on, everyone, let's eat," Jaylee yelled, forming the line. They placed the holiday meal on the bar, buffet style, and everyone served themselves before heading to the dining room table.

The conversation centered on the bonding ceremony. It would be the first one ever celebrated on a Christmas moon and being a Wilson made it that much more special.

Tucker rested his head on the back of the chair, his hand over his stomach. "I think I ate too much."

"That's too bad. I guess your brothers will have to eat the brownies I baked," Lucia said, and he lifted his head and looked across the table, grinning.

"I don't think so." In his sprint to the kitchen, his chair fell back on the floor, but no one seemed to notice.

Growing up in a family of competitive males, his brothers knew better than to get between him and his brownies. It was attempted, once, and if he remembered correctly, Hayden said it was like "wrestling honeycomb from a bear's paw." When he walked back into the dining room, everyone laughed. "Thanks, Mom."

Tucker righted the chair and pulled Jesse away from the table to the small loveseat across the room from the Christmas tree. "This is the best view," he said, pointing at the tree with the brownie he was holding. "Want one?" He held out the wicker basket.

Waiting as the others finished their meal, Jesse snuggled against his side as the younger siblings gathered around the tree. Once the rest of the family had joined them, Lily Rose carried over two gifts, one for him and the other for Jesse. "It's for you," Tucker said, seeing the uncertainty in her eyes.

"But..." Jesse bit her lip as she looked around the room.

"I already took care of everything. I had Hayden bring the gifts back with him the day he picked up the tux. That was my proof I'd be here for Christmas." Tucker pulled her over and kissed the top of her head. "Now open your gift."

"So what you're saying is you were pretty confident I'd come with you?" Jesse asked as she pulled the ribbon off the present.

"No. I expected I'd be here alone, but I was prepared either way. Mom, this is for the den," Tucker said, lifting the large gift over to Hayden who passed it to his dad.

"Thank you," Jesse said as she draped the handmade purple scarf around her neck and placed the matching hat on her head. "It's perfect."

"Come, you'll want to see this," Tucker said, and he and Jesse walked over as his parents opened their gift.

Jesse gasped when she saw the large picture of her and Tucker sitting on Sallee's Rock. She looked up at Tucker, and he motioned her down the hall.

"This is the den," he said as he opened a set of large wooden doors, exposing a room that was dimly lit by low wattage lights that highlighted framed portraits on each wall of the room. He closed the doors behind them and led her over to the first picture hanging nearest the door. "It's our family tree, sort of."

"This is amazing. Now I know where the locket idea came from." Jesse walked the room, going from picture to picture as Tucker told her about each of the wolves and where they lived. "So every time there is a pair, you put their picture on the wall?"

"Yes, and after our bonding ceremony, we'll be added too. We're like celebrities now." He chuckled and pulled her into his arms. "You made this the best Christmas ever."

Twenty-Nine

Jesse

Jesse sat on the deck as the last traces of daylight
disappeared behind the mountain. The evening breeze
chilled the air, and the pine scent reminded her of home.
What would she be doing at that very moment if she were
back in Cloverly? Considering the hour, she would
probably be helping her grandmother clean up the supper
dishes, or maybe having coffee with her dad and Sonya.
Oh, heck, who was she kidding? After accepting the bond,
she would probably be snuggled up with Tucker for the
evening, at either her place or his. Probably his, in front of
the fireplace, cozy and warm... *Get your mind out of the
gutter!* She glanced over when the backdoor opened.

"Just who I was looking for," Alyssa said and sat
down on the step beside Jesse. "I'm so glad Tucker found
you. I know all this seems a bit much, the family and all,

but we look out for each other and we'll look out for
you as well." Alyssa shrugged when Jesse smiled. "I've
never seen my brother as happy as he is right now. I hope
someday I find a mate that looks at me the way he looks
at you." Alyssa's eyes held a dreamy gaze as she stared
out over the mountain.

"That's sweet of you to say. Thank you," Jesse replied.
"And I'm sorry I didn't introduce myself when you were
at the store. It's a little embarrassing, but I thought you
were Tucker's girlfriend." That made Alyssa laugh, and
Jesse nudged her with her shoulder "You think that's
funny?"

"Considering I was wondering which one of you was
Gina, yeah, it's funny." Alyssa rolled against Jesse, falling
over in her lap.

"You're as nutty as your brother." Jesse laughed and
looked back as Tucker walked out the door. "Shh. We
have company," she said, leaning against Alyssa's back.

"Aww, can I play?" Tucker dashed across the deck,
joining the two females. Pinning Alyssa down with his
forearm, he leaned over and kissed Jesse.

"Excuse me, but I don't need to see this." Alyssa
pushed her hand between the two and squeezed Tucker's
chin. "There are some things sisters should not be
subjected to."

"Then I suggest you close your eyes." Tucker pushed
her hand down and gently laid Jesse back on the deck.
"Ignore her; she'll go away." The soft rumble of his voice
as it swept across Jesse's ear sent goosebumps down her
spine. And as Alyssa rolled out from between them,
Tucker instantly slid over to take her place.

"I hope you know I'm taking notes," Alyssa said,

tapping her boot in the snow. "I didn't realize I was supposed to let the male pin me down." She chuckled when Tucker looked over his shoulder.

"Do and die," he growled.

"Pfftt, you don't scare me." Alyssa jumped down the steps when Tucker reached for her. Laughing, she swatted back his hand and took off around the house.

"You can't tell her not to do something, especially if you do it yourself. She has a point, you know," Jesse pushed herself to a sitting position.

"Well, she'd best forget her point." He chuckled and laced his fingers with Jesse's. "So are you nervous?"

"Maybe a little, but I'm mostly excited." She leaned against his shoulder and wrapped her arm around his waist. "I wish my family could be here, though."

"You know we don't have to have the ceremony tonight." Tucker lifted her chin, and she nodded. "We can wait."

"I know, but I don't want to wait. I think we've been through enough and it's time we do what's right for us. I want to do this. I've been so unsure about my future and what I expect will happen, but this, us being together, feels right."

"I'm glad you feel that way because I promise to support you in anything you choose to do. You are my life now, and nothing will ever come between us. Right?"

"Right." She smiled.

"Good, because I've got one more surprise for you."

"Tucker, no. I don't need..." Her mouth dropped opened when Sonya's SUV pulled around the side of the house and her eyes brimmed with tears.

"Surprise!" Tucker stood and pulled her off the steps

and they ran out to meet her family. "Did you really think they would miss this?"

"Dad!" Jesse threw herself into his arms, sobbing into his coat. "I can't believe you're here."

"Alpha Wilson called and invited us. I couldn't very well turn down his offer. It's not every day your only daughter gets bonded."

"Congratulations, Jesse," Sonya said, moving around the car. "Your grandmother couldn't make it, but she wanted you to know you were in good hands."

Hearing another door slam, Jesse jerked around, not sure whom she expected to see.

"Did you really think this could happen without me?"

"Lori!" Jesse squealed and ran around the car. "How did you..."

"It was an inside deal we made months ago," Lori said, fist bumping Tucker over the hood of the SUV.

"You knew?" Jesse asked, and Tucker shoved his hands into his pockets.

"I had no choice. She threatened me," he said, exposing his dimples.

"That is true. And now I know where you live." Lori winked.

"See what I'm saying? Call me a sissy, but she's fierce. Have you ever heard her growl? It's not good. Not at all." Tucker laughed and followed Dr. Williams and Sonya up to the house.

"I cannot believe you're here," Jesse said, holding onto Lori's arm as they walked across the yard.

"Well, don't expect too much. I plan to stay inside where it's safe and warm," Lori whispered and looked up. "Geesh, this place is huge."

"Wait 'til you see the size of his family," Jesse said, pulling Lori into the kitchen to introduce her to Tucker's parents. "Thank you, both, for inviting my family to be here tonight. It means the world to me." Jesse quickly wiped her eyes.

"You're welcome," Alpha Wilson said before leading everyone into the family room.

"Tucker, would you do me a favor and get my bag out of the car?" Lori asked and grinned when he skirted the room and walked out the door. "So, what's the family really like?" She leaned to the side, hearing laughter in the front room.

"Come on; I'll introduce you to the others. Wait until you meet Lily Rose. You're going to love her," Jesse said and motioned for Lily as they entered the room. "Lily, this is my friend Lori."

Lily looked up and smiled sheepishly. "It's nice to meet you, Lori." She curtsied, causing her new lime-green tutu to flare out over her red tights.

"She's adorable. Can I keep her?" Lori asked and stooped down to run her hand over the tutu and then up into Lily's hair. "We have the same color hair." That made Lily smile, and Jesse grinned.

"Can you be my friend, also?" Lily asked, and Jesse bent down and whispered in her ear. As Lily's eyes widened, Jesse stepped away from the tiny tornado as she threw her arms around Lori's neck, knocking her to the floor. "I'm human too because I don't have my wolf yet."

The excitement in Lily's voice made Jesse smile, but the sight of her straddling Lori had Jesse laughing so hard she had to turn away to stop the giggles. She snorted and looked up as Hayden rushed across the room and lifted

Lily into his arms.

"Lily Rose! You can't just plow down the guest!" The look on his face had Jesse slumped against the wall, holding her stomach. Again, she snorted.

"She's my new friend. She's human," Lily protested and wiggled against the thick arms holding her, but even Hayden wasn't any match for the little twister. As she dropped to the floor, Jesse bit her lip and looked around for Tucker. She needed a distraction, and quick.

"Are you okay?" Hayden asked. Stooping down beside Lori, he lifted her into a sitting position, his hand resting on her knee.

Lori just stared.

It wasn't often Lori was speechless, but then again, Hayden was a hot guy, and she was practically drooling. Jesse rubbed her forehead to block out the rosy glow that covered Lori's face.

"Lily, you need to be careful," Hayden said, pulling Lori to her feet as he stood. When he realized he was still holding Lori's hand, he quickly stepped away and shoved his hands into his pockets, muttering, "Sorry," before he turned and rushed out the front door.

"Who was that?" Lori asked, slumping against Jesse.

"That was Hayden, Tucker's brother."

Nearing the midnight hour, Jesse grew antsy as Lori stared out Alyssa's bedroom window. Tucker, Hayden, and Sawyer stood on the deck below, next to the alpha, as the crowd gathered in the yard. Slipping on her shoes, Jesse glanced over at the frown on Lori's face and chuckled. "What are you so sour about?"

Lori had been quiet most of the evening, even during

dinner when Jesse expected she would hold her own against the Wilson males. But since thinking about it, she wasn't even sure Lori had eaten. Lori wasn't usually a shy person, but being in a house full of wolves, maybe she was a bit skittish.

"Who's the Tracy wannabe?"

"Lori!" *So much for skittish.* Jesse walked over to the window and narrowed her eyes. "That must be Katherine. According to Alyssa, she's determined to snag a Wilson male." Jesse wanted to roll her eyes remembering what Tucker told her about the snotty she-wolf, but instead, her wolf just bristled.

"I'm guessing she doesn't know there's a bonding ceremony, judging by the way she's flipping around in front of the guys. I mean, three Wilsons are standing there; which one is she after?"

"From what I understand, whichever one that will give her the time of day," Jesse said moving over to the mirror hanging on the bedroom door. "Alyssa said she's chased Tucker for years and when he's not around, she goes after Hayden."

Lori wrinkled her nose. "Well, that changes everything. I was going to watch the ceremony from up here, but I think you might need back-up." She looked down at her clothes. "I didn't bring anything dressy. Sorry." The baggy jeans and the oversized sweatshirt hid her shape and made her look like the tomboy she was.

"You look fine, and besides, you'll be wearing a coat," Jesse said as she followed Lori down the stairs.

Walking into the kitchen, Jesse wrung her hands as she looked toward the backdoor. All afternoon she had been excited about the upcoming bonding ceremony, but now as she waited, her mouth went dry. She shook out her hands and closed her eyes, drawing in a calming breath. "I didn't think I would be this nervous." She opened her eyes as Lori peeked out the window.

"Just keep your eyes on Tucker. Megan said it would be a short ceremony, a few words and then it's over. You'll do fine. Now if you'll step to the side, I'll let them know you're ready." Lori smoothed down her hair and winked.

Jesse leaned against the wall as Lori walked out the door and her dad walked in. "I'm right here if you need me," he said and kissed her on the forehead. "You look beautiful. Tucker's a lucky man."

"You're just saying that because I'm your daughter." The ceremony was a last-minute decision, but thankfully, the alpha had invited her dad and he brought Lori along. Having her best friend there eased her mind, especially since she brought a dress from the boutique for her to wear. Smoothing out the pale pink gown that touched her ankles, there was no way she would ever wear anything as boring as plain white. The lace sleeves hid the goosebumps that covered her arms, and that was a good thing. She looked up as her dad presented her with a beautiful rose bouquet. The tiny pink and white flowers, nestled in baby's breath, matched the ribbons that streamed to the floor. She held them to her nose, inhaling the sweet fragrance. *Concentrate on the roses and this will be a breeze.*

"Well, this is it. The last time I get to call you my little girl. You grew up fast. Way too fast," Dr. Williams said, and Jesse placed her hand on his arm.

"Oh, Dad, don't. You'll make me cry. And that's all I

seem to do lately," Jesse said, and he scowled. "Dad, you know what I mean." She laughed as a tear rolled down her face. "See?"

Dr. Williams pulled her into a crushing hug. "I love you so much. And I'm sorry about everything."

"I'm not sorry about anything. Well, maybe a few things, but this isn't one." She kissed her dad on the cheek as the door opened.

Jesse wasn't sure what to expect from the ceremony, but Sonya had told her it wasn't nearly as formal as an actual wedding. That was a relief, considering most of the people attending were people she didn't know. She glanced up as she walked out the door, and Tucker winked. Moving over beside him, Alpha Wilson nodded and turned to the pack.

"Quiet down, everyone." The alpha lifted his hand. "Rarely do we enjoy a full moon and celebrate Christmas on the same night, but when we do..." Sam looked over at Jesse and grinned, "We like to make it memorable for all."

Jesse suspected the alpha was a jokester like Tucker when she saw the grin spread across his face. She chuckled and looked down at the roses, not daring to see if Tucker were also grinning.

"So before we start the run, I have an extra special bonding ceremony to perform." The crowd erupted, and Tucker nudged Jesse with his elbow. Alpha Wilson raised his hand to quiet the last of the whispers. It was clear the pack loved their alpha if the way they responded to him were any indication. "I would like to introduce the newest member of our family, Jesse Williams. She and Tucker share a bond."

Jesse focused her attention on the gray, satin shirt

that molded to Tucker's chest. Not willing to look past him, her skin prickled, and not in a good way. The hair rose on her neck, and she fought the urge to turn and glare, choosing instead to look up at Tucker. He winked again. Being a new blood, everything she thought she knew had changed. But thankfully if she had to be part of the shifter world, she would always have Tucker by her side. *Sorry, ladies, but he's off the market.*

"Care to share?" Tucker smiled at the grin on her face. She shook her head as the alpha moved over to stand in front of them.

"Tucker, Jesse, as the alpha of the Smoky Mountain Pack, I ask, do you, Tucker Wilson, accept Jesse as your bond mate, uniting the two of you until your time on this earth is over?"

Tucker dropped to one knee and kissed Jesse's hand as he looked over at the alpha. "I accept Jesse as my bond mate, now and forever." He grinned and looked up at Jesse when she squeezed his hand.

"Jesse Williams, do you accept Tucker as your bond mate, uniting the two of you until your time on this earth is over?"

Jesse looked down into Tucker's eyes, ignoring the surrounding crowd. "I accept Tucker as my bond mate, now and forever." She lifted his hand to her heart. "You're here. Always here."

He stood and placed his hand on her cheek, and she leaned into the warmth. "I'll always be there," he assured her and then lightly pressed a kiss to her lips.

Wrapping her arms around his neck, she deepened the kiss as the crowd cheered. Then for no reason, she giggled and pulled back. The smile on his face was brighter than the moon, and she traced his bottom lip with her thumb. "We really did it." Her breathing came fast as she looked around, and he draped his arm over her shoulder.

Alpha Wilson nodded his approval before turning back to the crowd. "As the alpha of the Smoky Mountain Pack, let it be known, Tucker and Jesse Wilson have sealed their bond. May their union be blessed and may they bring new life to our pack."

It was apparent the pack readily accepted her like Tucker said they would, and at that moment, she felt the pack connection binding them all together. Electricity pinged throughout her body and she turned to Tucker. "Now what?" Her eagerness made him laugh, and she swatted his chest.

"Now comes the fun part. You get a personal tour of the mountain." He led her out into the crowd.

"Wait," Lori yelled as she ran to catch up. "Not in that dress. Hand it over." She flicked her brows and grinned as Alyssa and Jaylee snickered behind her.

"Well, this is a surprise," Katherine said as she walked over and looked up at Jesse, causing Lori to frown. "What did you do, pick up the first stray mutt crawling out of the gutter?" Her singsong voice made Tucker cringe.

Lori pushed around Jesse to confront the ballsy blonde. "You did not just call my best friend a mutt." She fisted her hands on her hips.

Katherine flipped her hand as if shooing away a fly, and Lori glared. "You're human, go back to your kind. Why is she even allowed here?"

"Katherine, I would advise you to watch your mouth," Hayden warned, but before he could move forward, Jesse had already moved in front of Lori.

"Do you have a problem with me?" Jesse asked, the tone of her voice cautioned Katherine to tread lightly.

"As if I'd waste my time on the likes of you." Katherine looked over at Tucker. "Why would you do this to me? You knew how I felt."

"Do not speak around me to my husband. If you have issues with me, address me, not him." Jesse stepped forward, and the blonde snarled.

"Husband? See? That's proof she's not one of us." Katherine sidestepped closer to Tucker as a low growl rumbled, and Jesse narrowed her eyes.

"This is your final warning. Do not address my husband as if I'm not here. It will not bode well for you."

"Please, you may be from the city, but that only means you've crawled through more sewers than most. You are not good enough for a Wilson male. It should have been me, and he knows it." Katherine placed her hand on Tucker's arm, and his eyes flashed a warning, but it was too late.

Jesse grabbed Katherine around the neck and lifted her off her feet. "We are bonded now, so unless you want the pack to find your bony ass dangling off the side of the mountain, I would suggest you keep your hands to yourself. I've taken all the shit I'm going to from females like you." Tucker held his hands up to hold back his siblings as Jesse's eyes flared red. "Do I make myself clear?" Katherine nodded as best she could, and Jesse released her grip, causing the blonde to fall to the ground, rubbing her neck.

"You... you're a..." The fear in Katherine's voice made Jesse smile, and Lori snicker.

"I am Jesse Williams Wilson. Do not challenge me, or you will see exactly what I am."

Katherine stayed on the ground, smacking away any hands that tried to help her to her feet. She was wrong to confront Tucker, especially after the bonding ceremony and Jesse knew she had every right to stand up for herself. She and Megan had discussed the issue after her run-in with Gina, and she knew exactly what she was allowed to do under pack law. Jesse could have laid her out cold if she had wanted, but not wanting to ruin the night, the threat would suffice.

"I'm sorry," Jesse said, looking up at Tucker. He tugged her to his side, and they walked further out into the yard, leaving Katherine on the ground.

"Don't be. You just proved to the pack that someday you will be an alpha female."

"Hold up, you two. I'm not letting you off the hook that easy," Lori said, stalking up behind them. "I mean it. Give me the dress or else." Lori held out her hand, and Tucker snickered.

"Fine. Unzip me." Jesse may have stood up to Katherine, but when it came to Lori she wasn't risking it. She stepped out of the dress, and Tucker whistled.

"Don't get ahead of yourself there, buster. Drop 'em." Tucker blushed as Jesse crossed her arms over her chest and waited for him to undress. Handing Lori his slacks and shirt, he stood there in a pair of camo boxers that matched the boy shorts and bra Jesse wore. "I really don't know what the big deal is. It's not like anyone can see you." Lori laughed at her own joke, and then headed back to the house, passing Tucker's siblings along the way.

"That was crazy!" Sawyer said, running up to join

Jesse and Tucker. "I don't think I've ever seen anyone put Katherine in her place like that."

"Yeah, there's no mistaking who you are now," Alyssa said, "and that should teach her not to mess with a Wilson female." She bumped Jesse's shoulder and then glanced over as a silver wolf shot past. "Catch you later." She winked and phased.

"I'm watching you," Tucker yelled and then turned to Jesse. "Let's get this night started."

Jesse's wolf was in heaven as it explored the mountainside. Hill after glorious hill, she followed Tucker, reveling in the freedom she felt as the wind swept through her hair. It was overwhelming at times, the changes she'd faced, and who knew when Dr. Stevens said she would become stronger, he actually meant physically stronger? Her body, although firmer, seemed no more muscled than normal, and it wasn't until Katherine put her hand on Tucker, that Jesse dared stand her ground. It was weird, like a volcano erupting through her veins, and she was more than willing to take out anyone in her path. She never considered herself a violent person, and still didn't, but she would fight for what she believed was hers. There would be no more playing nice when it came to her family.

Her ears flicked as Tucker led her across a wooden walkway, to a small cabin that overlooked the mountain. His footsteps, silent in the night, came to a stop and he looked out over the trees. Rubbing against Old Clumsy, she then phased and looked up as the moonlight cast shadows over the area. Her heart raced from their run, and she drew a deep breath to fill her lungs. She sat down beside Clumsy and kissed his nose while running her arm up under his neck. She leaned into the massive wolf. "The view is beautiful," she said, and he phased and sat down beside her.

With a smile as wide as the mountainside, Tucker leaned in and kissed her cheek. "My wolf is in love with you." He lifted her up off the deck and placed her in his lap.

"You're not jealous of Old Clumsy, are you?" She looked up and batted her lashes.

"Are you kidding me? That's the conclusion you came to?"

"Well, yeah. I mean he was on his game tonight and would make an excellent snuggle buddy, so warm, soft, and protective. Yeah, he's a definite ten in my book."

Tucker tightened his grip and nuzzled down her neck. "I can be warm and soft and protective. And as soon as the others clear out, I will show you," he said, and Jesse squealed at his subsequent caress.

Thirty

Tucker

Tucker rolled over and stared out the large window that showcased the mountainside. Newly fallen snow blanketed the mountains overnight and sparkled like tiny diamonds in the early morning light. He snuggled deeper beneath the covers, with Jesse nestled against his side— her warmth teasing his wolf. She was at peace, her face no longer creased with worry. He lifted a strand of her hair, her chicory fragrance now more prominent and filling his nose. She was his mate, their wolves, bonded together just as fate had intended.

His thoughts drifted to the day he returned to Cloverly, after denying the bond he held. He had little hope in his heart, of ever being happy again, but still, he planned to tell Jesse he loved her, even though his wolf would never claim her as its mate. But luckily for him, she had her own bond to share. Destiny's way of correcting the wrong and reuniting old souls back together, or so he was told. He could live with that, and with Jesse at his side, he was more than excited to start his own family at their cabin in Berkley.

Most of the renovations were complete, and with Jesse's flair for design, there was no doubt she could turn the rundown cabin into an interior masterpiece that would reflect both of their personalities. He glanced down at her and smiled. That was still a few months away, but as soon as Tucker's alpha training was complete, they would be moving to Berkley where he would oversee his own pack with Jesse at his side. His breath hitched when he thought of her as his alpha female. In more ways than one.

He rolled onto his side and gently tugged Jesse against his chest. Skin to skin, her body molded to his perfectly, everything about her tugged at his heart as fond memories of their bonding replayed in his mind—igniting a fire that urged him to rock against her.

Their ceremony, shared with his Tennessee family, was unexpected but now his wolf was fully content. Standing in front of the pack, binding his life to hers, he was a proud male, and she was the most beautiful female he had ever set eyes on. Her flowing, pink dress against her lovely dark complexion, and her long black hair drove him wild just thinking about it. And as magical as it had been, nothing could have prepared him for what took place in the cabin later that night.

As he inhaled her scent, his heart drummed in his chest, and he debated watching her sleep or waking her.

He peppered kisses from her ear down to the crook of her neck. She tasted sweet, and he wanted nothing more than to devour every last inch of her, again and again.

She snuggled into him as a soft smile formed on her face. He loved knowing he was the reason for her smile.

He glanced back to the window. It couldn't be more than an hour after sun-up, which meant they probably hadn't slept more than four hours the night before. But with his mate lying in his arms, sleep was the last thing on his mind.

Tucker and Jesse had split from the pack sometime after midnight and spent the early morning hours getting better acquainted with each other. A wide grin crossed his face, picturing how sexy she looked straddling his waist—his definition of heaven. His hand trailed down to her hip, and he drew in a sharp breath. He wouldn't wake her, she needed the sleep. Instead, he would wait, and as soon as she awoke, he would remind her just how much he loved every glorious inch of her body. He closed his eyes, satisfied with the knowledge she would always be there with him, no matter what.

Three days later, Tucker and Jesse finally left the comfort of the small cabin and joined the Wilson family for breakfast. Expecting to be hounded for details of their bonding night, especially from Hayden, he was surprised to find the morning fairly quiet.

"How was your stay at the cabin?" Lucia asked as she placed a large plate of bacon and eggs on the counter.

"It was very nice. Thank you." Jesse blushed when Tucker grinned. Boy, how he loved to make her blush. A shiver rolled through his body, and he drew in a calming breath. But what he really wanted to do was slip between the sheets, and show her exactly how much power she held over him.

"Anytime you all want to visit, just let me know, and I'll have the cabin ready," Lucia said as she walked past Tucker. She poked him in the ribs and added, "Behave."

"That sounds great. I would love to see the mountains in the spring or the fall. I bet they're really beautiful," Jesse said.

"You should see the mountains in the winter." Tucker jumped away from the spatula his mother pointed at him.

"Tucker!" Lucia scolded.

"Yes, ma'am." He cut a glance to Jesse, and she snickered. "Here, Mom, I'll get that while you and Jesse plan our next visit," Tucker said, taking the spatula before his mother could threaten him again. Looking back at Jesse, he slapped the utensil against his hand and waggled his brows—her blush deepened.

"Now this is what I'm talking about." Tucker dipped a crisp piece of bacon into the pancake batter and dropped it into the skillet. His stomach automatically rumbled.

Watching his younger siblings out the kitchen window, building a snowman, while listening to Jesse and his mother make plans for another visit in the spring, he smiled. Something he was doing a lot of lately. Yeah, his life was perfect and hearing Jesse laugh, his wolf hummed with delight. Old Clumsy had a major crush on their mate.

"Thank you all for welcoming me into your family. I have a half-brother that lives with my mom, and I don't see him as often as I would like. So being here is like a dream," Jesse said.

"I'm glad things worked out for you and Tucker. He

was so heartbroken over you after he denied the bond. You were the only reason he returned to Cloverly. He intended to tell you how he felt," Lucia said.

"But I thought if you denied the bond..." Jesse frowned and glanced back at Tucker.

"That you moved on? Usually, that is what happens, but in this case, the wolf was able to, but Tucker couldn't." Lucia looked up and grinned.

"Mom, would you stop telling her all my secrets?" Tucker scolded and walked over to plant a kiss on top of Jesse's head.

"She has the right to know how you felt about her. It was sweet."

"Yeah, because I'm a big ol' ball of sweetness." Tucker rolled his eyes, and Alyssa laughed behind her hand as she opened the door and yelled to the others to come in for breakfast.

"I think so," Jesse said, and Tucker couldn't resist leaning down to nuzzle her hair.

"Don't make me send you back to the cabin," Lucia threatened.

"You heard the lady. Don't make her send you back to the cabin because I can't guarantee they'll see you again before spring," Tucker warned as Jesse buried her face in her hands.

Once Tucker had enough bacon-pancakes made, he carried the large tray over to the bar and sat down beside Jesse. "These are my specialty." Placing four on Jesse's plate, he handed the tray off to Alyssa and said, "Fend for yourself." He swiped a pancake off the tray, and laughed.

Watching his family, it was still hard to believe that Jesse was now a part of it. He reached down beneath the bar and pinched his leg. "Yep, it's real." He chuckled, and everyone looked his way. "Did I say that out loud?" Alyssa rolled against Jaylee and the giggles spread around the table.

"Wait a minute; where's Hayden?" Tucker asked, tilting his head as if he expected to hear Hayden tromping down the stairs. Looking across the table, Alyssa bit her lip and shot a glance at Jaylee, who had dropped her head, snickering. Sawyer shoved half a pancake into his mouth as he got up from the bar and walked over to the refrigerator. The younger siblings had taken their plates and were watching cartoons in the family room. Alpha Wilson cleared his throat behind his newspaper.

"Uh, Hayden took your car... well, with the snowstorm coming, and Lori needing to get back to Cloverly, he left yesterday to take her home. He said he would drive your truck back," Lucia said, cutting into her pancake.

"Why? Lori was supposed to ride back with us," Tucker said.

"I don't know why. She seemed agitated and threatened to drive herself, so I made Hayden take her home," Lucia informed them, but Tucker still felt as if he were missing something.

"Alyssa? Jaylee? What's going on?" He drew down his brows. If anyone knew what was going on around the mountains, it was those two.

Alyssa glanced at Jaylee.

"I don't know exactly what happened, but Lori and Hayden spent two nights out on the porch, talking after the rest of us came in," Jaylee said.

"As cold as it was?" Lucia interrupted. Jaylee looked

over at Alyssa and giggled again.

"It's not that cold when you're snuggled up against a werewolf," Alyssa reminded, and Jesse's jaw dropped. "Anyway, he took her into town the day before yesterday, and showed her around, introducing her to his friends. Then yesterday, they were out walking the mountain, and evidently Katherine somehow caught up to them. Lori came barreling up on the porch, swearing a mean streak. She had some choice words for Hayden after he walked off with Katherine. By the time Hayden got home, about fifteen minutes later, Lori had already loaded her bags in the car, and was about to leave when he rushed up behind her and took the keys."

"I can imagine how that played out," Jesse said, shaking her head.

"It wasn't pretty, but it was Hayden's fault. He chose Katherine over Lori and had to deal with the fallout." Jaylee shrugged.

"Jaylee, Hayden wouldn't do something so rude without reason," Lucia said.

"I didn't say he didn't have a reason. Katherine will say and do anything to get Hayden's attention, now that Tucker's bonded." Jaylee rolled her eyes.

"Well, hopefully, Hayden was able to make peace with her before she got home," Tucker said.

"I doubt it. Lori was sitting in the back seat, turned toward the window. She didn't look like she would ever speak to him again," Alyssa chimed in as the backdoor opened and Hayden stomped into the kitchen and slammed the truck keys down on the counter.

Hayden stormed back out the door, without saying anything to anyone, and mumbled below his breath. His clothes were wrinkled, and his hair stood out in all directions, a clear indication that he had run his fingers through it multiple times.

Tucker jumped up from his seat and looked out the window. "Wow, he's pissed."

Lucia walked over beside Tucker as Hayden phased, his clothes blowing up around him. The large, mahogany wolf bolted down the side of the mountain and Tucker looked over at his mother. "That doesn't look promising."

"Well, you know how your brother is; he likes things to run smoothly. It will work itself out. It always does," she said, turning away from the window.

It was getting late, and Tucker knew they needed to get on the road, but concern for his brother made him hesitant. He'd never seen Hayden so angry... well, there was that one time in high school, but Hayden was twenty-three now and much better at controlling his temper. "Should I go after him?" Tucker looked back at his mother.

"No. When he's ready to talk, he'll come home. As for you, you need to get your things packed and head out. I don't want you anywhere near the mountains when the next storm comes through," Lucia said as she took her seat next to Alpha Wilson.

"If he's not back in an hour or so, Sawyer and I will go after him. He's an adult; he knows these mountains better than anyone. He'll be fine," Alpha Wilson insisted.

Tucker was confused by Hayden's reaction, and for him to just blow up, and for no apparent reason, made Tucker uneasy. But Jesse's safety was now his first priority, so he decided to let his dad deal with his brother. "Well, I guess we'd better get going, but if you need me..."

He and Jesse said their goodbyes and within thirty

minutes, they were heading down the mountain road. Glancing back through the side-door mirror, Tucker purposefully drove slower, hoping Hayden's wolf would appear at the top of the ridge. It wasn't like his brother to take off in a tizzy, and definitely not like him to not say goodbye. They were thick, the two of them, and often one pretty much knew what the other thought. Concern creased his forehead as his eyes scanned the mountainside.

"Tucker." Jesse turned in the seat and placed her hand on his arm. "I know you're worried about Hayden, but I don't think there's anything you can do. I could be wrong, but I think he kind of likes Lori."

"Of course he does. He likes everyone." Tucker looked through the rearview mirror, again.

"No, I mean really, really likes Lori."

"What makes you think that?" Tucker asked, glancing over to her, before looking back at the snow-covered road.

"I don't know. It was just a feeling I got the other day when he helped her off the floor. He was holding her hand a little longer than necessary, and then he acted embarrassed by the situation."

"I don't remember Lori falling. When did this happen?"

"It was right after they arrived. While you went out to get Lori's bag from the car, I introduced her to Lily, and well, Lori ended up on her back." Jesse chuckled.

"Okay, so he helped her up. That's what any polite male would do in that situation."

"Well, it wasn't just that he helped her up. There was something in his eyes like he homed in on her and she stood there practically drooling, as I did with you." Jesse's

eyes rounded and she slapped her hand over her mouth as
Tucker slammed on the brakes, the truck skidding
sideways.

Remembering his own mistake, his heart dropped to
his stomach as he looked over his shoulder, but it was too
late to turn back.

"He has a bond with Lori but didn't tell her?
Dammit!"

Acknowledgements

To my family: Thanks for listening to my incessant droning over the years.

Thank you, Teri at editingfairy.com. I look forward to working with you again.

Thanks to my beta readers. You know who you are.

And a huge thanks to the readers. If you like this story, please consider leaving a review.

About the Author

B. S. Todd lives in a small western Kentucky town with her husband, son, two dogs and a ferocious feline. A nature enthusiast, she has always drawn her greatest inspiration from the natural world around her. Her hobbies include reading, writing, and on certain nights throughout the calendar year, she can be found watching meteor showers or lunar eclipses conveniently from her backyard.

You can follow me on Facebook at: B. S. Todd
For updates on Always Hayden, book three in the Cloverly Wolves Series. Due out August 2018.

www.ingramcontent.com/pod-product-compliance
Lightning Source LLC
Chambersburg PA
CBHW020334180626
46812CB00001B/193